The
Crocodile Hunter's Widow

by Peter Dearlove

Published by Kindle Direct
for Flatdog Books of Rhodesia and Zimbabwe
Contact email: adwrite72@gmail.com
First published January 2017
Second Edition January 2020

ISBN 9781520452807

About Peter

Peter Dearlove is a former journalist and copy writer who lived and worked in Rhodesia through most of that country's civil war years, serving as one of the 'occasional soldiers' he writes about in this story.

He worked in London for Reuters and Associated Press, and later edited a number of trade journals including *The Rhodesian Farmer*, *Tobacco Today*, and *The Rhodesian Chamber of Mines Journal*.

In South Africa he was for eight years editor of the *Montagu Mail*.

His advertising career began as a copy writer with Lintas. He worked as *Creative Director* at Barker McCormac before moving on to start his own agency, Adwrite, which ultimately became DDH&M, and still operates in Harare, Zimbabwe.

Flying, gold mining and farming are among other activities and interests of his long and varied career.

He is married, has two adult children and one grandchild, Willa.

For Helen, Jake, Lucy and Willa, and in memory of our Sally.

In a nutshell

The country called Rhodesia no longer exists. Where it was is now the Republic of Zimbabwe, a landlocked chunk of Africa lying somewhat south of the Equator, somewhat north of the Tropic of Capricorn, east of Namibia and Botswana, and west of Mozambique. But for something like 90 years it did exist as an outpost of the British Empire. It was named to honour Cecil John Rhodes, an Englishman who came to Africa in the middle of the 19th Century and made a vast fortune from diamonds.

Among his many other qualities he was ambitious for Africa and proudly British; he wanted to use his great wealth to civilise the continent and its people under the British flag. He began by sending a small military force and a few hundred prospective settlers to occupy the eastern half of what was then Lobengula's kingdom, Lobengula, son of Mzilikazi. To do this with nineteenth century respectability he first contrived a 'concession' from Lobengula, allowing him to settle and search for gold and other precious metals in a part of the realm occupied by the vassal 'Shona' tribes who were not militarily well enough organised to resist him or the coming Europeans.

In the hands of white settlers Rhodesia flourished for much of its short existence, developing a complex infrastructure based on agriculture, mining, tourism and industry, and, as Rhodes had hoped, the land was 'civilised' in the sense that its indigenous people absorbed much of Western culture - more than enough to know that they wanted to have their land and their freedom back. It was not long before they demanded to be included. It seems a strange thing, now, to record that the settlers and those that followed them and their descendants turned the frequently repeated request down on the grounds that they were not yet civilised enough.

Frustrated after many years of patient application, succeeding black leaders and their young followers eventually took to the bush and began a deliberate program of violence against the whites, minuscule in its effect at first, but growing slowly until the entire country was involved in what was recognised as a civil war. It was to lead, inevitably, to black majority rule and the birth of a new identity for the country which became Zimbabwe.

Chapter 1

When I recall the tangled web of our mingled lives and how they were affected by the war that was going on around us I think of other sudden blossomings and tragic terminations of human relationships, of love affairs just beginning or about to end, of others already in full bloom, alive with joy and confidence, that had the malign fortune to be set against a background of angry people and flying metal. And for a fleeting instant I feel almost ashamed to suggest that our own romantic wartime catastrophes in the heat of one of the world's least known civil wars, should merit a mention. And yet we are surely all members of the same sorry club; without a war behind our every fumbling touch, none of what follows would have happened quite as it did.

In a sense then, this story could have been set in any human conflict anywhere and at any time, yesterday or a hundred years ago, here or in another country, but, as a matter of fact, it all took place in Rhodesia, what you might describe as a hand-made country with a hand-made name. At the time Rhodesia was in the throes of a civil war pitting white settlers of European and South African descent against indigenous black nationalist forces.

As civil wars go it was a picnic outing in the bush for some of the soldiers involved on the white side. These, mainly men over the age of 35 (and later much older), were the 'occasional soldiers' of the war. Called up by the Police, the Army, or the Air Force, they served regularly for short periods at a time in whatever unit they had been trained for or assigned to. When the system was introduced in response to the growing need for military manpower the length of service was six weeks every four months. Later, as the military pressures began to mount, it became 'six weeks in and six weeks out'.

As you may easily imagine this made life something of a challenge. Yet most of the men involved found themselves almost enjoying these stints away at the front-line – sometimes in the face of great danger, more often doing nothing more than camping out in the bush with other men, making friends, smoking, drinking a little, and generally being a bit more masculine than they ever were at home.

It was on one of these six week military call-ups that I met Smuts.

In the usual army way we were ordered to report at the mobilisation depot before daylight at 4am for onward transit to somewhere at the military front, otherwise known fondly as 'the sharp end'. Fully kitted out in standard camouflage uniform, and each carrying a kitbag, we arrived in dribs and drabs, most of us dropped off by wives or girlfriends. We gathered on a wide veranda at the depot to await orders. Most of the men were known to each other but I was a stranger because it was my first full call-up. Years before I had taken part in the usual four months national service scheme at an army barracks near the city of Bulawayo, followed by a year of occasional weekend army drills and exercises. This was interrupted when I left the country to improve my career prospects as a reporter. I went to London for two years and so managed to miss much of the early build-up of the war. Nevertheless I was considered to have had military training, especially since I knew my way around the FN Rifle which was then the Rhodesian Army's standard weapon issue.

In my naiveté on that first day at the depot I thought we should have been standing around like tightly coiled springs, ready to fly to arms at the first word of command, but, as the wait grew longer and there seemed no reason to get excited, I began to relax and take in the surroundings. Most of the men were sitting or lying down with their kitbags as pillows, smoking lazily and trying hard to look relaxed and unconcerned. It may be that many were not worrying much about the coming six weeks, they had done it all before. As for myself, I was hiding my nerves, a definite case of dread and foreboding, for I had no real idea of what to expect – despite the dozens of personal reminiscences and assurances of a boring time ahead from my various friends, I feared the unknown. Worse, I had a hangover of sorts from too much to drink the previous evening when I had argued drunkenly and furiously with my wife Tina, who chose to see my departure for the war front as the start of an unearned holiday, abandoning her for six weeks to furnish and arrange the decoration of a new and empty house by herself.

No doubt other men were thinking through their last evenings at home too, for, all in all, there was little chatter among the 30 occasional soldiers waiting at the depot that morning.

I noticed one man propped up against a wall with his *camouflage* cap – we called them 'cunt caps' because with their long shade flaps and pointless little peak they made you look pretty stupid – pulled down over his eyes, smoking a cigarette and blowing tiny smoke rings by tapping rhythmically on the cheek with his right forefinger.

Now that, I thought, is cool, calm, and collected.

All I could say was "How the fuck do you do that?"

Untroubled by my uninvited and probably slightly provocative interruption, he carried on tapping until he had run out of breath for it.

"Do what?" he asked, fixing a mildly curious look upon me with his penetrating blue eyes.

"The smoke rings, hundreds of them, every one perfect. I've never seen anything like it," I said.

"Oh that," he said casually, "that's the sum total of my sporting achievement. Olympic smoker."

Long pause. Then, "I haven't seen you around before, are you new?"

Before I could answer, he added, "I'm Smuts. Smuts Brander. What's your name soldier?"

"Hunter Hill." I said. "Or to give you the full five-shillings' worth as laid on me by my careless parents, Francis Hunter Rowland Hill. Most of my friends call me Hunter, some use Francis, and I answer cheerfully to both, but never to Frank or Rowland."

"A mouthful indeed," he said. "Much too much to remember with the hangover I have brought to this occasion, Dog," he said. "Mind if I call you Dog? It's easier, and you look like a good dog to me. We're all good dogs around here. Have a seat, have a smoke and don't volunteer for anything if anyone asks."

I laughed. "Fine with me Dog, call me anything you like."

And thus it was that we became Dog and Dog for the duration of a short but happy friendship. Two dogs against the rest.

I told him what I did for a living. I was a species of Public Relations Consultant. I say 'species', because I was doing that sort of work, but without any formal training. In reality I had been a newspaper journalist for some years but while working in London had switched when I found I could earn more money telling people how to make their self-serving stories and business reports look like news, and get them published in newspapers and magazines more or less for free but with a nice fee for me.

We called it Public Relations, or PR for short, styled it 'image building', and dressed it up with an overtly formal work process, sprinkling just enough fairy dust to make what we did look like very deep stuff indeed.

I had been fudging my way through this career building process when I suddenly decided to go back home to Rhodesia only two years previously. During those two years I had not bothered to register for military service since I was already close to the cut-off age and was in any case trying to get a new business going. Latterly, however, the age limit had been raised, putting me squarely back into the eligibility bracket for some years to come, and I was trapped. And so it was that I belatedly presented myself for registration and service.

Smuts laughed when I told him this short story.

"In Rhodesia you will never be too old for the army Dog, not until Bob Mugabe comes roaring into town waving a red flag and sitting on a Russian tank, or in chains behind a South African one."

The short scene is embedded forever in my soul.

After about an hour of idle loitering, the Company Sergeant Major, Jimmy Rogers, arrived. Like the rest of us he too was an occasional soldier; in real life, a senior executive in a local oil company, but he had some history in the Territorial Army, and he was militarily wise and super-efficient. Better, unlike some of his colleagues, he understood that the men under his command were not first-time recruits needing to be dominated and broken, but mature individuals, some of them successful businessmen. Instead of barking orders like the legendary parade ground tyrant, he was far more likely to stroll into the midst of the men, clap his hands softly to draw their attention, and say something like 'OK guys, listen up, here's what we are doing today.'

And that, more or less, was how he opened proceedings as we waited on the veranda for the next step in what was to be my first experience of wartime soldiering.

Rogers revealed that we were going to a remote camp in the north-west of Rhodesia, taking over from the platoon that had now completed their six weeks. Our function was to provide a credible military presence in an area where the African liberation forces were trying, with so far only limited success, to penetrate. There had been few incidents and little action, but intelligence warned that the mood in the area was nevertheless beginning to boil. We would man the camp and daily send out small patrols to various villages in the vicinity, fire off hundreds of rounds of rifle ammunition, and send mortars flying into the nearby hill country. "*Waving the flag and terrifying the shit out of the locals*," as he put it. Although it was not yet a 'hot spot', he said, the analysts expected it would become one, and very likely soon.

"The guerrillas against us are infiltrating the country in greater numbers," he said. "And they have changed their tactics. For the most part they spend their time moving around at night, politicizing the locals, threatening, even killing those who appear reluctant to become involved. At the moment we don't think they are looking for a major scrap with us. They will take out any soft white target they can, farmers, farmers' wives, even children, and they will do it for maximum publicity by inflicting the most barbarous death and carnal damage that they can. But they are also looking for newspaper headlines and the prestige of international TV

11

coverage, so every now and then they will take a stab at something bigger, particularly if at the end of it they can claim a military victory. It's important for their credibility with the locals, and their financial supporter base overseas in China and The Soviet Union. So they are putting land mines down on military routes regularly these days, and when they have numbers, they will have a go at a weak or sloppy army camp. Don't be one!

"What I am going to say next is not official army policy, but you must be aware that they have already largely succeeded in converting the locals in many parts of the country to their cause. Whereas a few years ago the villagers were either on our side, or at worst indifferent to the nationalists, today we are the people's enemy and the gooks their liberators. That means that, almost without exception, every black person you come across in the tribal areas is on their side, and they are their eyes and their ears. Unless you know otherwise, you must look on every local as a potential informer, indeed a spy, for the enemy.

"In the hours when you are off-duty, don't go walk-about alone in the bush. Have a shower as often as you can or as you like, but do not use highly perfumed soap, and never ever cover yourself in aftershave or sweet smelling hair concoctions – you won't believe how far those scents and odours carry out there in the bush. It's like walking around at night with a great big spotlight mounted on your head, advertising 'here I am, a white dandy from Salisbury" he said. "Easy meat. Shoot me".

"I will be acting CO of the camp for the time being. We'll be doing regular patrols on foot and in mine-protected vehicles. We have an element of Intelligence Corps bunking down in camp with us although they will be in a separate section with their own tents and messing arrangements. They will not be sharing guard duties, so don't let them catch us out.

"If you want to stay alive and go home to your families in six weeks' time, stay alert and stay sober. There will always be beer available at the end of the day in camp, but only an arsehole will get pissed - remember that you can be called out for a duty any time and you don't want to be rotten with booze in the bush.

"Meanwhile, relax. Take it easy, the transport is on its way."

For now, all we had to do was draw our rifles, have a cup of tea in the canteen, and wait for the transport to arrive.

"Hurry up and wait," *"Greatcoats ON, Greatcoats OFF!"* – these soldier expressions have, I suppose, been used, oh, since way before the First World War, mocking an essential truth of wartime army life, and, sure enough, having had to be up and ready for action at the depot before daybreak, it was not until mid-morning that anything of a vaguely military nature other than the short briefing, began to unfold.

Those otherwise wasted five hours changed my life. For Smuts, henceforth to be known as my friend Dog, they may have been a death sentence.

I do not want to give the impression that our meeting had any great significance for either of us at the time. It was simply that we seemed to have so much in common. I liked him from the start, and his quirky ways of thought and speech amused me. It is true that we became friends, and that, for a short period of time, we enjoyed each other's company, almost to the exclusion of other, older friends. The life-changing aspect of it was simply in the sense that so much of what happened later could be traced back in a straight line to our meeting that morning.

"If you had never met him, none of this would have happened," I sometimes said to myself, more in wonder than regret.

On that day, however, I was thinking nothing more about Smuts than his elegant artistry with smoke rings, his quick wit, and the fact that I had become Dog.

The platoon travelled to the destination beside a distant river on the backs of five ten-ton supply trucks. We lay on boxes and spare tyres between crates of vegetables and various other food stuffs. It was a long trip and the sun beat down so that it was uncomfortable in our hot, green, camouflage uniforms.

13

We smoked, of course, the whole way. Conversation was difficult with the road noise, so we basically kept our mouths shut. When finally we arrived at the camp it was almost dark and there was little time to prepare for the night. All of us, with the exception of our temporary CO, the Sergeant Major, were billeted in one huge tent pitched on a corner of the vast square of ground bulldozed into a rough fort formation. Three sides were six-foot high earth walls of some considerable thickness, the fourth was made up of two overlapping piles of earth providing a protected way in and out for both vehicles and men. At the centre of the fort there was a higher look-out platform with a thinly thatched lean-to roof – just enough covering to prevent a drenching for the occupying guard in case of rain.

Our predecessors had obviously not been particularly house proud: the tent was sloppily raised and badly pegged to the ground, and, since the whole contraption was on a slight slope, any rain at all would have meant the tent interior rapidly becoming a mud hole. With an hour to go before dark we all pitched in fast to secure the tent, and cut a shallow ditch all round to draw off any rain that might fall. Then we laid out our sleeping positions with a little space on each side, enough room to spread out the contents of our kit bags.

In no time it was all quite cosy.

Burned by wind and sun we were ready for bed as darkness fell. Food for that first night came from a standard ration pack known to us with more menace than good humour as a 'rat' pack; two biscuits, one small tin of bully beef, a wedge of something resembling cheese, and a small tin of peaches. We ate in the gathering darkness. Only the insect sounds of the dense Africa bush disturbed the stillness. Few uttered a word.

Each of us had a small torch to be used to read under the blankets, or to tell the time. Otherwise, for obvious reasons, no lighting was permitted in camp.

CSM Rogers had allocated guard duties in such a way that the man on duty would be followed by the man in the bed next to him, clockwise. The duty was two hours at a time and it was the current guard's responsibility to call the next one five minutes before he was due. Guarding was hardly onerous; a boring round of peering into the dark, sharpened a little by the realisation that whether the gooks attacked in daylight or dark, if they chose to attack, the guard would be their first target.

As it turned out, nothing of *that* sort happened for the full six weeks of our river-side camp. In the course of our many patrols we came face to face with death in several unpleasant forms, but whatever the action, it had already missed us by miles. We were not even always contemporary onlookers. More like undertakers, we were sent to pick up the bodies and, if they were white, send them back to Salisbury; if they were black, dispose of them some other way.

Until then, the first body I had ever seen was that of a new-born baby. I was fourteen years old at the time at boarding school in Johannesburg. The baby was wrapped in several sheets of newspaper, and it had been dumped in a ditch across the road from the school's main rugby field. It was on a Wednesday, a 'free' afternoon, and some of the boys were kicking rugby balls from one end to the other. One ball sailed over the small fence, and when someone went to retrieve it, the little corpse was discovered. Word spread like wildfire, and within minutes, or so it seemed at the time, half the school was clustered around the sad little figure. What I remember of it was the bloodiness of the swaddling newspapers, the beatific smile on the baby's rosebud lips, and the soft blue vacant staring eyes. It appeared to be resting easily, but it was quite dead. Someone called the police and it was not long before we were dispersed to go back to school and talk in muted tones about death and all things dead. The occasion was commemorated in a way that only small boys can do. For Wednesday dinner, every Wednesday dinner, the menu was and always had been the same – a pale looking salt beef with carrots, awash in a thin, but tasty pale gravy. We re-christened it, and forever after, as long as I was at school anyway, the salt beef and carrot menu was known as '*dead baby*'.

War-time casualties were never so disarming or frivolous.

The morning after we arrived at the camp the CO took a radio message from headquarters about a couple of white civilians who were missing in our district. Twelve of us were sent out in two armoured cars to look for them. They worked for a black granite quarry company and had come from town to do a routine inspection of a new deposit then being surveyed and evaluated. They were armed and supposedly *au fait* with the security situation in the area. Not sufficiently *au fait*, however, for we found their bodies on the veranda of the makeshift offices at the quarry. They had been executed Chinese communist style; that is to say they had been made to kneel on the floor with their hands tied tightly with wire behind their backs, looking at the ground, probably praying. They were both shot in the back of the head at point blank range. You could see that the hair was scorched around the bullet holes.

Apart from the bodies, the place was deserted and there was no one to question. The entire labour force of quarry workers had disappeared, their belongings left behind in the crude huts they occupied. There was no way of knowing then, and we never did find out, whether they had gone at gun-point, or simply left of their own accord – either to join the revolution or escape the white retribution that was sure to follow.

About half-an-hour after we reported the find to Army HQ, two helicopters arrived at the scene and dropped off two small units, 'sticks' we called them, of army scouts. Compared to us occasional soldiers, these were all youngsters, seemingly fresh from school, not more than 18 or 19-years-old, troopers of the Rhodesia Light Infantry. Yet they looked the part of seasoned, menacing and professional killers. Dressed only in khaki shirts and shorts and wearing rough rawhide shoes and floppy *camouflage* caps, they were all heavily armed – two with machine guns, the rest with rifles, extra magazines, and six grenades each,

16

attached to a double over-the-shoulder harness. These 'boys' gathered around the corpses, conferred for a few minutes, scurried around the general area looking for tracks, split up into their two original sticks, and soon set off in different directions, apparently chasing down two different sets of footprints.

We loaded the bodies aboard our transport, then watched in awe as first one, and then the other chopper accelerated to full power and took off in that ear-splitting clatter of swinging blades and blinding blur of dust and trash that are the unforgettable trademarks of helicopters at war.

Driving back to camp in our mine-proofed vehicle was for the most part a silent experience as each of us digested the events of the morning. One man, I don't remember who it was, let out a sort of agonised half shout: "bastards!" he cried out suddenly. Another, more reflective, and no doubt referring to the two dead men rather than the people who killed them, said more softly "silly, careless cunts".

Some hours later back at the fort as the afternoon wore on, we again heard the sound of helicopters approaching. Soon they arrived overhead, the same two. Suspended below one was a huge bag like a sea-going fishing trawler's net. Full of black bodies, it was lowered to the ground and released. The young white soldiers had done their work well; there were eighteen black dead in the bag. Aboard the second chopper was a haul of arms and ammunition retrieved from the engagement. No white soldiers were killed or wounded in the engagement.

The dead were quickly cleared away to the Intelligence Unit part of camp, there to be gone through and pored over, pockets emptied, documents examined, faces photographed, and then, finally, buried naked together in a mass grave with nothing else tangible that might later identify them, except perhaps their teeth – assuming any of them had ever had dental work done.

Later, Smuts and I were waiting in line to shower before turning in for the night.

"Shit, Dog," he said. "That wasn't funny was it? There is something so much more than awesome about a day like this, weird, worrying and tragic. For me it crystallises what I have been thinking about for a long time. We're bullshitting ourselves. This resistance to majority rule is absolute bullshit. Smithy tells us on TV that we can win the war, and sure, these young buggers from the RLI or Scouts, whoever they are, go out after this gang of gooks or that gang, and they come back with dozens of the bastards dangling dead in a bag below a hovering helicopter. And tomorrow they'll have to do it all over again. And tomorrow, and tomorrow, and tomorrow after that. There are more of those black buggers than there are of us white buggers. We're all buggers. But you and I, Dog, we're on the side that cannot win. At least I don't believe we can win. But we'll go on giving it a go. There's nothing else we can do. We're in for a lot more pain before our side finds out for a painful certainty that we can't shoot our way out of an argument with our own people like this. To stay sane, and to stop myself from just running blindly off into the bush, I have to shut my mind to why we are here and just get on with whatever we are doing."

I nodded, sadly. "I was working in England when this shooting war truly began," I recalled. "I had never thought all that much about the black white divide to be honest. It was just the way things were, and while I was growing up and at school I don't think there was much tension day to day between whites and blacks. My family lived on a small gold mine, far from any town or city. There were more black people around us than white. We all seemed to get on alright. My brother and I played with the black kids. The only thing unusual about it all was that there was no real adult mixing. My parents had no black friends. No black adults ever came to visit us for a cup of tea or a drink. It was weird really, quite feudal, although I didn't even think about that until much later.

"Once I did become politically aware I became a liberal, but the rest of my tribe, previously, like me, quite unconscious of the winds of change, slowly developed the other way. As politics hardened in Rhodesia, they all joined the Rhodesian Front. I guess they saw it as the only way forward. Anything else was surely simply to hand over to the black masses, and lose everything in the process.

"Watching the trouble growing from afar in London one day I came to the conclusion that whatever the future, I would rather be with my own people than against them. I came home. Eventually I joined the army. And here I am, deep in the shit like they are."

"Deep in the shit like all of us," my new friend Dog corrected me.

Chapter 2

When you truly come to grips with the proposition that you could get killed doing what you are doing every day at war, time does strange things to you. At those moments when you actually perceive yourself to be in immediate danger, the minutes drag by and you wish them away, but they resist. Then, when you lie awake under your blankets at night waiting for sleep to claim you, and you think back on a day of concentrated apprehension, the kaleidoscope of events that war, no matter how small by the yardstick of international conflict, can sometimes deliver, makes the whole collection of events seem short, to have gone by in a flash, and you wonder if it can be true that you were really there all the time. As I look back now I realise that our small army unit was never in any great danger on that, my first call-up, but we did not know that at the time and I confess there were many minutes and many hours of a gnawing kind of inner fear, a steady apprehension of serious threat.

On our second day we were again called out early to provide armed support – this time for policemen investigating a landmine blast. No immediate danger there, for it had all taken place in the darkness before dawn. A small farm truck had been destroyed in the blast. There were three dead, all black, although it was not easy to say for sure because the remains were limbless, headless, floppy bundles of torso in dirty rags. The power of the land mine blast is phenomenal, reducing whole vehicles to bits and pieces of metal, and people to unrecognisable lumps of muscle and bone. If there is anything to be said for such a manner of death it can only be that it is swift and sudden. No one in that small vehicle could have suffered in any way. One moment they were all there, nicely dressed for a day in town, and the next they were gone like ants underfoot, instantly destroyed, blasted out of existence and scattered who knows where, scattered pieces of protein to feed only the tiniest of scavengers.

While standing as perimeter guards for the policemen investigating this incident there came the sound of a huge blast just over the hill from where we were working. Looking in that direction we could see a column of black smoke rising fast. Within seconds came the rattle of machine-gun fire. Then a short break, and then more firing. That was a testing moment for all of us. You never saw a police team finish their investigation quite as rapidly as ours did, and they were off. We were about to follow suit when a radio call from HQ ordered us to re-deploy over the hill to the scene of the explosion and gunfire.

Strapped firmly in our Hyena, which is what our particular type of mine-proof vehicle was called, we tore up the rocky, dusty road as fast as we could, nervous of course, wondering, and at the same time dreading, what we might find on the other side. As we crested the rise we were able to heave a combined sigh of relief, however, for in front of us, stalled by the leading truck which had indeed hit a landmine, was a long military convoy of at least twenty vehicles of various descriptions – all Army, of course, all ours.

The driver and two other soldiers in the lead truck were injured; one, unconscious, was receiving attention from a medic. The Captain in charge of the convoy dismissed us, for there was nothing we six could possibly do to assist fifty or sixty fully armed men. The machine-gun fire that we had heard had been purely precautionary. That officer was a man who operated on the principal that an ambush was likely around every turn in the road, and he believed the way to deal with it was an immediate answering charge left and right, guns blazing. There was one casualty from his immediate reaction on this occasion, a cow that had been grazing peacefully in the long grass took three direct hits in the hindquarters, and bled to death.

I was standing with Smuts while the driver manoeuvred our Hyena around the twisted metal that was all that was left of the lead truck's driver cabin.

"Pure comedy Dog, pure comedy," he said. "I wonder how the Captain's going to write this one up? *'In the cross fire there was* one casualty, one black and white Frisian female killed preparing her mid-day meal..."'

"Drama yesterday, tragedy and a touch of farce today. What will tomorrow bring I wonder; any chance of opera?" It was a wisecrack that proved to be not that wide of the mark.

In the contact that led to the killing of the 18 on our first day, there were in fact 19 black casualties. The last was a tall young man, boy rather, for he could hardly have been 17-years-old. He was badly injured but conscious and able to be questioned. None of this, naturally, did we ordinary riflemen know at the time. The fact is however, that in the contact he had taken a clean rifle shot that entered the soft tissue of the abdomen on the left side, and emerged in parallel fashion on the right, missing the spine by an inch or so, but destroying both kidneys. He would not live long. His interrogators had to work fast. What they may have done to extract the information from him no one would say, but he had given them some indication of a massive arms cache which the gang had been heading for when surprised by the follow-up troops.

So once again we were bundled off in our Hyena to provide an armed escort for the intelligence detail sent to look for the cache. They took the boy with them on a stretcher on the back of an army Land Rover. He lay there quite still, naked but for a broad white swath of elastic bandage around his middle – no doubt to support his mortally injured shot-to-pieces organs. To us, travelling behind, it seemed as if he was dead already, or at least wholly unconscious.

Over rough roads the journey went on and interminably on, kilometre after kilometre, until at last we came to a long sweeping bend, one that the prisoner presumably had identified, for the Land Rover pulled up and a uniformed man got out of the cab to get further directions from the stricken boy. We parked, and the six of us quickly formed a protective ring around the little convoy. I was particularly close to the scene and saw and heard what happened.

To begin with the questioner spoke softly, but with some urgency, in the local African language, to the young man who reacted at first only by lifting a tired hand to his head as though trying to think. The questions became louder and more like angry demands. Suddenly, seemingly galvanised by something the man had said, the boy sat bolt upright and let out a fearful, prolonged and piercing jumble of sounds, somewhere between a scream and a lengthy rattle. Then he collapsed, quite lifeless, back onto the stretcher. At this the questioner appeared to lose his temper and become incredibly agitated. He jumped onto the back of the truck, shook the lifeless body, slapped the face a few times as if to try to awaken him, and shouted out in utter frustration, "not now you fucking cunt, not now!"

But the boy was very obviously stone dead and of no further use or interest. Like a tracker dog that has lost the scent, the army man scurried around the immediate vicinity, looking for a footpath or track, anything that might lead somewhere, anywhere. But there was nothing to go on. After a while and a hastily brewed cup of tea, we drove slowly back to camp with the boy's dying aria ringing in our ears.

Learning to deal with a daily dose of death and the callous inhumanity that often goes with it in wartime is an obstacle course that all soldiers must work through for themselves. As for me, my first reaction was a stunned sense of disbelief; some incredible error had occurred, but it would right itself and I would think through it all again in more detail when it stopped, as it surely must. As the days went by and the bodies piled up it became clear that there was no 'error' and that this was the real thing, WAR. I veiled it for myself in a cloak of righteousness; these people being hurt and killed were merely paying the price for trying to hurt and kill us. Brushed away in that fashion, the deaths of so many young black men became no more significant than the imaginary wallpaper of our bush lodgings.

The next day was damp and discouraging. Thick grey clouds hung over us, a light drizzle falling, then fading, falling then fading.

I couldn't help hoping that the war would be rained off until further notice, like a game of cricket. Smuts and I were taking a smoke break, sitting on some empty boxes just outside and under the overhanging canopy of the tent.

"Bad weather for shooting people don't you think?" I said.

"Hope, Dog, not think, just hope. I've had enough of dead buggers. I want to go home right now and never see another dead thing ever. I've been on any number of call ups over the past three or four years but none of them were anything like this. I have a bad feeling that this picnic is going to get very bloody indeed. Casualties will not be only on the other side. We will lose friends. If not this call up, then the next."

"Bloody depressing isn't it," I said. "But in the meantime, here's hoping for a quiet day of reading, smoking, and blowing smoke rings."

And for a blessed change that's the kind of day the fates delivered. Indeed it was almost as if the rain had washed out the war, and the next few weeks passed almost uneventfully, one dead body or two notwithstanding. At something over 18 killed in the first few days of our call-up, the bar had been set high however, so that when the numbers of dead dwindled, we occasional soldiers lapsed into a state of agitated boredom, constant background apprehension, and a desperate kind of wish, or hope, that if worse happened, we would be able to face it, manly and brave.

Chapter 3

A few days after coming home from that first call up, it may have been a week, fresh 'call-up' papers began to arrive with an almost patterned regularity. The occasional soldiers had found their own source of contemporary relief, and they worked it for all it was worth. To any event that would normally warrant a simple invitation, there would be a 'call-up'. The first of these that I received was a printed requisition to 'report for duty' at 6.30pm on a given day at a factory in the city industrial sites, a "military occasion for military men only", the papers read, "to celebrate your safe return from a spell at the sharp end".

"Dress – Casual".

"Security – Tight".

"You will be required to furnish proof of your identity, (flash this invitation) and upon interrogation by the gate guard, to all questions you will reply

'Snoopy sent for me'."

It was an invitation too tantalising to miss, and clearly not for discussion with mothers, wives, or girlfriends. When the day arrived I said nothing to Tina except that I would be working late on an army project, out of the office and certainly out of reach by telephone. She gave me one of those slightly sideways looks that said she understood I was hiding something from her, and we left it at that.

The 'call-up' hour meant there was time after work for a drink or two with Smuts at *The Watering Hole*, a nightspot in town. I had called him in the morning to make arrangements. He had also received the invitation. Strange to tell, but after so much time in the bush together I still had no idea whether Smuts was married or single. I assumed he was in a relationship of some kind and that he would have made some equally lame excuse to explain his absence.

At 5 o'clock that afternoon we met at *The Hole*.

"What's it all about?" I wondered.

'"An hour or so of harmless pornography, I guess," he said. "*Debbie does Dallas*, or some other example of the latest and hottest skin flick. Six weeks away from their home comforts, which by the way may be real or imaginary, the buggers become fixated on flesh.

"That's what I think at any rate, but it could be more complex than that," he admitted. "Time away from home on call-up is almost like a term at boarding school or college. All lads together, and the subjects are cricket, rugby, and sex; Sex 1, Sex 2 and Sex 3. At least it is a way of shutting out Death 1, 2 and 3."

"I can't wait," I said, and I wasn't lying. Smuts was right. Being in exclusively male company for weeks at a time did bring sex closer to the surface. As for myself, I hadn't thought much about it for a long time; it was like many other things I had eventually abandoned – model aeroplanes, sports cars, all-night parties, even the occasional joint. I suppose much of this was the response to an indifferent marriage. Tina and I had been together for eight years. No babies. And little else to keep us together apart from the loyalty left over from the fresh young years when we thought we were building a partnership for all time. For the first three years we were devotedly on the pill, no room for offspring yet, and we rattled away madly. Then, when Tina decided it was time to breed, nothing happened. For two years we tried everything. Useless.

Eventually we gave it up, the trying that is. But with it, even the very occasional recreational shag disappeared as a lukewarm affection grew up between us. I took up golf, Tina carried on with her teaching, and joined the Women's Institute.

Army life certainly stirred something inside me, though I wasn't entirely sure what. Not that is, until the *Snoopy Sent for Me* event.

I suggested we go in one car, but Smuts declined. "I may have to leave earlier than you will want to," he explained.

Arriving at the venue, the gate guard responded with a broad grin and a salute to the flashed invitation and the verbal "*Snoopy sent for me*". I parked, waited for Smuts to arrive, and the two of us were shown into the office portion of a large factory. There were already about 15 men in the company hospitality centre, a euphemism for a rough and ready office 'pub'. Bottles of whisky, rum, gin and brandy were neatly and prolifically arranged on shelves behind a thick mahogany bar, glasses on racks overhead, big glass or copper ashtrays everywhere, cases of beer stacked up against the wall.

Most of the men were casually dressed, a few had come direct from their offices and were in formal suits. They were all of a similar sort of age and there were no young 'troopies'. Evidently it was a fair sample of the town's businessmen revelling in their role – one of the perks of life as occasional soldiers.

"Occasional soldiers be damned. We've all become occasional bastards if you ask me," Smuts commented.

As if underlining their brief return to boyishness, almost everyone was drinking beer straight from the bottle and chatting happily away to each other, talking deep. I had met one or two of them before, Smuts appeared to know them all. Slowly the room filled up until about an hour after we had arrived there were more than fifty of us waiting to enjoy whatever was to come. The chatter was incessant, so loud that you could really only hear what your nearest neighbour was saying to you, mainly about war incidents, rumoured or real. We were enveloped in a dense blue fug of tobacco smoke – it was still a few years before the American Surgeon General started to get serious about the war on tobacco, and puffing away was as natural as breathing fresh air.

The sharp striking of a bell on the bar was the signal that an announcement was about to be made. The hubbub died to nothing and a man of somewhat more than middle age, no doubt the owner of the factory, and thus our host for the night, welcomed us.

"Thank you for coming," he began. "I am Snoopy. This is a 'need-to-know' occasion, not for discussion beyond these walls. The fact that you are here by invitation makes you a friend, or at least a friend of a friend of mine. Please honour me by saying nothing. You can imagine what the papers would make of this if they got even the slightest whiff of our harmless fun.

"And now, if you will fix your eyes for the moment on that double door over there, I will introduce you to a couple of other friends of mine who have come all the way from Paris to entertain the troops tonight.

"Gentlemen, let's give them a hand of welcome, I give you Mesdames Suriya and Babette!"

A hand of welcome the two ladies certainly were given. Amid prolonged cheering and wild clapping, these two visions of loveliness appeared at the doorway, grandly dressed in the brightest colours, both with their hair done high, and heavily made up as for the stage.

I looked at Smuts and he looked at me. "Another evening of opera, perhaps?"

"Bring it on!" He was getting into the mood.

The room that had seemed so full before was now hollow at the centre; the troops had retreated *en masse* to press together against the bar and three walls, leaving a large enough space for the ladies to entertain us.

Suriya and Babette advanced, Suriya leading, and with a grand gesture, holding her left hand high and open, she began a loud and tuneful trilling which she kept up for a surprisingly long time without a breath. Then with another grand gesture her partner, Babette answered the call. She was the smaller of the two, but her voice was deeper and even more musical. They trilled together.

As the trilling ended, a few sharp piano chords played over the sound system, announced the start of some popular number of the day. The ladies held hands and bowed deeply to the four corners of the room. The men went mad, which they did again a second or two later when Suriya and Babette suddenly stripped off their outer stage garments and high hair-do's, flinging wigs and gaudy costumes over the bar. Now they stood at the centre of the ring in sweet white and flimsy little-girl dresses, short boyish hair, and bare feet.

It was the start of an hour-long show the like of which I never saw before and never expect to see again.

Split in two halves to allow the troops to fetch more beer from the bar, the first part of the show was highly erotic, I will say little more, but the girls kept their clothes on. In the second, the clothes came off almost immediately and the act became more explicitly sexual. Towards the end one man was pulled protesting from the crowd, most likely he had been set up for the event. I close out the scene simply by telling you that as their 'prisoner' on the floor, and in wondrous tune to the decibel beat, he gave everything he had to his two tormentors.

Smuts had not stayed to see the end. Ten minutes earlier he had nudged me, said goodbye with a surreptitious wave of his hand at belt height, and slipped out the way we had come in. When it was all over and the applause had died down, I followed.

It was still early, and, not wanting to get home before Tina was asleep, I dropped in at *The Hole* for a drink. There, to my surprise, I found Smuts, alone. I joined him at the bar.

"What happened Dog," I asked, "I thought you had to get home?"

"What a cock-up," he said. "I was supposed to meet someone here for a drink but I arrived a bit late and she obviously decided I wasn't coming. Or maybe she just changed her mind, I'll find out tomorrow."

"A blind date?" I asked my friend in some surprise, for I felt sure he had a partner, whether wife, lover or merely mess mate, I did not at that time know for sure.

"Oh someone I just met," he replied. "I thought there was a touch of chemistry between us, but I guess I was wrong. We definitely arranged to meet here at eight thirty."

Then he tapped the side of his nose which I took to be a way of closing an unwelcome line of conversation, so I changed the subject.

"Man it's hot in here tonight," I answered, "can I get you a drink?"

"Whisky and soda," he replied with a smile of appreciation.

The next day I was expecting Tina to ask how the evening had been, but she said nothing and I did not refer to it. I felt no tension in the air. Neither did I feel any guilt; only a slight sense of unease as if I had finally passed a point of no return in my marriage.

As I sat at breakfast I was thinking of the show and wondering if my enthusiastic presence there could be called infidelity. I was eating in silence, staring out the window, quite unprepared for what came next.

"Let's pack up and go to South Africa," Tina said without warning. "You were away for six weeks, you've been back less than two, and in another few weeks you'll be gone again for six. What kind of a life is that for us? We don't owe this country anything and now I begin to think there is a good chance you could be killed. My friends at the Institute all tell me that the war is going badly for us.

"From a very practical point of view, Hunter, what am I going to do if one day there's a knock on the door and some man in uniform tells me you've been blown up, shot, ambushed, killed, and you're dead? All I have is a job and a car. The bank will pretty damn quickly come and take the house away."

"I don't think it's as bad as all that yet Tina, but if you're worried we'll talk about it. Only just now it isn't possible. There's the bank overdraft, still massive. If we go, we go with nothing, walk away from our debts. As for losing the house if I die though, it is insured and you would probably end up better off with me dead!"

"Oh don't say things like that," she said. "What you say in jest has a way of coming to pass."

"Oh rubbish," I said. "That sort of superstitious nonsense is just another form of witchcraft for which we despise our black compatriots."

"Well I believe it," she said. "And I don't want to risk tempting fate.

"Anyway to continue with what really is behind my worrying, I do understand that leaving right now would be difficult. I didn't know it was impossible, we rarely talk about anything these days. But can we work towards it? Lots of people are leaving. Every new school term you can see it, kids you were expecting who simply don't come back to school – almost certainly because their parents have got sick of the war and have just packed up and gone."

"Dear Tina," I said in a sudden little flurry of affection for this wife of mine grown distant, "if it matters to you, we will work on it from this moment on. Perhaps we could make it a longer term project. In the spirit of my new military involvement let us call it an 'operation': *Operation Great Escape.*"

As I left for work next day Tina gave me a kiss and a hug such as was unknown for many months in our house, and I felt distinctly uneasy about my part in the performance of the night before. Actually I wondered quite seriously for a moment if she had guessed something, or even had a tip-off from a friend. Nah! I shrugged that thought away. No chance, but I was left to conclude that even if it did not amount to five-star infidelity, my enthusiastic participation in the show was certainly something like it, particularly as I knew I could not have discussed it with Tina. Not in a million years.

The day passed for me in a completely unexpected cascade of fresh ideas. I was thinking of what it might mean to leave Rhodesia and make a new start. Perhaps Tina and I might even get a second chance. I took out a pen and notepad and listed all Tina's good points, those that I think most men would consider in working out the ideal mate. The list was short to start with and as I chewed the back end of the pen I scratched out one thing after another. Those were all distant memories, hopes and dreams from the past. Nope, I concluded, there was no long term hope for the two of us. Life with her was to some extent meaningless. And yet I owed her an effort. We had once been lovers, maybe even friends. I decided however that this was not the time to break anything up, I would talk further with her about leaving. Yet in my heart I think the so-called *Great Escape* was already stillborn.

At the office towards afternoon I was trying to pack up early to get home and be there for Tina at what I recognised was a difficult time, when a client telephoned, wanting to meet me for a short briefing session at *The Hole*.

"Shouldn't take more than about twenty minutes," he said. "Or two gin and tonics, whichever comes sooner."

"I'm on my way, Ross," I promised, slightly irritated but thinking 'what the devil', I would still be home sober, still sober enough not to be irritated if Tina did want to nag me into definite long term plans.

Ross worked for one of the larger advertising agencies in town. He was a partner in the business, very much an opinion leader in the field and well respected by the business community. From time to time he hired me to do some specialist PR jobs for his clients. His proposition over drinks that afternoon was interesting, but it wasn't business in the ordinary sense. He was offering me an opportunity to be transferred to a new army outfit then being formed, a Psychological Operations Unit designed to bring a new dimension to the war.

Someone, somewhere within the government or the fighting forces, had come to the conclusion that we, that is 'we *the white Rhodesians',* were in a war we were losing because the opposition were offering the vast majority of the people of Rhodesia a 'better product', the hope of a better life, a life in which they would no longer be ruled in their own land by people they still thought of as foreigners. It should not have taken much thought to realise that what the Nationalists were promising was indeed a more attractive offer, and the wonder is that it took so long for the penny to drop.

Ross explained that it was to be the new unit's mission to counter their view of a liberated future by saying and demonstrating that they were liars, and that they could not make it happen even if they wanted to. They would lose the war and many more innocent people would be killed in the process, and that the war itself was using up the very resources that the government would otherwise be able to apply to making life better for everyone.

We talked about the war and where we thought it was going, but by the time Ross had to leave to go to another appointment, I was still undecided, a full glass in my hand, lost in thought, thinking of Tina and wondering what she might feel if I wanted to stay and take up the new army job.

As I shook off the thought and was about to leave I noticed a young woman looking at me from across the horseshoe bar. It was by no means a provocative examination, yet it was quite frank, and to me a little disturbing for she was tall and attractive and exquisitely dressed, like Joseph, in a hand-embroidered coat of many colours. By raising my glass and my eyebrows and cocking my head all at the same time I tried to convey an invitation to her to come over and join me. She hesitated only a moment.

"I am sorry if you thought I was staring at you because I want to add you to my collection," she said with such easy charm as she sat down beside me that I felt I had known her all my life.

"You remind me of someone I met quite fleetingly about twenty years ago, and have often thought of since," she said. "In fact I am still thinking it is indeed you. I will never forget the face, or the long, leggy body. Tell me, did you once work on a dairy farm in the Midlands near the town called Hartley? And did you on one lazy Sunday morning spend a few idle minutes showing a little girl how to milk a cow?"

The scene came back to me in something like a blinding flash.

"You?" I asked in astonishment. "Gangly, skinny, freckle-faced, flat-chested, incredibly cheeky teenage provocateur extraordinaire. Give me a minute or two and maybe I can come up with a name."

"Barbie Darby," she answered without waiting. "Now Barbara Flanagan, the widow Flanagan."

"Good grief! What a change. Who on earth would have guessed that after all, buried in that cheeky little bag of skin and bone there was this gorgeous swan waiting to be let out?"

"Well," she said, "so I was right, it is you, Hunter Hill. What a hoot. What an absolute hoot. "

She took my hand and looked deep into my eyes, bit her lip in a funny kind of wondrous smile, and told me:

"Sadly I can't stop now, but can we meet again some other time? Say same time same place a week today? And then I will tell you what the ugly duckling thought of you all those many years ago, and all that has happened in between. And you can tell me where life took you to leave you looking so fit and well and utterly gorgeous!"

"Who could resist such an invitation?" I answered. I'll be here."
And then she was gone.

Mentally turning the clock back as best I could, I tried to remember the details of that day on the farm, now so long ago. I lost myself in the thought, perhaps for only a minute, but the loss was complete. Next thing I found myself staring into someone else's eyes. It was Tina.

"I thought if the Hill wasn't coming to Mohammed, Mohammed would have to come to the Hill," she said, pleasantly.

Considering my recent evaluation of our marriage chances I was strangely pleased to see her; a little relieved too that she had not materialised a few minutes earlier.

I affected a casual and easy attitude to hide the guilt I felt at the deception I was about to weave, and I said rather weakly, "I am so sorry, I was miles away. Ross called me with a proposition, and we came here to talk about it over a drink or two or three. He has only just gone and I have been sitting here wondering what to do. Shall we go home now and I'll tell you all about how he and I and a handful of other people are going to end the war and save Rhodesia for the white man."

"I suppose that means the end of our *Great Escape*," she said, taking my arm and piloting me quickly to the door.

"Not necessarily," I replied. "Two projects can live together for a while. It's like a two-horse race. You put money on both, and wait to see what happens at the finish line. You can't lose."

"True," she said, "but neither can you really say you won."

Chapter 4

How I found myself in the position to teach anyone to milk a cow was an odd little spin-off of what today is known as a 'gap' year. Though there was farming in our family background I had no particular pull in that direction myself. My only experience came from fairly regular school holiday visits to a cousin who was himself fresh from school and working as an assistant on a farm near my home. It seemed to me that all he did was stand around in the fields under the blazing sun, watching the labourers at labour. He called it 'supervising'. I thought of it as an idle way of getting sun-burn of the brain. But then I was brash and perhaps a little arrogant. I could not guess that very shortly I would be doing something similar.

At 16 I was finished with school life. I had in my pocket the passes necessary to carry on to university if that was what I chose to do, but none of the teachers in charge of my final year's performance had believed I would pass; my father was equally negative. And so, in the certain knowledge that I would be going back to school for another year to pass what I was sure to fail first time, no other plan had been made for my future.

When the results came out and I had achieved very creditable passes in all subjects, most of those who knew me expressed their amazement and horror, *surely some terrible mistake,* they teased.

Sitting around the dining room table one evening shortly after the results were published, my parents and I discussed the future. My mother, wonderful woman that she was, insisted that I go to university. No one had any idea where my talents or interests lay, but she was determined that university should be involved, if only to prise open the oyster. Accordingly she sent for a prospectus from various establishments the very next day, and when they arrived we spent hours in close perusal, hoping to stumble upon my true path to a useful future. I was slow to decide, and it soon became obvious that a fruitful enrolment for the coming year was out of the question. And so it happened that I had the best part of another year to use up, and the question was what would I do with it?

My father solved the problem. He had been managing a rich little gold mine near the town of Hartley for years and he enjoyed a certain respect in the district. He was popular, a good drinking fellow and on favour-exchanging terms with everyone. At the local pub one day shortly after our inconclusive hunt through the promotional material of at least three South African universities, he asked if anyone of his farmer friends needed an assistant for a while. I think he thought that if I once started in that direction, inertia would keep me at it and who knew? Perhaps I might again surprise everyone with unexpected aptitude – he was not all that enthusiastic about the idea of university, although he himself had studied at the Camborne School of Mines and had good reason to believe in tertiary education. As it happened, one of his friends did need someone for at least six weeks. Urgent family business meant he had to fly to Britain and would be gone at least that long and maybe longer. His was a dairy farm that he said more or less managed itself. In other words, little or no skill was required. But his wife and two young children would be there while he was away. I would have my own little cottage near the family house. My main role, as he candidly admitted to my father, was to be little more than a white-skinned male presence in a sea of black farm workers, a form of protection and a white deterrent against unwelcome black adventure. It was still several years before the start of the political troubles that would lead to war, few whites had heard of Robert Mugabe, and Rhodesia was peaceful and quiet, but still there were occasional incidents of black-on-white crime. While the man was away, his wife and children would feel much easier for having someone such as myself, a physically strong and energetic young man, close at hand; a 'kith and kin' reassurance I suppose.

I moved in, pleased beyond speech at the thought of having my own little home with my own little bathroom and my own little kitchen. I rose each morning before sunrise and walked down a hill to the dairy where I was to assume a sort of supervisory role, checking that all the dairymen had freshly scrubbed and sanitized hands, that the machinery was sparkling, that the water was hot, and so on. It was pretty easy stuff, undemanding, and as the man had said, the process largely looked after itself. Milking machines did most of the work and only a few cows needed to be milked by hand; they were the ones that had recently calved, and their milk was still high in *colostrum*, unacceptable for mixing in with the commercial flow.

It was a Sunday soon after I arrived when Barbie Darby came to the farm. She was related in some way to the family and apparently enjoyed regular visits with her cousins there. She was 12 years old at the time; tall, skinny, plain and neither intellectually nor sexually of interest to any young man of my age and cocky teen-age self-confidence.

It was about ten in the morning and I was still hard at work in the dairy – I worked seven days a week. I had quickly got the hang of things and I was busy milking one of the high colostrum cows myself. It is hard work that requires much effort from your thumbs, for they must apply a firm and rhythmic rolling pressure, left hand, right hand, left hand right hand. I looked up, to find a small group of spectators watching me, the family children and this skinny little someone who could have been a boy or a girl, with short hair and apparently no discernibly female figure at all. I carried on with the work and they all left.

Much later when I had finished at the dairy and was back in my cottage there was a knock on the door.

"Hello," this little person said. "My name's Barbara. I was just watching you working with the cows."

I didn't invite her in and stood at the open door, hoping that my attitude made it clear that I was not in the mood for children. At 16 the gulf between myself and any 12 year old was vast. She was a persistent little beggar however, brimming with self-confidence. "What you doing?" she asked.

"Oh I said, I've been up since four and I am just about to take a rest with a good book."

"Can I come in," she asked, "can I see your house?"

"Sure," I said, a little grudgingly, and stood aside. She darted in, quickly putting her nose into all the little corners and features of my somewhat basic home. I left her to her own devices and sat down on the comfortable armchair by my bed, picked up my book and began to read.

"People call me Barbie," she said, interrupting my attempted concentration, "it's because of the doll more than just a short name for Barbara, you know."

"Oh," I said. "That's um, that's interesting," closing the book politely and hiding my irritation as best I could.

"I'd hate to have my tits pulled around like that," she said.

"You'd what?" I burst out, slightly stunned and not entirely sure I had heard her correctly. "What *are* you talking about?"

"Oh it's about the cows being milked. I said I wouldn't like to have my tits pulled around like you were doing to that poor cow."

"Don't worry," I said, recovering my equilibrium and determined to regain control. "You're not a cow and you haven't got anything worth pulling for milk anyway."

In a flash she had her top off, and there, revealed, were the sweetest little emerging buds I had ever seen in my own short life. There was much more to this scrawny little body that I could possibly have imagined, and to tell the truth, I began to feel awkwardly aroused, at the same time feeling dangerously guilty because of it. I realised I should end the episode before it could possibly go any further, although to be truthful, I had no real idea of what that might imply for I was without any real sexual awareness or experience at the time.

"I have to go now," I lied. "I need to check one or two things down at the dairy. You can come if you like and I will show you the machinery and explain how it works."

"Don't you want to kiss me?" she said.

Shocked again! Shocked and wrong footed. But I was already out of the chair and walking to the door so I ignored the question and she did not see my bright red face. She followed me, skipping and bouncing her steps in a happy way, unfazed, oblivious to the rebuff.

"How old are you?" she asked as we were going down the road to the dairy.

"Much older than you," I said. "Sixteen, seventeen soon," I lied.

"I'm nearly fourteen," she lied.

"You're very fast," I said.

"You mean running and that?"

"No, asking to be kissed like that. You could get into lots of trouble."

I didn't know for certain what that meant either; in those days it was the way people spoke of girls, and boys, who were sexually forward, in other words I supposed, easily taken to bed and made pregnant.

"Oh," she said, "does that mean you don't like me?"

"Hold out your hands to me, palms down," I said, deflecting the conversation. Taking her two forefingers in hand with my thumbs up, I squeezed each in turn, in the rhythmic motion of milking. "That's how it is done," I said. "And if you had any milk in your fingers it would now be coming out in a steady stream. Any questions?"

"Are you sure you don't want to kiss me?"

"I'm sure."

Now she was biting her lip, and a tear rolled down her face, which, for the first time, began to look ever so pretty to me.

"You don't like me," she said and she turned and ran off back to the family house. I was left to myself in the dairy, and I did not see her again for nearly twenty years, until that day at *The Watering Hole*. I was 36, and she, bloody hell, was an unbelievably beautiful 32.

Chapter 5

Smuts came from an unusual family background which may have explained his own ever unconventional, and to me at least, often sage-like personality. He seemed instinctively to understand issues, he was seldom openly emotional or unbalanced, always interested, never pushy. I grew to think of him as a rock and a genius.

He was an only child, the son of a mining engineer employed by one of the great South African mining houses of the time. Although of entirely English descent, he was named after an Afrikaner, the former South African Prime Minister, General Jan Smuts, for whom his father had unbounded admiration.

His father, Arthur, had gained eminence for some highly original approaches to the blasting of certain kinds of underground rock found in the mining industry of South Africa in the early 1930s. For that he was highly respected and highly paid, so that the family lived very well indeed, *most of the time*. The trouble was that in addition to being a brilliant engineer, Mr. Arthur Brander was an addicted gambler. Not just any common gambler, he had a rare and curious form of talent to mitigate the addiction. Without any apparent effort of will power he could stay away from any form of gambling for months, even years, at a time. There was no known trigger to send him off on a spree, and, equally, no explanation for the sudden end to that spree; he might quit while ahead or deeply in debt. In fact, when he married Smuts' mother Dot, he had been 'clean' for a year or more. He had confessed his problem to her at the time he proposed, but, being wildly in love, she said she understood, thought she could deal with it, and hoped to be able to help.

Then, while pregnant with Smuts, there was an unpleasant incident in which Arthur lost heavily in a game of poker and had to sell the house to settle the debt. The reality of serious gambling proved such a shock to Dorothy that she went home to her parents, leaving Arthur with the assurance that she was never coming back. He set about restoring his fortune and his marriage in the only way he knew, accomplishing both quite soon thereafter, enjoying such success in a steady run of poker that he was able to offer her a new and far more luxurious home to come home to, with the bonus of her own small car. It was an offer she happily accepted.

When Smuts was born Arthur was so delighted with family life that for a long time there was no further hint of trouble. It reached the point where Dorothy was more than happy to try for a second child, which they both hoped would be a girl. Life for the Brander family was grand. A new baby was created, but died at birth. Those in on the secret of Arthur's disease prophesied to each other that the shock of the loss would drive him quite soon to the tables, but it did no such thing.

Several years passed and there was no further sign of an addition to the family, nor of a return to gambling. Smuts reached the age of eleven, and it appeared to Dorothy that Arthur was cured. They were living well and Smuts was attending one of Johannesburg's most expensive private schools as a 'dayboy', that is to say a scholar who went home after classes each day, thus distinguished from most of the boys whose distant homes meant they had to be school boarders.

On his way home one Friday, a journey that involved twenty minutes by train and ten minutes on foot from the local station to their house, he had got off at the station and was walking the short distance home when a car drew up on the road beside him. In it were his mother and his uncle, her brother.

"Jump in"", said his uncle, you are going away with Dot for a few weeks holiday."

It turned out that Arthur had lost everything in a poker game that Wednesday and the house and two cars were being sold. There was no question of divorce for Dot, it was just that she recognised instinctively that Arthur needed the spur of loneliness to settle the debt, find a new home, and get back to normal family life.

Later, in his school report for the period, the Headmaster commented: 'Smuts is a clever boy who would have done better but for his long absence from school this term'.

They were gone for almost two months, taking refuge on a guest farm in the mountains of the Orange Free State. There are photographs of Smuts and his mother on this holiday, smiling happily as they fed the horses and other farm animals, but the whole episode was quite puzzling for the young boy. He understood little of the background, and to all his questions as to Arthur's absence from this unplanned family holiday, his mother merely replied that he was 'too busy'. Evidently Dorothy had come to terms with Arthur's curious lifestyle, accepting with confidence that even after the biggest bust, the good life would almost certainly be restored to her. A letter from Arthur eventually brought the 'holiday' to an end and they took a train back to Johannesburg. There at the station to meet them and hug them and kiss them, was Arthur, jingling with obvious pride a set of car keys. Parked outside by the main Eloff Street station entrance was a brand new Buick.

All Dorothy could say as she settled into the luxury of new and expensive leather, was "You! Oh Arthur! You!"

He beamed, for Dorothy was his life.

As far as anyone knew he had never once so much as looked at another woman with serious intent. Nothing gave him greater pleasure than to please her, except of course, when he succumbed to the lure of a turning number or flip of a card.

And so life progressed for the Branders. Years afterwards, when we talked of it, a few months after our first meeting, Smuts told me that much the same thing had happened on two or three other occasions in his school days.

"Dot always had a bolt-hole for the two of us. She was always ready, and as far as I know she never complained or threatened Arthur. We simply bumbled on, knowing that there would be other dramas of loss and then recovery. We only knew it would happen but there was no predicting when, I don't think he himself had a clue as to what drove him. He was just very, very good at the great gambling act that was his life."

When the time came for Smuts to think of University, Arthur encouraged him to consider a degree in Accounting, probably in the belief that a good and solid foundation in something so conservative and bound by form, rule and system, would insulate him against the chance that deep down, the joy of massive risk might be embedded in his genes.

It was advice that Smuts readily accepted. For all of Arthur's occasional incomprehensible behaviour, Smuts got on well with him, adored him, believed in him, and respected his considerable achievements. When he was old enough to know the whole story, he thought it a feat of extraordinary concentration and mind power that his father had always managed to more than recover his losses, however large they might be. How many times had he lost his home, his cars, and the complete family bank balance? And yet there had never been more than a few months at a time of the slightest sense of being destitute or needy. Arthur was indeed incredible.

Only one thing marred the outlook for Smuts as he set off for the cloistered life of accountancy at a small provincial university. He had had an excellent passage through school, easily passing from year to year without extending himself, playing first team rugby and cricket in his final year, and generally being liked and even admired for his cool detachment. But if there was anything that threatened a brilliant future it was this very thing, the cool detachment which could easily be interpreted as too casual an attitude of *couldn't-care-less*. The fact is that at school he did not have to worry nearly as much as he did at home. School life was tightly regimented, and he went from class to class, game to game, lunchtime to catch-the-train-home time, in an endless routine that was effortlessly endured.

From such an environment to that of University was a slide downhill to joy and rapture. A loose system governed attendance at lectures, tutorials and seminars, depending never on cane or rod, and always on willing compliance. Like myself, Smuts was 16 when he left school, and arriving at University at that age was for him a heady experience that easily obscured the target of education.

There was one other thing: the sudden and unexpected free association with girls, hundreds of them. There were girls in his class, girls lounging on benches in the quad, girls in the library, at the university café, girls everywhere, and most of them seemed to Smuts to be looking excitement, for friendship, even for love. They were easy to meet and get to talk to because for the first six weeks of life at that university, new students were obliged to wear a placard on the chest identifying themselves and the 'house' to which they belonged. No formal introduction was required; if he saw someone he fancied, he knew who she was and where to telephone her. And vice versa for all the many young girls who looked hard at Smuts and found him interesting, appealing, and probably a little mysteriously attractive.

It was not long before Smuts was in what we now call 'a relationship' or what was then known as 'pushing'. Smuts was 'pushing' Brenda. She had become his girl.

In some way like his father, he later told me, he pulled off a stunning balancing act. Despite missing days and even weeks of lectures in his first year, he passed all his exams with good marks, progressing as planned to the second year of a three-year degree course in Commerce. His girlfriend Brenda in that first year was known as Boo, and the two of them were quite devoted to each other. Unfortunately Boo did not manage the balancing act in quite the same way. At the end of the year she failed miserably and her parents declined to sponsor a second attempt. Boo took a secretarial job in a town unfortunately close to the university, which meant that Smuts was able to visit her most weekends, which he did. Driving to her home and back to university once a week proved to be too much for a successful repeat of his first year results, and for the first time in his life he failed his year-end examinations.

Arthur was phlegmatic. Doubtless his own feet of occasional clay kept them on the ground at least.

"My own experience of love has been happy with your Mum," he commented when the truth of Smut's year was revealed to him over a glass of wine one evening, "but I have known many men who made idiots of themselves chasing the crystal slipper. All I can tell you my boy is this: be true to yourself and choose your own focus. If you think this girl Boo is the most important thing in your life, do the damn thing properly. Marry her, give up your degree, and get a job, any job just sufficient to keep you both in reasonably fair shape, have babies. But don't, whatever you do, dither. Don't fiddle around somewhere in the middle ground between screwing your arse off and working to make yourself employable in the class from which you come."

It was as close as Smuts had ever known his father to be judgemental. He did not have to ask for Arthur's advice on the choice to be made. In his usual candid way, when he went back to varsity after the Christmas break, he called Boo and told her what he had decided. Their affair was over.

"I can't afford to love you any more you wonderful woman," he said. "And I cannot ask you to wait another two years while I beat this degree thing into shape. I have loved you dearly and you know with how much passion, I still do, but now it is *Good Bye, so long, tot siens, au revoir.*"

When, many years later, he told me this in the most matter of fact sort of way, I thought to myself, not for the first time or the last: *cool, balanced, studied – he can blow smoke rings under fire, a good man to be with when skull busting objects come flying at you from all directions.*

Smuts went on to two successful years of study after his one aberration, emerging with a respectable but undistinguished B.Com degree that pleased his parents but in no way excited him.

"Over the degree course," he told me, "I soon began to believe that the only thing it was preparing me for was a life of accountancy or auditing. I never really wanted to be a bean

46

counter, but that's what I was going to be unless I took early and direct action."

After Arthur and Dot had come to the University for Smuts' graduation ceremony, the three of them went out for dinner to discuss his next steps. Arthur, of course, was well placed to get him into an articled arrangement with any one of the best of the partnerships then running professional accounting in South Africa.

"Thanks, but no thanks," Smuts told them. "I am pleased and grateful to you for the opportunity and now of course for the degree, but it is behind me. With your blessing I am going to do something entirely different. I'm going into business."

"I have always liked your field of work Arthur, "he said, "and I am thinking of starting a mining supply business myself. Over the next few years I am going to learn everything I possibly can about mining technology and equipment. I want to become THE specialist. I'll look for up-coming equipment manufacturers and represent them. That;s it in a nutshell, what do you think?"

Dot was stunned, Arthur impressed. Naturally enough he was flattered by his son's admiration for his field of enterprise, and he said so.

"It is a canny move and I can help you, my boy. Mining everywhere is still somewhat in the dark ages. World War Two held it up for a long time but now, in this post-war period, the world is beginning to boom and there is a desperate search on for commodities. New mines will be opening up all over the place. I think there will be massive developments soon and they will continue over your life time bringing equally massive opportunities. I'll start working on a paper straight away."

And that was how Smuts started his business life. It wasn't easy, and it did not do particularly well for some years, but there was always enough to encourage him to continue, and being based in Johannesburg meant that he was able to carry on enjoying a degree of home life with Arthur and Dot.

At the age of 48 Dot was found to have a particularly virulent form of cancer and she died in less than three months. As was widely expected, Arthur did not long survive her.

With a good inheritance to back him and wanting to get away from the sorrow of his home situation Smuts decided sometime in the early sixties to move to Rhodesia, and there, amid the many political excitements of the time, he flourished. After the country's unilateral declaration of Independence in 1965, he found his way around the international economic sanctions that swiftly followed, and became a reliable supplier of important bits and pieces used in the mining industry. The only discouraging feature of his life was that in due course he was obliged to join the Territorial Army. Like myself, he was still well within the ever increasing army eligibility age bracket. But unlike myself, he obeyed the call as soon as it came. He had been in the army for more than a year by the time of my first call-up.

Chapter 6

I was trying to explain to Tina why I thought joining the army's new psychological operations unit was attractive to me and good for us. The conversation took an unexpected turn.

"I have no idea whether it is a good thing to do for the country, or for the outcome of the war, but it should be interesting and, to be absolutely honest, much safer for me personally. If you think that is hypocritical of me, say so."

"Well it is isn't it?" she said with obvious irritation and perhaps rather more honesty than I might have preferred.

"Not that I want you or anyone else to be in danger, but if you're doing it just to get away from the possibility of being killed or wounded, why not just do the more honourable thing and leave. Give up, leave now. That's what I would like us to do."

"Because we can't. I told you, it isn't that easy, we would leave with nothing and I'm not sure I could start up again quickly anywhere else. I'd have to take a job, which I am absolutely constitutionally unprepared for. But to be truthful, I am not sure that I am willing to go. I like it here, I like my job and I tolerate the army. Plus there is also the prospect that in this new outfit I will be working with my head instead of my gun-holding hands to improve life for all Rhodesians, black and white. I will be involved in trying to convince the black majority that we have seen the light, that we recognise their aspirations and that we want to work towards a common goal. If we can get them to withhold their support from the nationalist gooks and give us a chance to make a better place for them as well as for ourselves it would be the best way towards a truly better life for all."

"You mean you will be trying to manipulate them psychologically before sending them all to Auschwitz?"

"Hey," I said. "That is uncalled for. Just remember this. For all your idealism, which is now somewhat of a revelation to me, we are in a war not of our own choosing. It may be said that we are to blame for it, but only in the sense that we have not been prepared to hand over the management of the country to people we don't think are capable of doing it properly. This is not a discussion that I really want to have. We are here, we've been enjoying the life that Rhodesia has been so excellently able to offer us at what I personally never thought of as in any way being at the expense of black people.

"Do you know Tina what was the first thing the nationalists had to do before they could even think of making war to achieve their objective? They had to do some serious psychological manipulation of their own people. They first had to convince their otherwise reasonably happy and content fellows that they were badly dealt with and unhappy. It took them years to make people understand how unhappy they ought to be and even then they did not find it easy. They had to tell their people they were unhappy because they did not know it for themselves."

"Slow down Hunter, slow down. I know what you are saying, and yes we have taken the best of Rhodesia and so I concede, it might be indecent to bolt at the first sign of a bit of uphill. Anyway, who are all these people, where do you suddenly find hundreds of psychologists for a whole army company?"

"Thank you," I replied, easily mollified, "well, not everyone in Psy Ops has to be a psychologist. I don't know exactly what the structure will be, but I imagine there may be one or two qualified shrinks who help decide the tunes we must play, but most of us psychological foot soldiers will have been involved in psychological activity in a way, through, let us say, hidden persuasion, which is just another name or a different spelling for advertising and public relations.

"As far as I know the unit will be made up of people who are involved in marketing in their ordinary working lives. They will be writers and artists from advertising agencies, executives from big brand companies. They, 'we', will spend much of our time working to see if we can come up with really good and honest ideas to tell people there can be a better future for them by, say, following a conservative path rather than the madness of Marxism that we expect from Mugabe's people.

"And the best part of it, for me at any rate, is that for most of my call-ups I will be working right here in Salisbury at the army barracks. I think, but I don't know for sure, that I will be coming home at night most of the time, so in a sense I will just be changing clothes – civvies for six weeks, camouflage kit for the next six. And I'll still be able to look in at the office and make sure the business is carrying on. In every way that must be better for us. If the time comes for us to get out we will be better placed and the mortgage more nearly paid for."

"We'll see," she said, obviously not wholly convinced. "But anyway, here's to you and your new army. Just don't you dare try out your psychological arts at home. Leave me out of it; I don't want to know what goes on or hear what you are doing or where you are going. OK?"

We drank a toast in a fresh local red wine with an absurd Italian name, something like Da Vinci, which we both proclaimed to be utterly undrinkable but enjoyed it just the same, a pungent concoction that we agreed owed little or nothing to a vineyard. In truth it wasn't all that bad, but we had become ever so slightly wine snobbish in those days because good South African wines were usually readily available on the black market. Secretly I think we were also quite proud of Rhodesia's ability to make-do while fighting a war in which we had so few friends in the world, even down to the production of a sharp little red wine made from cheese or bread, or left-over tea, or indeed whatever else might ferment.

"Where did you find it?" Tina asked, setting me up for the old one-two.

"At the bottle store down the road, it's not hard to get."

"Doesn't travel well does it?"

And so the matter of my army future was settled for the moment, the first hurdle successfully negotiated. If Tina was not exactly on my side, at least she was prepared to hold her breath for a while.

I'd be meeting with Ross sometime next week to try to get the transfer moving smoothly along whatever channels were involved, and quietly hoping that it could be arranged in time for my next call-up due then in just a few weeks. At the same time I planned to discuss with him the possibility of making it a double offer and getting my friend Smuts involved too.

I told Tina of the meeting although I must confess I was thinking ahead in deceit, using the plan as a possible cover for my coming meeting with the widow.

"I'll take Ross to *the Hole* after work next Tuesday," I said. "I'll try to get everything resolved soon. I don't particularly want to go back to the bush. The last call-up was a horror story."

"Don't tell me about it, I don't want to know."

Chapter 7

By a quarter to five on the appointed evening I was at *The Hole,* feeling only mildly guilty because I was deceiving Tina, but nonetheless excited and looking forward with more than passing curiosity to a further meeting with the Widow Flanagan.

Barbie Darby arrived on the dot of five, more plainly dressed than the week before, but still striking. She was a well-tailored widow, a clothes horse if ever there was one.

She sat down with me at the bar. We looked at each other, both registering a silent 'what next' with well-manufactured smiles and raised eyebrows.

"Well, what next?" she said, reading the thought and giving it words.

"What next indeed." I said with a silly laugh. "Well, let's get a drink and lubricate the conversation," I offered, and that's exactly what we did. She drank Scotch whisky.

"You could start, if you like, by telling me more about who you are now and how you happened to be in the pub to pick me up last week."

"It wasn't a classic pick-up," she replied archly, "I recognized you. I remembered the day long ago, the only day we ever met. I was a brat for sure. I remember the incident well and the milking of the fingers. I must have seemed a proper little trollop to you, whipping off my top as I did. Believe it or not, that was my first truly overt sexual gesture, and I'm not so sure that it was really all about the mystery of sex. I think I just wanted to be friends and I thought *you* thought I was too little to be bothered with. And, of course, I was proud of my budding boobs. I thought they made me quite grown up.

"What would have happened if you had taken the chance for a kiss and a cuddle I am not sure at all. Anything was possible. I could easily have lost control, for I had then and still have, few inhibitions. You were a pretty boy, fresh, young, hair tightly cropped, tall, skinny, and, I thought, somewhat superior. You still are some of that."

"Grief!" I said. "Which part? Surely not fresh and young, not so skinny, certainly not superior…"

"Let's have another Scotch," she said, "and then you can tell me about yourself, where life took you after that single memorable day. Are you a farmer? Do you still milk cows?"

We ordered another drink and I ignored all her questions. I wondered how long it would be before Barbie asked if I was married. She never did.

We began instead to talk more about her. That was easy because she had called herself 'The widow Flanagan' as if there was some fame and frame to the title.

I asked. "Who was Mr. Flanagan, and what happened to him?"

"You're side-tracking me," she said, "but what the heck, if you want to know, I'll tell you."

She mused a second or two before continuing, almost as if she needed to put all the pieces together first, as if she had not yet really grasped the size of the story herself.

"Flanagan," she said with a gentle sigh. "My wonderful husband Jim."

"He was an old man of 47 when I met him, that seemed so old to me at the time but of course now I know it's not at all old; prime of life really, twenty-five years older than I was. He was a crocodile hunter and he lived in Zambia. He was born there when it was still Northern Rhodesia He wasn't a wolf, didn't seem to care much about women, but when we met at a party I liked him right away. He was quiet but he had an air of authority about him. He spoke, but not too much; he drank, but not heavily. He was cool, perhaps too cool, almost remote.

"I liked him so much after about a half-hour in his company that I did something I probably never have done since the day I met you - no I didn't take my dress off!

"We were standing in a little social ring around a woman playing the guitar and singing like someone famous who I couldn't quite name, when on an impulse I took his hand in mine and gave it a little squeeze. He looked down at me, for he was very tall, laughed

54

softly and returned the squeeze. Not long afterwards he said "Come, let's get out of here. Time to go." And of course we did, and we stayed together in a hotel, and we were married within a month. We were together nearly eight years and I don't think we ever had a fight of any kind. It was not a spectacular marriage but it was so wonderfully settled and happy. He made a lot of money and we lived well. Sadly, although I did not think it at the time because I was so happy to be alone with Jim, we had no children."

I was watching her as she told the story, looking for her to reveal some emotion. It had the makings of a sad ending obviously, but I was surprised at her composure. She had put the pieces together now, and she had no difficulty in talking about it.

"What happened to him?"

"He died. He was killed, actually. Killed in the most stupid fashion. I didn't kill him, but it was really my fault."

"Don't talk about it if you don't want to," I said. "I'll order another Scotch."

"Don't worry, I'm fine. I never blame myself, that's much too negative for me, an indulgence actually, one that would be neither true nor in any sense healing. And in any case my only part in the process was to distract him, but it cost his life. But order a Scotch I'm fine with that too."

We drank a few Scotches that night and we felt very easy together. I had pushed guilt so far into the background that it ceased to exist. My wife Tina too, simply ceased to exist.

"You know," she said. "The thing is that Jim was a strange man in some ways. He had been hunting crocodiles illegally for so long that he couldn't change. People were starting up crocodile farms left and right along the Zambezi and they were all doing well, in total safety. He could easily have started a farm himself, but he preferred a bit of danger, both from crocodiles and, I suppose, the police, although I think in Zambia the police knew all about his activities. They liked him and they looked the other way.

"We lived in a small town on the road between Livingstone and Lusaka, and he would go away hunting for two or three weeks at a time, never taking me with him. To be honest I didn't want to go any more than most wives want to join their husbands at work. It was enough to have loads of money in the bank, to be able to take holidays in Europe once a year, and buy nice clothes.

"Do you want to hear more?" she asked. "Just another life really…"

"Tell me everything," I replied. "I'm fascinated. I had no idea you could make a living killing wild crocs. I know you can catch them at night if you are mad enough. A fisherman golfer once brought a whole lot of small crocs captured at night in Lake Kariba and put them in a dam at one of the golf courses here. I think they are still alive and thriving, probably on a diet of frogs and fish, not to mention people's puppies..."

"All I know is that the way Jim did it was quite dangerous. And yes, you're right about it being night work. He had a boat and two Zambians working with him, and from what I heard, the crocs he was after were much bigger than the ones killed on croc farms for their soft young belly skin. I know little more except that he had his own agents in Europe, which is why we went over so often. I think he later had an arrangement with one of the farms to pass off his skins as theirs. We didn't speak much about those things.

"Anyway, a cousin of mine came to visit us for a couple of months. He was a brash little sod and he obviously felt that Jim didn't really work and that in any case he was much too old for me. Jim was slightly irritated ny his cocky manner but it did not rattle him in the way it rattled me. One day when Jim was away on a hunt, the little bugger made some disparaging remark to me to the effect that the old man was probably away at a gym on a physical training course so that he could cope with his young wife. It was meant to be funny I'm sure, but it pushed me to a little outburst and I told him that the 'old man' was twenty times the man he would ever be, and that I would arrange for him to see exactly what Jim did for a living.

56

"When Jim came home that time I did not tell him exactly what my cousin had said, but I begged him to take us with him on his next trip. I played a little on his pride and said how much it would please me to have my squirty little cousin see how dangerously physical the work could be.

"He agreed, to my surprise. "We'll do it then," he said. "We'll go soon."

"Jim had a place on the lake as I said. It was a hilly, almost mountainous area and his living there was rough, just a tent or two. The so-called boat was just a planked platform on oil drums with a big motor at one end and a couple of boxes for stowing stuff away, and for the crew to sit on while travelling and waiting for the real work. In the centre was a fairly large well, big enough to take the carcasses of two or three crocs at a time.

"Work never began before dark, and the darker the better. We didn't have to go far that night. You found crocs simply by shining a very powerful torchlight low across the surface of the water. In the light their bright eyes popped up like stars in the sky, you couldn't miss them. Then we'd ease up slowly towards those bright shining eyes, get real close to confirm the animal was of a reasonable size, and if Jim liked it, he'd shoot it, simple as that. The hard part then was to get the croc before it sank to the bottom and was lost. One of the men had a long gaff attached to an even longer rope, and the instant the shot hit home, it was his job to gaff the croc and hold it while it was thrashing around – if he could. The hook was barbed so that it did not matter too much if he couldn't hold on because the croc would run out the length of rope and then most likely die in the mud below; to be heaved back on board. The bigger the croc the tougher that man's job. Smaller ones were easy, but then Jim was mainly after the big brutes.

"So that's how it was that night with my young cousin. I suppose we must have done five or six and returned the bodies to shore for skinning. Then we went out one more time, the last time ever for Jim.

"About five or six meters from the shore in a little creek we found a croc that Jim considered ideal. Carefully he set up for the shot up and gently pulled the trigger. The man with the gaff did his job too, but the croc was bigger or stronger or less dead, and was thrashing around more than usual. Without waiting to be asked for help my silly cousin rushed forward to lend a hand, but somehow he slipped on the wet deck and got in the way. In the general chaos that followed he managed to fall into the water. Jim shouted and swore and immediately jumped into the water to get the boy out. The gaff was dropped, the croc vanished and the water was erupting. I watched in terror, but quickly Jim surfaced with his arm around my cousin, and he pushed him up into waiting outstretched arms on the platform. Then he tried to lift himself up but couldn't do it. Even in the torchlight I could make out that he was in big trouble. He looked drawn and grey. Someone helped him up. There was blood everywhere. Jim had the time and strength only to say in a half-whisper 'Hippo'.

"That was it. A hippo, disturbed by all that was going on, had lashed out and bitten his leg, almost severing it and opening the femoral artery. In the warm water his heart swiftly emptied him, pumping his blood out in what must have been a single massive gush. It took no more than a few seconds and I was a widow.

"He was a good man and I loved him more than my own life, and that's why I still wear the widow label so proudly. It's like my personal identification card. I like to be known as the Widow Flanagan. It keeps me close to him in a way that still manages to surprise my friends. They all think I'm crazy, and perhaps I am."

Lost for words, I mumbled artlessly "what a thing to happen, what an unbelievably tragic end to a real love story".

Then, still mumbling, I said. "Maybe now is a good time to change the subject. Shall we eat?

"Here?"

"No, no one who has had a meal here ever eats here again. Great as a watering hole, desperate as a diner. How do you like Chinese?"

"I like it fine," she said. "Are you free?"

"I'll need to make a quick call, but yes, I'm free."

I called home.

"Sorry Tina, I am tied up, I may be out for a couple of hours. Don't wait up."

I could tell she was irritated by the strange little cough she always had when really aroused to anger, and I wasn't surprised. She hung up with a cool "Good night".

We dropped in at the Golden Dragon, some called it the Golden Cockroach, but the food was good and it was fairly private with head-high cubicles for diners.

"Don't you want to be seen with me?" Barbie asked as I piloted her into one of these cubicles.

"Hell no," I lied. "One of my hungry men friends is bound to take a look at you and want to cut in, and I'm not having that when we've only just met."

I knew she would take it as a fairy story but I hoped she would also see it as the compliment I intended. In any case she did not push it any further.

We drank a little and we ate, and then we drank some more and ate some more, the conversation trivial. One of the topics, naturally enough, was about my business. She seemed interested in Public Relations.

"It's my own field, I'm a natural," she told me. "I've been working for a PR company in Lusaka since shortly after Jim died, but, look at me, I have been studying image projection all my life. Why don't you employ me and I'll show you some real skills."

"Serious?" I asked, "Looking at you I wouldn't have thought you needed a job."

"I don't really, but I've had enough of Zambia and I think I'd like to work with you."

It was an invitation to disaster, but I was far too flattered and aroused to see much further than an hour or two ahead.

"It was your wife you called wasn't it?" she asked.

"Christina May," I admitted, "and now I am wondering how to explain myself; what big lie will I be able to conjure up for tonight's long absence. Not that it matters all that much, it is a marriage in cold storage, but I do try to avoid confrontation."

I took her hand and squeezed it, just a gentle little squeeze.

"You sod," she said with a happy giggle, "you absolute sod, you don't miss much do you? But I can help you with your story if you like. Tell your wife you were actually out with an investor, someone exactly like me, a widow with lots of money and a deep desire to be involved in the country's youngest, most important public relations company. That should hold it for a while."

"What a good idea, but how do I explain how this has come about so suddenly, where did you hear about my business, and how did we meet?"

"Tell the truth, or as near the truth as you can. Tell her you knew me many years ago and that I just popped out of the woodwork, we bumped into each other in a bar, oh, just the other day. You thought so little of it that you didn't think it worth mentioning. Then I bumped into you again this evening and we talked, long and hard, about business."

"Now," she said, "this project will have to wait. I too have some explaining to do and it is time I went home."

"Boy friend?" I asked, assuming that if she still called herself the Widow Flanagan it was highly unlikely she was married again.

"No, sadly not," she returned, "but I do have a dying mother at home, and she gets quite agitated if I am out late without warning."

We drove back in silence to where she had left her car. As I opened her door for her, she leaned forward and kissed me, lightly.

"By the way," she said, "I really do want to buy into your business. That part is true."

"You're on," I said on an impulse. "Let us meet soon to speak of terms, but I am interested. I think you would be a great partner for the business.

"If not tomorrow then the day after," she answered. "There is someone I need to consult."

It was not quite the ending to the evening that I had hoped for, pleasantly piqued but mildly confused. I thought back to a time in Hong Kong, years before, when I was taken to a bar in Wan Chai. My male friend and I had ordered drinks from a tall and elegant woman in a room that looked nothing like a bar, and were then shown through to two little cubicles, each with a young Chinese girl waiting iside. As she left us, the *Mama San*, for that is what she was, turned to me and said, "by the way Sir, the girls are not allowed to make love."

But that is a different story.

Chapter 8

It was no surprise to me when I got home late to find that Tina was awake, sitting with her feet up, snug on the couch in the lounge, hugging a mug of coffee and staring out of a window into the blackness beyond. She did not look at me as I came in. Evidently she had rehearsed the scene.

"OK," she said, "do you want to tell me all about it now? What is going on? Who were you with? Why do I feel that I am being lied to and badly used?"

"In the first place," I told her," it isn't as if any of this should come as a surprise. It is not as if we are the world's most loving couple. In fact we are hardly a couple at all. And haven't been for God knows how many years. And in all that time I have only put a foot wrong twice – once to go to a boy's night out that proved to be a bit of a porn show, which I didn't tell you about. And tonight, sort of. I bumped into someone I knew when first I left school. A child she was then, but a widow now. We found we had a lot in common and much to talk about. But that's the extent of my lying and wife abuse so far. Would you like to hear it in a little more detail?"

"Go ahead. Sounds like you are making your story into nothing more than a memorial to a dead horse, but I may as well hear it all."

I did not hold back. As best I could I recounted the story of my meeting with Barbara at *The Hole*, and later.

"That night when you came to me at the pub, I had just said good bye to her, Barbara Flanagan. As planned, I had been with Ross discussing the army thing. He left, and I was about to come home when out of nowhere this rather visible woman materialised and asked me if I remembered her, if I was Hunter Hill.

"For the life of me I couldn't remember her at first, but we had a drink and she reminded me of a day on the farm when I had just left school, and then I did remember, but she had to go before we could really chat about it.

"It was all very curious, I was piqued and interested and I agreed to meet again about a week later to fill in the gaps and to get to know each other. She introduced herself as The Widow Flanagan, or Barbie Darby, which is who she was when we first came across each other as little more than children. I won't say we met all those years ago because we were only together for about an hour or so and since she was so much younger there was not much in the way of a formal introduction.

"You know Tina, meeting up with her now has been quite a shattering experience. She has an exceptional presence, I don't think she is particularly beautiful, but she has something very compelling, and the experience rocked me, I am still in a mess about it and I can't get her out of my mind. I went out with her again tonight to hear her story, the upshot of which is that, in a way, I think I have been head hunted. Mrs. Flanagan is a Public Relations executive in Zambia and I think she has been looking around to buy, or buy into, a public relations business here because this is where her dying mother now lives. She has money, PR experience, and she needs to pick up her life again after the death of her husband. When the name Hunter Hill and Associates came up as one of the contemporary PR outfits in town she remembered me. I think she is genuinely interested in the company, but still she is smart, and finding there was something personal in our backgrounds, she was not above using it. I'm hooked. Haven't yet had a chance to wriggle, but I'm hooked. I can only ask you to hang in there and see the business through. I will meet with her again and we will discuss the company. Who knows, this could mean a way out, the end of Rhodesia for us. If I get enough for the company we can go, and I'll not have to look for work straight away when we leave."

Well, up to a point it was the truth, and I thought it was convincing. There was little that Tina could legitimately complain about, except for the fact that I had not told her the evening it first started. And yet she must have seen more into it, more even than I did.

I certainly had not mentioned the squeeze of the hand and the kiss on the cheek, nor had I said anything about the beating of my heart or the rushing of my blood.

"Are you alright with it?" I asked.

"I really don't know. I'll have to think it through. Why don't you go to bed now, I'll just sit up awhile. Just one question. Do you want to sleep with her?"

I didn't hesitate.

"Yes," I said. "I can think of little else."

It had been long day with much emotion and mental changing of gears. It worried me that with all that was going on with Tina, I could still only think of Barbie, but I was tired enough to take the hint, and minutes later I was wrapped in the arms of Morpheus, unburdened for the moment, but nothing like easy in my mind.

When I awoke next morning Tina was gone. I wandered around the house in a state of quiet shock. It had been stripped of her presence. Her cupboards were bare; there was nothing left of her. The wedding photograph of the two of us that sat on the mantelpiece in the lounge was gone.

Had I behaved that badly, I asked myself, was my performance worthy of a walk out? Was it only the fact that I confessed to wanting to sleep with the widow? That would do it, I thought. So there I was. Alone, troubled and confused, but yet oddly excited by what now seemed to be an open highway to where I wanted to go.

Chapter 9

First thing I did at the office was to call Tina's school and ask if I could speak to her. Was it important? Not really, I said. Good, she's in class at the moment, can you call again at break time, between ten and ten thirty? Certainly I could. It was a relief to know that she was at school and hadn't done anything wild. Not that I thought she was the kind of disappointed partner to kill herself for love, let alone love *for me*, but I had worried a bit without being able to tell myself exactly what I feared. It was unlikely that she might have flown home to her family in South Africa at such short notice, but then, anything was possible. I called again at ten and she was friendlier than I expected. Friendly, but firm.

"I'm alright, "she said. "You don't have to worry about me. I've got somewhere to stay, no I won't tell you where or who with. I'm safe, I'm as happy as I possibly can be at a time like this, and I don't want to be in your way, which I would be if I was at home with you. Good luck with the Widow Twankey."

"Flanagan."

"Wanker."

"Oh all right, I get it, just bang away at me, make me feel bad. I'll call every day," I said. "Let me know if you need anything."

"I will thanks." Click. She hung up.

And then I called Ross to ask him about the army. Nothing doing just yet, he told me.

"Very unlikely to come through before your next call up in fact, but don't worry we'll keep a place warm for you after that.

"What about Smuts?" I asked.

"Haven't you heard," he asked.

"Heard about what?"

"Smuts has put in for a transfer to the Scouts."

"No!" I was stunned. "He seemed keen when last we spoke. I wonder what changed his mind..."

"Ask him, it hasn't happened yet as far as I know, and probably won't for a while so you'll likely be together for your next call up at least."

I tried to call Smuts but he was away from the office. I would call him later.

I wondered what had made him do such a thing. *'The Scouts'* meant The Selous Scouts, according to legend a tough unit of fearsome individuals if ever there was one. Well, that was what I thought, and most of my contemporaries thought so too. The Scouts, it was said, were somewhat of a private army within the Rhodesian Army. They were chosen for toughness, determination, independence and self-sufficiency. They could operate together, in small groups, or alone. The naked African bush held no terrors for any of them, for they were trained to survive in any situation. When they ran out of lunch they could catch and cook a lizard or a frog and munch away quite happily on some hideous reptilian portion. In fact their selection course was reputed to be a course of privation, deprivation, and very unusual meals, of which frogs and lizards were only the most nauseating to the ears of ordinary mortal soldiers. Aspirants might be sent off for days, even weeks at a time, with no rations, no radio, no back-up, to make their way alone from Point A to Point B a hundred miles away with a pack full of carefully marked bricks that must at the end be returned to the Quartermasters store on pain of failure.

Not surprisingly those who made it through the course were welcomed as brothers, and soon became so absorbed in the activities of the unit that they held most of the remainder of humanity in a kind of unsympathetic scorn. From what little experience I had of any of them they were not arrogant, merely private. They never spoke about their missions outside of their own company, they did not boast, nor did they dine out on their membership. What might have been going on inside a Scout's head you were left to wonder. He offered no clues.

I tried several times to reach Smuts that day, and Barbie too. No dice. I struggled through the endless hours and left for home early, telling my small staff to carry on without me. They had lots to do, and I, said I, had the mother and father of all headaches.

Back at home I fidgeted for the rest of the afternoon, pacing from one room to the next, seeking consolation from the empty walls and uncurtained windows, from flowers in the garden, the bees and the trees. I covered the property from one end to the other in an absent- minded hunt for certainty and direction. One thing I could have done but did not, was to phone Tina again. From the moment I parked the car I put that thought right out of my range of possibilities. I knew why. It had to do with the Widow. She was on my mind and I wanted to know her better before doing anything definite.

That first night without someone beside me in bed was a challenge. At length, at about two am, I said to myself if sleep will not come to the sleepy, then the sleepy must find out why. I had a good idea of course, so I found three more pillows and my army overcoat and made up a body to lie beside me. I lay down and put my arm around my little dummy and hugged her good night.

When I awoke the sun was already high in the sky, I was late for the office but I did not care. My mind was still on other things.

For a start, I decided that I would not broadcast the fact of my separation from Tina. If she wanted to let everyone know, that was her business, but I thought it better to keep the news to myself, even from Barbara and Smuts. It was something I could not easily explain to myself other than the vague idea that I wanted to keep things open and let events unfold as they would.

And then I was mildly worried about Smuts. I could not get used to the idea that that he so suddenly wanted to be a wanted to be a Selous Scout and take what was to my way of thinking such a lonely path to the hardest possible of all army challenges, with, at the end, the chance of a lonely and violent death. As always though, he surprised me.

I saw him later in the day and he told me all about it; making the decision appear so rational and matter of fact that I toyed momentarily with the idea of following him. Sanity prevailed and I soon realised that the thought was fathered only by the state of my mind at the moment. What I really wanted more than to join the Scouts was to find a retreat, some relief from the unravelling threads of my suddenly very confused life.

Smuts told me that the choice he'd had to make was not between Psy Ops and the infantry battalion that was our current army posting. It was much more fundamental; it was whether to stay in Rhodesia or to leave. He said he wanted to stay on in Rhodesia, but he would do so only on condition that his time in the army would be valuable and worthwhile to him as well as to the war effort. He wanted his time to mean something more than being a spectator at a bull fight.

"Our last call-up was enough for me," he said. "I can't be such a passive onlooker in all of this mad bloodshed and terror. Either I'm doing something very active myself or I'm not prepared to do anything at all. I suppose we might have been more physically involved if the situation had been different, but only the gooks could have made it different. We were just reacting to whatever they chose to do. The Scouts, on the other hand, really do take the war to those who want it. They go out looking for them, they want to make contact. That's what I want to do. If I'm in this war I want us to win and we'll only do that if we take the battle to the enemy wherever they may be hiding.

"I'm fit, strong enough, I think, and still good enough for a tough selection process. And I like the idea of the Scouts, especially, because the nationalist cadres are more afraid of them than maybe of all the rest of us put together."

* * *

Mrs. Flanagan arrived at my office in the afternoon, bringing with her a cool older fellow she introduced as Maurice Feinstein, her accountant.

"I thought we should begin discussion right away if it suits you," she said. "Maurice will want paper work later on but for now he just wants to look at what you have got and get a feeling, and he

68

is very good at that. He will quickly suss out whether you are running a good and profitable enterprise or an affair that he wouldn't want me involved in. Ha Ha!"

Hey, I thought, this is fascinating. The Widow deal is for real.

When she first mentioned the possibility of joining me in my business I had taken it very lightly indeed, even though I had managed to present it to Tina as the actual and tangible reason for all this bloody hoo-ha. I had not imagined that the Widow would take the initiative so quickly and in this very forward and faintly aggressive manner.

After a few minutes she dismissed Feinstein. "I'll come by your offices tomorrow after lunch," she told him. "I'll bring some figures which Hunter here will no doubt have ready for me first thing in the morning, and we'll take it from there."

Feinstein left with an old-world little bow and a handshake.

"Nice to meet you Mr. Hunter," he said.

"Hill," I replied.

"Oh yes," he said, "Hill."

Barbara seemed confident the meeting had gone off well.

"I can tell he likes you and the way you go about things," she told me. "Maurice is a hell of a man, he is a number machine from top to bottom, and vastly wealthy himself. He was Jim's accountant and the Executor of his estate, but he also fancies himself as a good judge of people and character. He thinks he is infallible in his opinions of his fellow man, particularly those he is likely to find himself in business with. So far I have found him a brilliant counsellor, and he surely has been good to me since Jim's death: stopped me from making some silly mistakes and getting me out of a few personal scrapes.

"Have you got a list of your client base and what they pay in retainers? Do you trust me enough yet to hand over that stuff? But first let me just show you some of my past history in the business. You understand that I married quite young and had only done a little in PR when that happened. Nevertheless my credentials are good in that they come from some good people in London."

She showed me a letter of appointment and another of farewell from a top London PR Agency. I had heard of the people involved, they were industry celebrities. It would be easy for me to check it out. The letter of farewell was particularly impressive, offering Barbie an unlimited assurance of employment if things in Zambia did not work out, and a promise of free accommodation for a month and complimentary airfare to London from wherever in the world she happened to be.

There was no doubt in my mind, she was the genuine article. If I could make a deal with her I felt sure she would be a first class asset, and a magnet for new accounts.

"And then," she said, "there is the question of how much of a shareholding you are prepared to let go and at what price?"

So far I don't think I had said much at all; a nod, a smile, two handshakes with Feinstein, one coming in and another to say goodbye.

I punished her for it, opening and closing my mouth several time like a drowning guppy.

"Have I stormed the ramparts?" she asked. "Is all this too quick for you? Say something."

"Twenty five per cent. Twenty five thousand dollars. Both to be held in suspense for three months pending ratification by both parties. In the meantime you will work here at a salary to be agreed but not less than a thousand dollars a month"

"Yes, yes, and yes please. That sounds fine, but if after three months we both want to carry on, then I must have a way of getting to 50/50. Obviously at a price, but I won't invest my time and money in something that later on I can simply be fired from or voted out of."

"I can think of a way round that," I said. "When the time comes to ratify and go forward, I would be prepared to sell you up to 48%. At the same time I will sell, or give away, 4% to a third party, someone perhaps like Feinstein, but not him, someone we could both trust absolutely to use their vote for the good of the business rather than for you or I as individuals. That way we would both have the same shareholding. I couldn't invite you out, nor you me."

"Where might we find such an impartial person," she asked. Do you know of anyone?"

I thought of Smuts.

"Yes, there is someone whose opinion I value very highly, but I won't introduce you or tell you more about him until the time comes. You may also suggest someone yourself if you like."

"Fair enough," she said. "I'll put the whole thing to Feinstein tomorrow, with the figures you give me in the morning."

We agreed, and shook hands on it, although I would have preferred a long, lingering kiss and an encouraging hug. *Bastard*.

If I thought my carnal luck might match my business fortune in the fading daylight I was wrong.

"I won't see you socially until this thing has been tied up one way or the other," said the widow. "I don't want anyone to think I might have applied, or been under, the undue influence of lust, love, desire, or alcohol to do this deal with you," she said.

I laughed heartily.

"Does it matter to anyone what the motives and methods might have been?" I asked. "Apart from the staff, there are only the two of us to worry about," said I, ignoring for the moment that Barbie had no idea that I had been abandoned by my wife. And I chose not to break that news to her just then either.

"Good idea anyhow," I said, aiming for the firm voice of authority of the senior 48 per centre, "let us sleep on this deal, but not together," which I thought was quite witty.

"Yes sir," she replied. "Let us never confuse business with pleasure nor business rights with those conjugal. Check mate I think?"

"Check mate."

I stayed at the office late that night working on the figures for Feinstein. Then I went home to my three-pillow companion.

Chapter 10

As promised I delivered the figures to Barbara two days later. Her home was not far from my own. I waited until nine and drove around in less than ten minutes. She had a penthouse flat overlooking the city's main sports' club and golf course. After letting me in to a lounge furnished as beautifully as she was dressed, we exchanged the usual pleasantries.

Then, "How was the rest of your evening after I left?"

"Not bad under the circumstances," I told her. "I ended up in a threesome and slept soundly all night."

"Bad. Bad!" she said. "I should never have left you so early."

"Not as bad as it sounds," I replied. "I'll tell you all about it when we are free to meet socially again. Call me when you've seen Feinstein and we can talk about your first day at Hunter Hill Associates."

"Soon to be Hill, Flanagan and Company I hope. It has a certain ring of class about it don't you think?"

"Oh yes, very upmarket; should bring in another fifty grand a month at least."

As I was driving off I looked in the rear mirror and saw her frantically waving at me to come back. No room to turn around, so I slowly reversed up the winding drive.

"I forgot to tell you," she said. "Feinstein says his gut tells him that you are an excellent specimen of a man – to quote his exact words – and he thinks that as long as the figures hold out, you and I, and he, will go a long way together. He controls one or two decent PR accounts himself, so things are looking good. I thought you would like to know that."

"Certainly worth the perilous journey in reverse," I said. "See you anon."

With $25000 as good as in the bank, I thought it was almost time to make another effort with Tina. At the very least it would go some way towards vindicating my performance. But I hesitated. Do that now, I said to myself, and you can forget any rude and lustful ideas you may have about the exciting Mrs. Flanagan. Wait a little longer, see what happens, my inner self cautioned.

By pure chance I did not have too long to wait.

Not especially anxious to get back to my double pillow companion I chose to spend the evening at the Quill Club where I was an associate member. It was the local journalists' hang-out, and you could usually count on a happy hour or two among the many scribblers who gathered there to drink among their own kind.. Poker Dice, and more especially Liar Dice, was the popular drinking man's sport at that time and I soon found myself involved in a drawn-out game at something silly like ten cents a round. In a long and unlucky session you could lose all of four or five dollars. Peanuts, I thought, to a man who has just as good as sold a third stake in his struggling business for twenty five grand. The game went on until after eight, and the boys were beginning to break up when a giant of a man came into the club, someone I had not seen before. He was black, which was not unusual in those days, although his size and bearing were distinctly so; equally his easy self-assurance.

He introduced himself as Norton James, a correspondent for one of the international wire agencies.

"Where you from?" I asked.

"Originally? Right here in Rhodesia, now based in Lusaka actually. I'm here on an assignment."

"Did you ever work in Rhodesia?" I asked, scratching around my memory cabinet. Surely I must have come across him before, I thought.

"Remember the old African Gazette? Now banned? That was my first job. I was just a trainee and still staying at home. After Rhodesia declared independence my old man, who had been a parliamentary secretary in the old Federal government thought it best for us all to withdraw, so we left and went to live in Zambia. That's where I took up scribbling earnestly and how I happen to be here now. I had arranged to meet a Zambian friend here for a drink, Barbara Flanagan, does anyone know her? Has she been in? I forget exactly what time we were to meet so I could just as easily be late or early."

"I know her," I volunteered, not particularly surprised by the news since they were both from Zambia, although I did feel a twinge of uneasiness at the possibility that there might be something between them. "I met her recently. She hasn't been here tonight as far as I know."

"Ah well," he said, "it is still early. Let me buy you all a drink."

To which drinks we were just devoting our undivided attention when in swept the Widow, looking her stunning best. Where, I wondered, does she have to go to get all these exquisite clothes?

"I hope I'm not late Norton," she said before noticing that I was of the group. Then "Oh, this is nice, what are you doing here?" to me. "I didn't know you know Norton!"

"Actually I don't," I protested, "We've just met this evening here and now, I'm absorbing my first drink with him. This is it. The first of many to come. My turn next."

"Great, great, why don't we all go out to dinner after that? It's on me."

I was happy with that, Norton was happy, and my three Liar Dice companions were leaving for home anyway, and so, after one more drink at the Quill, Barbara, Norton and I went to dinner at *The Burgundy Room*.

Does anyone remember *The Burgundy Room*?

The *Burgundy* was on Union Avenue, or was it Baker? Wonderful restaurant, terrific style. The Maître D', was Senhor José Santander; tall, Latin, impeccably mannered, always in a white topped Tuxedo. José was the quintessential host who, as I remember, had a uniquely gracious way of palming whatever tips you left for him. It was from José that I first learned to show off my would-be urbane and cosmopolitan side by asking for particular red wines and turning down others equally expensive. That evening, I recall, it was a Château Neuf Du Papé that we drank rather more of than was good for us.

Of the conversation I remember very little. I know that at some point I began to be completely at ease and confident that there was nothing to worry about between Norton and Barbara. I realised that they were not even close friends; rather business acquaintances who shared only the fact that they had lived in Zambia.

I took to Norton. His manners were impeccable, his conversation educated and interesting. Never once was the subject of local politics mentioned, nor of the war, nor of Rhodesia's growing isolation.

We said our goodbyes in the darkened street outside the nearby Quill Club. Barbara lingered.

"I had a lift here," she said. "Can you take me home?"

Of course I could. And of course she asked me in for a cup of coffee when we reached her penthouse block.

"Now," she said as we relaxed with our coffee, "tell me about your threesome, I am quite green."

"Longish story, do you have ten minutes?"

"Only ten?" she protested. "You promised me a story not a simple explanation."

"Well then, here goes, although I must first remind you that we were not supposed to meet socially until the deal is sealed or abandoned!"

"Oh just get on with it," she said. "As for the deal, it is as good as done. Whatever Feinstein comes up with, I'm with you. Let us seal this deal here and now with a firm handshake." Which we immediately and rather formally managed to do, despite the copious amounts of alcohol I had managed to dispose of in the previous three hours.

I had not yet mentioned the bust-up with Tina and I wasn't sure this was the right moment, but still I plunged right in.

"Welcome to the world of Hunter Hill," I said.

Then, dropping my volume down to little above a confidential whisper:

"You asked about my three-some..."

"Dying of curiosity."

"OK. Stand by for the expose of the year! It was the night I was out late with you, and we were discussing how I would explain that to my wife Tina. Your suggestion was to stick as near the truth as I could live with. Well, I followed that advice and guess what? In less than 24 hours I found myself single again. How's was that for a good idea?"

"No kidding? She left you?

"She did."

"Because you were thinking of selling some shares in the business to me?'

"No. It was because I said I would like to sleep with you."

"You told her that?"

"I did."

"Why? Why would you say something so, so, I don't know, hurtful?"

"Because she asked me if that was in my mind. And you know what? It just came out. Sorry."

"Well then, I'm not surprised she left, and I don't want to hear about the three-some anyway. Your wife walks out and you get the girls in. Much too cold and calculating for me."

"Whoa, whoa, whoa. It wasn't like that at all. The threesome was just me and two extra pillows lying by my side so I could get to sleep."

"For heaven's sake, what a story."

I looked up and Flanagan was shaking her head in disbelief.

"Oh rubbish, you're just making yourself look good. What really happened, who were these two stunning items anyhow?"

"That was all there was to it, the naked truth, just me, and two pillows for company," I answered.

"And now? Maybe Tina is just cooling off, or rather trying to cool you off."

"Don't think so, she has taken every last thing that belongs to her. The house bears no sign of her ever having been there."

"Oh no!" The Widow seemed genuinely distraught. "Surely this can be fixed. Let me fix it for you – I'll call Tina and take her to lunch or something. I'll explain. I hate the idea that I might have broken up your home. We must fix it."

"Don't worry about it. It will have to fix by itself or bust by itself. This with you is an excuse. The fact is that Tina doesn't really want to stay on in Rhodesia and I do. Apart from the army, I am so much enjoying my business, and now, meeting you and looking forward to the prospect of vital new energy, I can't possibly think of going. Tina must fit in or make her own life. I can deal with the trauma of being single again, to tell the truth I am quite looking forward to it."

"Well I know one thing," said Barbie, "you don't have to go to an empty home tonight. You can stay right here with me. Don't argue, it is decided. You sleep in my bed, I'll make up something on the couch. OK?"

"As long as you have enough pillows."

"I might manage better than that," she said.

We went through the honourable pretence of making up a bed on a couch in the lounge; I helped spread the sheets and blankets.

When all was neat and tidy she said "Go on then, off you go to your room. Oh! I still have to show it to you." She led me by the hand.

Enough to say that neither of us could wait to get into bed together. The simple process of undressing seemed to take forever, and I am sorry to say that what came off stayed on the floor where it fell. It was a fumbling, exulting race that ended, for me, in a Hiroshima instant of blinding joy. We spoke little but we held on tight and did it again and then once more. It was as if two people had found each other after years of frantic searching and frustrating endeavour. For myself I knew I was home at last, and I cared not a cent in that moment for whatever hurt and anguish I might be creating in the broiling wake of my exultant emotion.

Lying in bed next morning, cuddled up and still feeling ridiculously elated, I tore my mind away from the feast and thought of other things.

"Tell me about Norton," I asked. "I liked him a lot and I wouldn't mind seeing more of him. He is so unusual in that he seems to have absolutely no reserve with or against white people. I wonder how he achieved such racial calm in the face of so much bloody superiority."

"I don't know much about him. Because he is a journalist we met a few times at news events and press conferences. We exchanged cards and so on. Other friends of mine thought he was politically well connected, that he was bright, charismatic and likely to go a long way. We bumped into each other a few days ago and made the date. I was quite surprised to see him here partly because I would have thought the Immigration people would not have let a black journalist from Zambia into Rhodesia. I don't know if you heard him telling me at dinner that he had come in on a flight from London and that he would have to go back the same way."

"I did hear that," I said. "It was while I was looking at José's Wine List. I meant to ask him more about it but the wine must have got in my way. I wonder where he's staying."

"Oh I think he said Meikles."

"I'll give him a ring later. Meanwhile I must jump around. Can I buy you lunch? Shall I see you after work? Will you have heard from Feinstein by then?"

"No to lunch, yes to supper, and 'maybe' to Feinstein. Here, take a kiss. I'll be home by five."

I left her then, went home, cleaned up, dressed in my best suit, and drifted in late morning into the office. I dithered with the idea of phoning Tina but was easily distracted and the call didn't happen. The day passed in a state of great emotional confusion. I was on a drug-free high, my excitement only occasionally interrupted by nagging twinges of guilt so intense that the

78

compound spoiled me for work and I accomplished nothing at all. It was a weird state.

I half-hoped Tina would call, and then again I dreaded that she might. I wanted to hear from the Widow but instead she sent me flowers which came early and effectively stopped me from launching a similar token of joy in her direction. Then I scratched my head for what I could do to assure her that the night had been so stupendously happy and exciting for me that I was impatient for the return match. I sent her a Gorillagram.

At exactly ten past five the gorilla, a clown named Joe dressed in a gorilla suit, knocked on her door. When she opened it he first shouted 'don't shoot, I'm friendly', then gave her a bottle of the most expensive champagne I had been able to find in town, and the 'telegram' - a note from me: PUT IT ON ICE, I'll be with you at 7. Hunter. She was amused. It put her into a good mood. The gorilla's parting antics left her bubbling.

Meanwhile, I remembered to call Meikles, but Norton was not in. I would try again next morning.

At seven prompt I arrived at Barbie's flat, wild love and boyish enthusiasm all over my face I expect. She seemed equally happy to be with me, and we enjoyed a second night of glorious indulgence, of which I will say nothing more than that it dealt a damning blow to any fleeting thought I might have entertained about my marriage to Tina or of any prospect of calling her any time soon.

Chapter 11

Next day I remembered to call Norton. He sounded pleased to hear from me, but a little surprised.

"Great stuff," he said, "so chuffed to hear from you. Are you available for lunch?"

We agreed to meet at his hotel. I called Smuts and suggested he come along too. He too took an immediate liking to the tall, good looking and thoroughly charming Norton. He was, however, more forthright than I perhaps might have been.

"It is a terrible thing to admit in the middle of Africa even if there is a war going on," he said, "but few whites mix much socially with your tribe. I don't like it and when I meet someone like yourself I wonder more and more what it is that keeps us so apart?"

"I don't like it either," Norton replied, "but I do understand it. We were fatally polarised from the start. When whites came here they considered the people primitive because they had no written language, believed in and practised witchcraft, and had easily beaten armies. No wonder your people with their newspapers and magic fire-sticks thought themselves superior. Where they went wrong, if I may presume to judge, was in behaving as if those inequalities would last forever. When a growing number of blacks became educated and trained to do all manner of things, from driving to doctoring, they did not hold out much of a hand of friendship or welcome. Instead they institutionalised the idea that the blacks were primitive, far too primitive to have any kind of a say except in their immediate tribal affairs, and even those were pretty well white-regulated. I suppose they knew that if they did relax and allow the black people into the system, their days in control were numbered – as this war will I am sure prove. Whoever wins, and it is hard to see how it could be the whites, the result will be further polarisation. I suspect we are doomed to be apart for years and years to come. And as for your 'when I meet someone like you' comment, I have to say it sounds frightfully condescending, even racist, as if I were some kind of a freak because I dress, speak, and hold opinions much the same as you do."

"I'm sorry if it sounds that way, "Smuts said. "I can see why you think so but it is not meant to be. It is a reflection of the fact that after, what, eighty years or so, the vast majority of your people still appear to us to prefer their primitive tribal environment and they really are resistant to the way of life that whites find absolutely essential. If I haven't been your friend before it's because I did not meet you before. Good Lord, I'm not even friends with the vast majority of my fellow whites, and when I meet one I like I would probably make the same kind of comment that you call racist."

"Touché," cried Norton. "The gulf is wide, but there is something to be said for all sides. How you solve it I just don't know, but I will tell you one important thing. This war is nothing more nor less than a power struggle. In the oldest, most old-fashioned sense, and as ever, the winner will take all."

With that the conversation moved on. We finished our lunch and left. As we reached the street outside, Norton put his arm around Smuts' shoulder to reassure him that he had taken no offence.

"Good bye for now," he said. "Fascinating talking to you. Let's do it again before I finish up here."

We agreed to meet again that evening at the Quill Club. When we were alone I said to Smuts, "Interesting man don't you think? Close your eyes and he's one of us, not just another Rhodesian, but definitely a modern sort of fellow. I like him."

Smuts agreed.

"But when the times comes," he said. "Put your cash on him to jump into the nationalist camp, if he isn't there already. I wonder what he is doing here – we talked so much of other things I forgot to ask. He's a journalist so I guess he's tracking a , I wonder if we will be in it..."

"Now, Dog," I said, changing the subject to what was becoming a matter of the most urgent importance to me, "Tina and I have split. I wanted to tell you earlier but the chance never came."

Although he had met Tina once or twice he did not know her well, and so the news was by no means shattering to him.

"That makes you the third of my friends this year to be fired by his wife. Soon I will have no married friends at all. Sorry about that, what happened?"

"Continental drift, I guess. We've been slipping away from each other for years. All it took in the end was a small personal earthquake. I met another woman and I'm afraid the reaction was explosive."

"Great luck! Who is the stick of dynamite?"

"You'll meet her at the Quill this evening if all goes as planned. Barbara Darby, a crocodile hunter's widow from Zambia. And I can tell you that the mere mention of her name gives me butterflies in the pit of my stomach."

"I know her." he said to my surprise. "Not well, but we have met. I am not surprised you found her irresistible. She is quite extraordinary. But you, my friend, for all that, are a bad dog. I can see that the poison has finally got to you."

"Poison?" I asked.

"Testosterone," he said with a half-laugh. "It builds up fast in an unhappy marriage. How long has this been going on?"

"The affair? Oh, days, only days. In fact it has only just started. Tina left me early in the process, when my naughtiness was only an ambition. Nothing had yet happened and might not have. But once she had gone, one night of loneliness was all it took for me to break every promise I ever made to her. The eye-watering speed of her walk out – on the face of it only because I admitted to finding the widow lady quite desirable – makes me think she hoped to bring me to my proper sense of responsibility before it was too late. She has always been her own woman, never meekly following in *my* cloud of dust. You could say a bit of a control freak. She wanted us to leave the country and she was not above trying to create conditions that would compel me to go her way.

"And you know what Dog? I'm going to leave it like that for the moment. Our next call up starts in two weeks' time and I am away on a two-day trip to the lowlands of Limpopo day after tomorrow, so for now I am just going to enjoy getting to know the widow. The future for Christina and I will have to wait at the back of the queue."

"Atta boy Dog. Head down, foot flat, go like hell. You'll be fine. What takes you to the lowveld?"

"A rich client. An American who sells farm chemicals. He is having a big cotton promotion with a farmer down on the banks of the Limpopo who gets all the water he needs from the apparently dry bed of the river. Billions of gallons of it. If my client can get a hundred or so other farmers to grow cotton on a similar huge scale down there his company will make millions. I have to tell the world about it – with pictures. He's chartered a light aircraft and we are flying first thing Wednesday morning."

"Lucky dog, Dog. Did I ever tell you that my old Dad Arthur once owned a plane? Flew it himself and was crazy about it. Whenever he heard the drone of a small plane in the sky above us he would turn to me and say 'look up son, look there. Some lucky bugger is flying'."

"I'm looking forward to it. I'm sure it will be fine, though in war time I do feel a little nervous about the whole idea of being up there like a duck."

I headed for the office to phone Barbie. I wanted to know if she had heard any more from Feinstein, and then again I wanted to know if she wanted to see me that night.

It turned out that Feinstein had not finished his figures but still sounded positive. As for my romantic intentions, they happened to coincide very much with her own. I told her that Smuts and I had been to lunch with Norton and were meeting again later at the Quill.

"I believe you have met the Dog, but not with me. It's time you got to know him, he is my new best friend, "I said. "Why not let's start the evening together there? I think you will find him a hell of a fellow, and he blows the most amazing smoke rings…"

"Smuts?" she said. "Smuts Brander? Yes I know him a bit. I'll get hold of Feinstein. Hopefully we'll have his enthusiastic support to celebrate. Pick me up on your way to the club."

When I arrived at her flat after work I found she was still busy entertaining Feinstein to tea – he never took anything stronger (on business grounds, he liked to say).

"As for the business immediately in front of us, Mr. Hill, I have found it extremely difficult to value what you have offered Mrs. Flanagan. There are no real assets to speak of. At the same time, your books show a steady and reliable income, even if your so-called contracts which I have briefly looked at could be broken at any time. For these reasons we must go a little bit with our instincts here. Mrs. Flanagan is of course well known to me. You are not. And yet I judge from your books that you are a steady hand. I think you must be working very hard, and that is in your favour. Since Mrs. Flanagan wishes to throw her lot in with Hunter Hill Associates, as her advisor and friend I am happy to support her wishes here. I offer you both my very best wishes."

I thought it important not to be too bubbly about this good news, especially as he had not gone so far as to congratulate us. I wanted to look business-like and thoughtful and so I merely nodded and tried to look profound.

"Thank you for your kind remarks and your personal support in this negotiation," I concluded. "Barbara and I will talk it through in close detail. I'll get my lawyers to come up with a proper agreement and we'll go on from there. I'm away Wednesday and Thursday, then off on a six week call-up in a couple of weeks' time, but I am sure we can get it all together without wasting too much time. For myself I would like it if Mrs. Flanagan would be with us by the time I next have to go off to the army. I will be away for the whole of the six weeks because my transfer to a town job with the military has not yet come through."

"That then is our aim," said Feinstein.

With the meeting closed, Barbara and I went on to the Quill where Smuts was already at the bar.

I started to introduce them but Barbie reminded me they already were acquainted. For all that, I could see that Smuts was slightly overcome; the only moment so far that I had seen him discomfited. Barbara was dressed as usual most unusually. She wore a bright red jacket, white frilly top, black leather trousers and a pair of sharp gold high heeled sandals. The effect was oddly masculine and formal yet it whispered too of elegance, character, sex and charm.

"The no-show Mr. Brander," she said, taking his hand gently. "I have been looking forward to meeting you again, and before the evening is out you must demonstrate for me the Smuts way with smoke rings. This dog here," she said, pointing at me, "works up quite a good story about it."

I was looking forward to hearing more about how they knew each other when Norton arrived and the conversation moved aimlessly along for a while in other directions. At some point I asked Norton what particular project it was that had brought him to Salisbury and whether he had any difficulty in getting through the tight immigration cordon.

"No," he said, "I've got a Rhodesian passport, they know I am a journalist, and I have good credentials and impeccable contacts.

"Actually what I am here to do is a story on how the two countries are managing to work together on keeping Kariba and the power supply out of the war. That's all I can say about it for the moment, but it will probably appear in the local Herald one of these day. It is not particularly controversial, just surprising really. Something like the English and the Germans playing football between the trenches one Christmas Day in the Great War."

"And you fellows," he said." How are you managing to fit your jobs into this very busy call-up schedule?"

"Good question," said Smuts. "It's incredible really and may only go to show how little we are needed in normal times. Seriously though, there is a great sense of togetherness in shared trouble. I cannot imagine any of my clients firing me for not being able to put quite as much effort into his problems as I would be expected to in normal times."

Trying to steer the conversation away from call-up issues I asked Barbara what she thought of the way the economy seemed to be booming through the challenges.

I think she sensed what I was up to and played the subject down.

"Apart from losing sight of your friends for weeks at a time it is hard to see anything abnormally complicated for most of people," she said. "You can get what you need in the supermarkets, in fact there is an abundance of literally everything. Very different from Zambia I can tell you. Apart from a permanent abundance of Scotch Whisky, they have acute shortages all the time, everything from toilet paper to fresh milk."

"Is that why you came back?" Norton asked.

"Partly," she answered. "But then too there was some difficulty for me to stay on in Zambia after my husband died. We had lived an isolated life and apart from him I had only my sick old mother in Zambia. I've brought her here where we have other family and so there's more of a support base for the old girl."

"That's good. I'm glad to hear it," said Norton, and I felt he meant it. We were just four friends out for a few drinks. Only the circumstance of war and too much alcohol could threaten our perfect amity. And it happened quickly.

Our presence and obvious pleasure in each other's company was too much for one club member. This burly stranger, red-faced and angry, clearly with much alcohol circulating throughout his oversize body, strode aggressively into our immediate circle at the bar.

"I have been listening to you lot," he said, "and I am shocked and disappointed that you could discuss call-ups and the economy in front of this fellow here," pointing to Norton. "Don't you know we are at war? Don't you know he could be an informer? Don't you know about GAG? I want your names, I'm going to make a report," he said. "This is going to the top!"

I could see that Norton was astonished, but he kept calm. Before he could respond in any way Smuts stayed him with a movement of his hand and then launched a counter attack of his own.

"Excuse me, Bud," he said, rising, and with only the slightest hint of aggression placing himself uncomfortably close within the other man's space, "but who are you Buddy?" putting a somewhat belittling accent on the word Buddy. Then, as if to underline his superiority, he straightened the man's tie and jacket, and ordered him to 'smarten up'.

"Even in civvies you're a disgrace," he said. "Now, if you are a member here you should know that this is an international club, and people of all nations are welcome. As for our conversation, it is none of your business, Buddy. But just for the record, this man who you refer to as 'this fellow', could be a member, and a distinguished one, of the armed forces of our country, good enough to fight and die for you and your disgustingly prejudiced views. Now, be so responsible as to apologise and we will overlook your woeful behaviour and crazy interruption."

I am not sure that Norton enjoyed the suggestion that he might be a commissioned officer of the Zimbabwe Rhodesian army, but he accepted it graciously, understanding no doubt that the incident might otherwise have become ugly, particularly if Smuts, or he himself, or the intruder, had lost the plot and started throwing punches.

The stranger seemed shaken, evidently taking Smuts to be an army officer. He stammered a few garbled words of apology before leaving the club. We judged it a good moment to move on too.

As we were leaving and laughing a little at the brief incident, Norton asked: "What did he mean when he asked don't you know about gag?"

"Oh," I recalled. "Years ago there was a government campaign warning people to 'Guard Against Gossip' aimed at promoting the security of the efforts to beat British economic sanctions."

"Looking at your bustling economy now I suppose those efforts must have paid off. It is quite astonishing how the Rhodesian economy has responded to the world's attempts to kill it off."

We all went home to our various beds; mine as it turned out to be for the last time for a quite a while with Barbie, 11 floors up in her luxury penthouse flat.

We had scarcely had a chance to discuss the expansion of Hunter Hill, but with Feinstein's positive thoughts to cheer us on and Barbara's official hand-shake later, we toasted the development appropriately between the sheets with our warm and enthusiastic bodies.

Chapter 12

Tuesday dawned cold and wet so that the thought of early rising and going home to shower and dress for the day was easily sidelined. Instead we toasted the business development once more. By the time that was all over and I had regained control of my responsibilities, I was late arriving at the office.

Jo, my receptionist, was agitated. Normally I kept her informed of my movements. She correctly perceived that something was amiss.

"I've been trying to call you for the last hour and a half," she complained. Tina's been calling between classes all morning wanting to know where you were, and all I could say was that you hadn't come in yet. There are urgent messages from three clients. A Mr. Feinstein wants you to call him. Senchem's office phoned to say Bill wants to bring forward your flight arrangements and leave for the Lowveld this afternoon at three if possible."

"Don't worry Jo. I'll tell you more later, but first try and get me Bill while I read the messages, then I'll call Tina. Feinstein will have to wait until I've cleared the rest."

Bill came on the line to ask me if I could handle the change of plans. I said I could. I would have to be at the airport at 2.45pm at the latest.

Then I called Tina, but as expected she was in class, so I left a message with the bursar to tell her I had to fly to a field day in the lowveld that afternoon rather than the next morning which she and I had discussed. The simple fact that I had left a message for her eased my conscience a little, and next I called Feinstein, wondering what he might have to say to complicate what had so far been a relaxed and easy progress to partnership with Mrs. Flanagan.

"No there's no real problem Mr. Hill," he said. I was just wondering if you could get a draft agreement to me this afternoon so I can work on it while you're away the next two days."

I said I would try, that I would at the very least dictate the heads of agreement to my Secretary and she would type them up for him.

"Flight plans have changed a bit and we're leaving this afternoon," I told him. "But the agreement is my top priority now and I will get on with it right away."

I called Jo into my office. She was a Dutch girl from Amsterdam, fluent in English, and well trained to handle most office needs. She was working her way around the world taking on temporary jobs as they became available. Tall and slim and neat and tidy, Jo had a nicely structured air about her. I liked her and found her attractive, and most of my male clients did too. She willingly stayed on late at the end of the day when anyone was coming to our little office pub for a drink. Much as I had fantasised about her I had so far managed to keep myself firmly in check. We were friendly to the extent that there was no reserve on either side but we had never spoken much about our private lives. Of course she had met Tina on her occasional visits to the office but we did not mix socially except for client drinks.

"There are a couple of things I need to tell you Jo, please come in and take a seat."

First I told her about the plan to take in a partner and expand the business.

"I have been in negotiations for a while," I said. "The prospective partner is a widow with a really good CV and PR experience, probably better than my own. She may come in later this morning if I can get the agreement headings. I will introduce you to her. I am hoping that everything will be sorted before my next call up in a few weeks' time so that she can keep the clients happy while I am away. She will also bring a bunch of her client friends in, so all in all this is a good development for Hunter Hill. As soon as it is finalised you can look out for a new Secretary Receptionist and you will move up to my personal assistant if that is OK with you. We'll come to that in a minute.

"The bad news in all of this is that Tina doesn't like it. In fact she has moved out and appears to be moving on. You are looking at a bachelor man, alone and fancy free. Now, tell me what your immediate plans are. Are you likely to be staying with me for another six months or so? Of course I would like you to stay on forever but I understand your urge to see the world."

She looked out of the window, thinking what to say.

"I'm happy with you," she said after a long pause. "You treat me nice, the work is interesting, and you pay me well enough. I like you a lot, and I am in no hurry to move on. I'm sorry about Tina, but then again that puts another great guy into the field for females such as myself always on the hunt! There you are. Take a bow Mr. Hill."

I did, and then I kissed her hand, and she kissed me lightly on the lips and then we both blushed. I tried to make light of it.

"Hell!" I lied, "That's the most sex I have had in months, and perhaps the best in several years."

She laughed. The danger was over. I dictated the agreement and asked her to type it up in time to be collected before the end of the day.

Then I called Barbie and told her of the changed flight plans and asked her to come into the office later to collect the agreement for Feinstein.

"Introduce yourself to Jo, my, sorry 'our' secretary receptionist," I said. "I'll call you the minute I get back."

My last call of the morning was to Smuts.

"I think I've been poisoned again, Dog," I told him. "I just had a very narrow escape. I must be mad. I look in the mirror and what do I see? Nothing but a great big walking talking, heaving bag of testosterone. Time for a massive rethink."

"Don't worry about it Dog. Life is short and who knows what happens next. To steal ideas from an old Latin poet, 'full many a buxom blonde may yet await you, or this may be your last. Kiss, touch, fondle and shag. Grab every opportunity with both hands. Live for the day. Live for love...'"

91

"Good advice Dog. I feel de-confused and decontaminated already. Now, the other reason I called was just to tell you that my flight plans have changed and I am off to the lowveld promotion this afternoon at three."

"Well," he said, "enjoy the ride, and if I hear an aircraft overhead this afternoon, I will look up and say for all the world to hear, 'look folks, there's a lucky dog in the air'."

Chapter 13

I went home, changed into something more relaxed for flying, packed my small case, and left in plenty of time to reach the airport as arranged. Bill was already in the hangar standing beside what appeared to me to be a ridiculously small aeroplane, and talking with our pilot, who he introduced to me only as John.

John was not at the moment in the mood for much chat as he was busy opening doors and compartments, pushing and pulling things this way and that.

"Ground checks," he said by way of explanation. "Making sure this little bag of bolts has everything she needs to get us safely to the river."

Then he stowed our bags, asked us to stand aside, and pushed the plane out of the hangar and into the open air. It looked more and more like a toy, small but pretty, a four-seater which he said was a Piper Tri-Pacer – as good as Dutch to me, for I had only ever travelled in aeroplanes with names like Viscount, Britannia, and Boeing. I was a little apprehensive, but nevertheless looking forward with much interest to the experience.

As the bigger of his two passengers John asked me to sit in front with him. He was in the left seat, Bill was behind. I made very little of the start-up formalities and almost before I knew it we were gathering speed down the broad tarmac runway which seemed to me to be separated from my backside by only a few inches. There was little wind and in the still air our little plane gobbled up the tarmac faster and faster. At length, which was probably no more than 40 seconds or so, but seemed ages to me, the Piper hauled us all off the ground and we were safely in the air. We turned right and headed south. I looked down in fascination at the beautiful green fields of maize stretching out below us. Then we were over the northern city suburbs and I was struck by the obvious affluence of the people below, for almost every home was at the centre of a large property with lawns, gardens and a bright sparkling blue swimming pool. Every road, every street, every tree-lined avenue was neatly tarred and paved. The traffic was slight: a car going somewhere, a boy on a bicycle, a couple playing tennis on a beautiful court in their own back yard. I felt a distinct twinge of guilt and hoped that the contrast would not be too great when we passed over the African townships, as soon we must.

When we did reach that point I saw that the difference was unfortunately disturbingly vast.

Salisbury's African townships at that time were already overcrowded. Seen from the air they gave an impression of arid and abject squalor. There were people everywhere, the dusty streets were crowded, the pavements were crowded, and, except for a field here and there where people were playing or watching soccer, only the smallest of spaces separated the hundreds of small homes; no gardens, no lawns, no trees, and certainly no swimming pools. It was a sobering sight, and without addressing anyone in particular I gave voice to my dismay: "There it is then, the haves and the have nots at a glance."

John turned to me and asked "Sorry, did you say something?"

"Not really," I replied. "I was just thinking aloud how perfectly hideous is the lot of so many of the people we are flying over in such luxury."

"Yeah, "he said, "it is not always pretty being people down there."

The painful reflection perished as our flight path once more took us over green valleys and farms and cattle in the fields, tobacco barns and tractors, a happy matrix that produced yet another involuntary spasm "God this is a glorious land, but you can see how it is divided."

"Enjoying the flight?" John asked.

"Very much."

Evidently he was a man of few words.

I looked over my shoulder to ask Bill.

"How are you liking it?"

"Oh, he said, "I'm an old hand by now. I do around twenty of these flights a year. They can eventually get quite boring unless you are interested in looking at the ground. But very quick and

94

convenient. We'll get to our destination in about two hours eh John?" John just nodded. "By road it would take us at least six, even eight, depending on road blocks and so on," Bill ended.

"And the cost?" I asked.

"Slim, very slim considering the time involved."

We landed at a place called Buffalo Range close on 5pm. I was surprised to see it was a busy air force base. Two Canberra bombers were parked in carefully camouflaged bays in case of ground attack. Several military helicopters were there to keep them company. Of military personnel there was little sign. Nevertheless it was all a ready reminder of the fact that we were a country at war.

We passed through the terminal building with little formality. John went off to the control tower to arrange a mid-morning take-off next day for our final destination, a place on the Limpopo called *Lookout.*

A car was waiting for us. The driver, a young African man with an immediately engaging personality, introduced himself as Gideon. He was friendly and polite. Making our way through the pretty streets to the sugar plantation head office complex and club, which was where we were to stay the night, someone asked him how things were in the lowveld – 'things' being quite naturally taken to be in reference to the war.

"Oh very fine sir. Very very fine, no war here sir. No trouble. No war." I imagined his answer was a combination of tact and professional tourist-pleasing patter.

We drifted off to our various rooms to patch up, clean up and get ready for dinner.

Bill had a meeting next day with a sugar cane farming company's crop chemicals buyer, so John and I loafed around after breakfast in the Club dining room. Gideon arrived at 10am to take us to the airport and we were soon back in the air, heading for *Lookout.*

As we were flying over one of the large rivers that flow south in that part of the country Bill spotted a large pod of hippo in a vast pool down below. He wanted to take photographs, and John seemed happy to oblige with some real life close-ups. Heeling the little Piper over to an angle of about 45 degrees, he let the plane drop very quickly and almost vertically through a manoeuvre he later told me was called 'side slipping'. Within seconds we were very low indeed and he righted the plane to fly leisurely over the surprised creatures below. I was mesmerised seeing these cumbersome creatures looking in obvious alarm at the bright silver apparition above. We made two or three passes, Bill took his pictures and John climbed again to regain height, and we carried on for *Lookout*. In all it had probably added no more than ten minutes to our flying time, but it proved to be a costly diversion.

We arrived at the farm which had its own private landing strip leading almost to the homestead back door. John hangared the little Piper and we went into the home of the owner, a man called Diedrick Geere. The field day promotion was to be next morning when it was expected that there would be a hundred or more white farmers from far afield coming to see what could be done with cotton crops fed with water from a dry river bed. That afternoon we were given our own private preview so that I could make notes to prepare the publicity material with the undivided attention of Diedrick himself. All went well. Later we were shown to our rooms, bathed, dressed and enjoyed a few drinks before dinner. The hospitality was warm and generous and we enjoyed fine wine with our lowveld cuisine of wild fowl and venison. I noticed that John our pilot would only take one beer before switching to something soft.

Next day the day's events were scheduled to start at ten but were inevitably late as the guests straggled in from all over the far flung district. I overheard John discussing take-off timing with Bill. We needed to be in the air by two thirty that afternoon, he said. It was a three hour flight direct to Fort Victoria where we would spend the night, and he wanted to be sure to be on the ground by six, a war time regulation for private sector aviation.

I remember thinking that Bill was a bit casual about it all, for when the time began to over-run, and John was pestering him, he shrugged him off with a 'yes, yes yes, we're going now' sort of reply. In the end we could only get in the air by three o'clock – half an hour past John's requested deadline.

Once in the air Bill apologised to John. I'm sorry," he said. "It was an important meeting for me and I was totally immersed in what was going on. We'll be alright for time though won't we?"

"Should be," said John, "provided we don't have too much of a head wind. I'll push it a bit. It's not the light we have to worry about, just the need to be on the ground before six. If we're later than that I'll get a bit of a rap over the knuckles but nothing too serious."

If there was more to it than that he did not say. But about half way into the flight the engine spluttered once, then coughed again.

I noticed John immediately reaching down to a switch on the floor between us and changing something there. The motor purred on and I no real idea of what had occurred until later, but I was mildly concerned that we might be short of gas. But John said nothing and as the engine hads resumed its steady drone, my momentary alarm dissolved and I was again scanning the ground below us, purely out of interest to gain as broad a picture as I could of the land below. For the most part it was made up of dozens of granite hills with few inhabitants. In the distance ahead I could see the land flattening out to become dominated by one large mountain which appeared to be the very point towards which we were heading. I was aware, more than I had been on either of our two previous flights, that John frequently consulted the flying map that he kept on a clipboard on his lap, making notes as he did so, but he still said nothing. The mountain ahead grew ever closer.

I was looking down and I noticed that we were passing from lightly populated tribal farm land below to more or less uninhabited land. Soon we were flying over what I could see was decidedly barren and inhospitable country.

Trapped in this gloomy thought I was brought back to a more stark reality when the motor coughed and spluttered, again and once again. John responded by turning knobs on the floor as before. The even beat resumed briefly and we roared on into early twilight.

Then: "sorry men," he announced, "we seem to have a slight fuel line problem here so it is possible we may have to make an emergency landing. Nothing to worry about, just a precaution while we still have good light."

He turned the plane sharply to the right as the engine coughed again, spluttered into and out of life and then, alarmingly, stopped altogether.

"Jesus Christ," Bill shouted from the back. "What the fuck now?"

"Now," said John calmly, "is no time to panic. Take it easy, Bill. "We have a problem, but I can put this thing down anywhere. What I need from you guys is absolute calm, just do what I tell you, and when I tell you. OK?"

I don't know what Bill was thinking just then, but for myself I was very much on the seat edge. My first instinct was to shout out as Bill had, but I had no idea what to shout, so instead I kept repeating a silent prayer to myself, 'Stay cool you fool. Don't make a fool of yourself, don't make a fool of yourself, don't make a fool of yourself you fool stay cool'; more or less.

John put his hand to the ceiling above his head and turned a small handle as we began what was at first a gentle gliding and circling descent. Then he saw something, a possible landing place, an old and now disused maize field along the bank of a small stream.

"We're going in there," he said pointing down at the spot, "and I have to get in quickly so the wind doesn't drift us away from the target. Stand by and remember, keep calm."

To me he said, "Just before we touch down, open your door a little and hold it open firmly just a few inches so that it can't buckle closed if we hit something unexpected. I will tell you exactly when to do it. In the meantime both of you check your safety belts and be ready for a quick exit."

With that he repeated the side slipping manoeuvre, dropping in towards the ground very fast indeed. Then, it seemed to me only feet above the ground, he righted the little machine and levelled off. He pulled back on the stick a little, told me to open the door, and suddenly we were rolling along, slowing down quickly, the smoothest landing and by far the shortest of our trip.

Bill and I applauded the successful effort in spontaneous clapping as the plane came to a stop at the end of the little field under a big tree. Both doors were now wide open and the three of us got out quickly and ran away from the plane as fast as our wobbly legs would let us, fearing instinctively that it might at any second burst into flames.

Nothing happened. And as we found out later, fire was unlikely because we had simply run out of petrol, there was nothing to ignite.

John gathered himself together fast. He signalled the two of us to be quiet and get close around him. Speaking in scarcely above a whisper, he told us: "This is not over yet. We need to be smart and on our toes. I couldn't manage to get a call in to Flight Control. There just wasn't time, the whole thing was over in probably less than two minutes, so no one knows we're down. And they won't know until we don't show up, and then it will be dark and I doubt that anyone will come looking for us until morning. In any case, we can't stay here because it is quite possible that local gooks saw the forced landing and may be on their way to us right this minute.

"I know roughly where we are – about 20 kilometres west of Fort Vic. I have a rifle in the plane, so let's get out everything we need and make an immediate move. The main road should be only about five or six km away, but before we get to that there is a big river to cross. We may have to swim.

"It could be a cold night, we can't make a fire, so let's get as far as we can while there is still light. Look where you put your feet down while you can still see so as not to crackle dead branches and so on, for we must walk quietly, in file about two metres apart. I'll take the lead, OK? And don't forget, no speaks. If you see something, give me a little 'Psst!' - just enough to reach me. Let's go."

With hearts beating even faster than the machine gun rate they had achieved on our unplanned descent from the sky, we fetched the rifle and some essential kit and set off, John in front, Bill in the middle, with me at the rear. We guessed we had about an hour of dwindling daylight and we hoped to find the road before nightfall.

It was hard going on stony ground, each stone separated from the next by a tough and unyielding bole of hardy veld grass. There were no animal tracks to follow, although I feel sure that if we had had time to cast around we must surely have found some evidence of life. Neither was there any sign of recent human habitation. Silently I marvelled at the fact that John had been able to find an old maize field in that wasteland; even more extraordinary was the fact that at some time in the distant past that little field had been cleared of the stones that so abounded there. Without that comparatively smooth surface, a landing there might have been fatal.

And so we padded on silently through the bush, stopping only once for a sip of bottled cold drink, of which we had brought along a few in case we might lose our way and be who knows how long in the bush without good water. With the sun now setting at our backs we came eventually to the expected river, mostly too broad to attempt to swim, for we feared crocodiles, but not flowing strongly at that time of year. After some time searching up and down we came upon a crossing place, a fairly shallow ford that we considered safe enough to attempt. Our brief discussion was conducted in hand signals, for John thought that the chance of alerting revolutionary ears was increasing the closer we got to the town of Fort Victoria.

Once through the river a fairly steep climb up a rocky slope landed us on the main Beit Bridge Fort Vic highway. But what to do next? There was a little traffic, but again John cautioned a conservative approach which took this form: he himself would hang back out of sight with the rifle cocked and ready, John and I standing side by side on the left side of the highway and trying by means of the universal rule of the hitch hiker's thumb to flag down some passing motorist. We hoped we did not look too much like bandits.

Several cars went by in the gathering gloom. The sight of two white men, obviously farmers or tramps, for we were dressed in khaki: shorts, shirts and the usual calf length stockings, plus simple farmer shoes, generally produced a rapid acceleration away from the scene rather than the slow down to a stop for which we were hoping. Who could blame them?

We carried on this performance for at least two hours and it was now as black as black could be. We conferred and decided that we would continue for another twenty minutes and if unsuccessful, then seek out some reasonable shelter for the night – perhaps under a bridge or culvert.

Minutes before our arbitrary deadline arrived, however, a vehicle approached from the other side. Seeing two ghastly white characters in front, the driver, thankfully, slowed down to a halt. It was a Police party in a Land Rover and they were actually looking for us. One of the people who had passed us in the gloom, too careful of their own security to stop, had nevertheless thought enough of the occurrence to stop off at the Fort Victoria Police Station and make a report. By that time, of course, Air Traffic Control had put out a bulletin on our missing flight and it was not difficult for the local police chief to join the dots. A warm glow of gratitude and relief settled over us as we bundled into the back of the truck and sped towards town.

Back at the station the police took separate statements from each of us, locked the rifle away for the night, and drove us to the nearest hotel where we booked in and immediately phoned our families and friends to report in and tell of our adventure.

I, of course, phoned home, but there was no reply. Evidently Tina was still away and probably unaware of anything extra amiss. Then I rang Barbara. "What a fascinating adventure," she said when I had given her a brief outline of what had happened. "I was bleak that you hadn't called, but I thought you probably had other stuff to deal with, I suppose you'll be back tomorrow. There's not much to tell. I passed everything on to Maurice and don't expect to hear from him for a few days, but it is definitely on, I promise you. Call me if you can when you get in tomorrow."

"I will," I said, adding the sound of an affectionate peck "Mwa".

In the morning the air charter company sent another small plane to take us back to Salisbury, and the circle was all but closed. John had one more piece of the business to discuss and clear up.

"If this story gets into the papers I will never get another flying job in Rhodesia," he said, "for it was my fault, or at least it will be found so. I wish I could say 'technically' my fault, and that is what the company will say if you sue us, but if we did not spring a leak somehow I must have made an error in my fuel calculation. We just plain ran out of gas. Could have been a leak, and there was a fairly vicious headwind. The diversion to look at hippo on the way down to *Lookout* didn't help. When the engine first misfired yesterday, if you remember, I switched over to the reserve tank which should have had at least an hour's worth of gas, but it obviously did not, or it leaked. I don't know why, only an investigation will tell us. I'm very sorry, that's all I can say."

Both Bill and I felt very warm towards John for the way he had kept his head, pulled off an astonishingly tidy landing on a tiny patch of earth, and then led us with certainty, confidence and authority to safety, and we promised him that for our part the story would not get out.

He was a great pilot and I wish I could report that he went on to bigger, better and much happier things, but a few years later he was killed in Angola when he crashed on take-off from a small town called Texeira de Souza. What he was doing there and who he was with I never found out.

(RIP John. I remember you with admiration. And, by the way, I have never told anyone the real reason for our shared adventure until now!)

Bill and I left the airport and went our various ways leaving John to file his report with the Civil Aviation authorities. Two days later he called Bill to tell him that the little Piper had been successfully tracked down and retrieved from its parking place under a tree in the bush.

At home I again tried calling Tina. No luck. Then Barbara. We agreed to meet after the lunch hour at my offices.

Had it all amounted to a brush with death, a warning from the gods to mend my behaviour? Juvenile and superstitious as was the notion, it crossed my mind, a sure sign, I suppose, of a guilty conscience. Natural attrition and the excitements of my hectic life quickly drove such melancholy ideas to the far reaches of my mind.

Chapter 14

When I did eventually get in touch with Tina it was only to find that she had not heard of my missing hours and when I told her the story she seemed unimpressed and unconcerned about what I thought of as an incredibly lucky escape in dangerous and harrowing circumstances. It was an awkward conversation that I found distressing, suggesting as it did to me that Tina had truly moved on and was easily able to cope with the death or loss of her husband of umpteen years. For all that I was to blame for the hiatus, I still cared for her and thought of myself as a married man temporarily out of control. Though still very much obsessed with the widow, I thought, perhaps naively, that the situation would eventually resolve to everyone's satisfaction and happiness. Scratching for clues to her true feelings, I changed the subject.

"I think I have some good news. It looks like the deal to sell a part of the business is on, and of course in that case you and I will split the proceeds. It will mean something like twelve and a half grand for each of us."

"Oh, don't worry about me," she said. "I have done nothing to deserve any of your money and I am surely not going to start being beholden to you now. I don't want the money, I don't need the money, and I won't accept it."

I was astonished. How was it possible for someone who just a few weeks ago had begged me to pack up and leave Rhodesia rather than risk being killed at the front, to care so little now?

"Really?" I asked. "Shit a brick Tina, if that's the way you feel perhaps we should put the money towards the cost of a divorce right away. I was hoping that all of this would soon blow over, that we both might eventually see it as nothing more than an early mid-life crisis and be together again, but if what little I said and did was enough to drive you out of the house and my life so quickly, and you feel so little interested in my life now then it must be terminal. Why not let's just call in the lawyers right now. I know a good one, but if you would rather choose your own, go ahead. It should be an easy case of an irretrievable break down with nothing for either side to claim or contest. No need for two lawyers, one will do."

"That's OK," she said. "That is how I feel and the sooner the better."

"My God you are angry aren't you...?"

"No, Hunter, I'm not angry. Somewhat surprised, slightly hurt, and bloody determined never again to be at your mercy or that of any man. Call your lawyer today. Now I *am* in a hurry."

"Good," or something like it, was all I could grunt as I took the phone away from my ear and stared at it as if it was personally taking sides in my destruction. Even at arm's length I could hear Tina crashing her handset down upon its innocent cradle. I shook my head, trying to clear the butterflies, bumble bees and cotton moths flying around inside there. Was this the real Tina? Was this the woman I knew and was for so long in love with? In all our years together I could only remember one occasion when I had angered her enough to provoke a rebuke – while she lay asleep one afternoon on the couch with her hair in curlers I sneaked up and took an unflattering photograph of her, and when I showed her the print she was furious, sulking for hours about it.

I rolled our shared history around in my mind, and slowly more memories of ill temper and sulking emerged; I had blinkered them. So perhaps this was more like the real Tina. I guessed she must by now know all there was to know about my affair and that too was likely to bring out the worst in her.

Edgy and irritable, I dragged myself reluctantly off to the office. It was early and my meeting with Barbara was flagged for after lunch. I didn't feel like going through the whole story with Jo. I wouldn't say anything, she couldn't possibly know what had happened.

Jo was bright as ever when I got in. My dreadful mood evaporated and I soon found myself charming her with my childish bravado.

"Good flight? Interesting visit?" she asked.

"It all depends on what you call good and what you think interesting," I said at my comic best. "How would you like running out of gas in mid-air, being lost in the bush, freaking out with cold as you have never been cold before, and peeing yourself with the fear of gooks with guns coming after you, all at the same time. That was my trip thanks Jo. How was your two days without me?"

"Are you serious?" she asked.

"Never more so unfortunately. That's a short list of the shit that actually happened, but that's all you're going to get right now because I am sure I have lots of work to do. Any messages? Any other disasters I need to know about and deal with? Did you meet the new partner?"

"She came in day before yesterday and took away the papers you left for her. And yes there are one or two unimportant messages on your desk, but absolutely no disasters that I am aware of. And lastly you've got to tell me all about the trip. I am dying to hear the whole story."

"You will get it dear Jo, it's much too good to keep entirely to myself, but later. Oh, and by the way, Mrs. Flanagan will be coming in for a meeting after lunch. She may stay for a drink and it would be nice if you could join us for a while too. Get to know her, she may be coming in as a partner, if we impress her."

Chapter 15

It was to be our last six-week call-up together. After that Smuts would be going off to join the Scouts; I would likely be heading for Psy Ops though I had not yet heard for sure.

In the usual army way, we waited interminably at the Depot on a Monday morning until eventually we found ourselves being trucked off to a camp in the hot and torrid lowveld, centre of the sugar industry and therefore home to a fairly dense white population. Apart from three big company sugar estates, all of which employed huge workforces with dozens of whites at the top, there were also perhaps a hundred or more 'settlers', white farmers who had been given land specifically to create a viable and growing centre of economic culture and white presence. The lowveld was naturally hot. Now it was unnaturally torrid, an obvious target for the enemy because it was close enough to the Mozambique border for reasonably easy entry, and there were plenty of lonely white farmhouses and families to attack and terrorise.

At our morning briefing we had been told to expect plenty of action, a forecast that was underlined for us when, after the first 100 kilometre leg of our outbound journey, our small convoy of five-ton trucks was provided with air cover in the shape of two Rhodesian Air Force light fighter planes flying back and forth at low level overhead, there no doubt to intervene in the event of ambush. A tour bus had recently come under attack in the general area, wounding two South African visitors and seriously wounding the tourism industry; another incident might kill it off completely. Aside from the excitement that our aerial protection provoked, the journey passed without incident. But of course we were late and the entire company bivouacked for the night by the banks of a fast flowing river in the ample grounds of a local golf club.

There was something crazy about that night. The clubhouse and bar was transformed into our company headquarters, mess, and barracks. We were a company of about a hundred men, and we laid out our sleeping bags and other kit on the wide verandas of the clubhouse. Officers and senior NCOs commandeered the insides of the buildings. Toilet arrangements were as good as we would expect to enjoy for the next 48 days, but slightly strained by the numbers.

Smuts and I queued up with a gang of other fellows to get a shower and clean up before the evening meal. Then we joined a bunch of men having a beer outside the bar on a neatly kept lawn and terraced garden overlooking the river.

If you exchanged the uniforms for the casual khaki shorts and shirts that in those days formed the basis of men's civilian clothing, it could have the nineteenth hole after any busy day of golf. Down below the terrace on the banks of the river some men were taunting each other into a turn at a unique Rhodesian army pastime called Bezant. Named very simply after a brand of tinned orange juice, the challenge involved a single attempt to strike an empty Bezant tin, set up on the bare ground about five feet away, with a stick, after spinning five times round on one's feet to the chanting of the onlookers: "One, Two, Three, Four, Five... Hit It!" The result was nearly always chaotic, frequently dangerous, and sometimes almost fatal. Totally disoriented by being spun around, the 'player' when he stopped, would see the can and try to move towards it and hit it. Instead he was more likely to stagger uncontrollably in any direction but the right one, in the process bumping heavily into whatever walls or other obstacles might be in is way. It was a madness of a kind.

That evening some bright spark had thought to turn the event into a money maker, offering odds of ten to one to anyone who would have a go.

"Come on," he was shouting, "Back yourself for a tenner, hit the Bezant tin and go to bed a hundred bucks richer!"

A few guys took him up on the offer. The first, after being spun around as required and then released to make the hit, simply charged off straight off into the river. He was pulled out quickly enough by the large crowd, soaked but laughing. Another man took the bait and bust his head on the terrace wall. Nosebleed.

"Funny thing to do on your way to war," Smuts said to me. "Could be a crazy way of winding yourself up for the occasion. Mad as it is though, it appeals to me, I think I'll have a go, I believe I can do it, not for the money, not for the gamble, just for the challenge. Ballet dancers do something like it all the time. They don't lose their orientation and fall down after every pirouette do they? I guess it is just a matter of spinning your mind the other way, and then aiming left or right of the mark by about five yards – against the spin.... I think."

"Mad dog, Dog," I said. "It's not worth it. It's bloody impossible, not worth a tenner, not worth a hundred."

"Watch me," he said. "If I end in the river you can fish me out and tell me you told me so."

I could see he was going to go for it and his confidence made me a little bullish too.

"OK Dog," I said. "Let's attack this together. I'll go first, and you watch me, I'll try your idea. You can fine tune your attempt from what happens to me. A quarter right, you say?"

"A quarter right if you spin to the left, a quarter left if you spin to the right! Go Dog," he said, and I went.

I declined the bet, the bookie just shrugged, he too was in it more for the fun than the money.

There was something in Smut's idea alright; either that or it was the mere fact that I was concentrating hard. I still missed the can, but only by a little, and though I lost my footing and fell down with the force of the miss-hit, I was fine, a bit muddle-headed, but fine.

Smuts strolled over to the bookie.

"Here's my ten," he said, "first time I've ever had a bet on anything in my life, first time lucky?"

He was dead on target, he smacked the can and it flew into the river. The little army of spectators went quite mad, crowding round Smuts as he collected his hundred bucks, patting him on the back and suggesting that he buy a round at the bar. But the game was over, and the bar closed; time for all good soldiers to be in bed, time for all good soldiers to prepare for whatever lay before them tomorrow.

We strolled slowly back to our veranda. Smuts pressed me to take fifty.

"I wouldn't have done it if you hadn't gone first," he said, "I wonder what Arthur would say," he mused. "Did we get lucky and beat the odds by chance or by design? I can see how gambling got to the old man. But hey, let's not take any more chances on this camp Dog, I'm fired up to do the Scouts selection thing, and I want to be there to do it."

"No chances, Dog. Definitely no chances."

Chapter 16

Next morning our convoy was away early, just after first light, no time for a quick cup of tea. The mood on board the trucks was sombre. We did not have to be told that the war situation was becoming difficult, it was becoming daily more obvious. Denied the sophisticated tools of combat that we had, like helicopter gunships, Canberra bombers, and Hawker Hunter jets, even motor transport, telephones, telegraph, and radio, the guerrillas were nonetheless making the utmost of the two advantages that they did have – endless numbers of willing recruits, and location. It was a home game for them, a hostile away match for us. The crowds of black Rhodesians who just a few years before, even months ago, appeared totally indifferent to a war of liberation, had now become zealous converts, patriots with a whiff of the possibility of victory in their nostrils. Now they were all Zimbabweans cheering on their team to win.

After four or five hours on the road we arrived at a place deep in the bush that must have been at one time a busy little centre of cattle commerce but was now quite deserted. There were dozens of well-made cattle pens surrounding a small parade ring with tiered bench seating for perhaps thirty people, the buyers at regular cattle auctions perhaps. A circle of lovely Msasa trees provided shade. Over to one side was a parking area with white washed stones marking out the bays. A brick under tin-roofed building proved to be a toilet block with seating for seven, showers for two, and a hot water boiler outside. In many ways it was a perfect spot for a bunch of men planning to map, or to search the surrounding landscape for diamonds, gold, *or men*.

I guess that's what we're doing here, I thought, and the notion was soon confirmed as we began to settle in for what was clearly going to be much more than an overnight stay. For the rest of the day we were kept busy pitching tents and digging perimeter trenches. By nightfall we had quite a little village: head-quarter tent, mess tent, and a literal forest of khaki bell tents to sleep in and be our homes. The perimeter was kept tight, but it still took a solid chunk of our manpower to patrol and guard day and night.

If this is to be my home for the next six weeks, I mused, at least it has beauty and a welcome feel, the sort of spot I would choose for my homestead if this were my farm, an oasis of warmth and spiritual refreshment to come back to each night after a hard day in the field. As a soldier in the bush, there was the added attraction of running water and decent ablutions. Heaven!

Next day, and for the following couple of weeks, it was indeed as if we were mapping the area for its wealth and natural resources. Actually we were combing the land for the presence of terrorists. Working on foot at first in 'sticks' of seven men each we pierced the surrounding countryside, making our presence and our military muscle known at every little cluster of village huts, of which there were many. It was a well-coordinated operation. Using our camp as the centre we moved out on random compass points, daily expanding our ring of investigation and gaining important familiarity with the whole, at the same time varying our stick routines in case we were being observed.

A persistent truth was emerging that rang bells with all of us common soldiers but as far as we could see produced no tactical answers from our military brains, neither the officers who were leading us on the ground or those they were reporting to back at HQ:

The enemy was nowhere to be seen, but felt and sensed everywhere, all around us in effect and perhaps in fact.

From our first day in that slice of rural Rhodesia where hundreds, perhaps thousands, of black families would normally be living, we came across no boys over the age of, say, fourteen, and absolutely no young men of military age at all. There were women and children and old men in abundance, but none of the tribal manhood muscle. And then too, all the huts we looked into were almost unnaturally free of anything to do with men; it was as if they had all been recently sanitized from mud floor to their neatly thatched roofs, cleansed of any kind of masculine content.

We found no weapons and no sign of anything subversive at all.

When we asked the women where their men were they simply shrugged and said they did not know - 'ang az' – or waved their arms vaguely in any direction and mumbled something like 'Salisbury'.

It was quite obvious that they had been coached, their answers to every enquiry were similarly vague and rehearsed. We had no means of further questioning them, nor were we trained to do so, and it would have been physically impossible to arrest them all and take them away for professional interrogation. In any case, our mission as far as we understood it, was only to note what we saw on the ground and make our presence felt. Later on, some of our more cynical members when slightly pissed and telling war stories, would say we had been held out like plates of smelly cheese to a truckload of hungry rats.

Eight days into our program of population probing we had reached the limit of where we could go on foot and get back to base in a single ten-hour shift. From then on until the great catastrophe, three sticks of seven would go out in different planned directions for five days at a time. As well as poking around for small settlements where the gooks might have a toe-hold, we would set up Observation Posts on high ground overlooking some feature that might conceivably be the nocturnal base of a gook or two. It was hard living and stressful work, unrelieved by anything resembling a comfortable night's sleep, and for the most part conducted in absolute silence. We ate rough and slept rougher; no question of a hot cup of tea or a warming fire at night. The only things we had to be thankful for were the weather and the absence of any kind of contact with an armed enemy. The nights were warm and dry and uninterrupted by anything more than the need for a silent pee or the two hourly wake-up shoulder shake indicating that it was your turn to keep watch for the next two hours.

Coming back from the second of these little sorties we were crossing the road that led to the cattle pens, now our base camp, when Smuts, who was leading our Indian file party, put up his hand to call a halt. We were close enough to base now to converse quite openly.

"Look," he said, pointing to some faint tracks in the sandy shoulder of the tarred road. "Have we seen a bicycle around here in all the time we've been on this camp? Have we ever seen a bicycle in any of the huts we've visited? But here are the tracks of at least three different bikes, and a couple of biggish footprints. Man-sized feet for sure. Anyone else think that's a bit odd?"

George Hales, our sergeant and stick leader agreed it was a bit 'fishy' and definitely worth a quick radio report to base camp.

"We haven't seen a soul away from the huts either," he said, "worth a bit of follow-up, though let's face it, in any other spot in Africa a few bicycle tracks wouldn't tell you a fucking thing."

All I could manage was "Good dog, Dog. Nose like a bloodhound."

"Get *your* own nose down Dog," he said. "Let's see if we can spot where these tracks came from or where they're going to."

And so, while our radio man was telling the operator back at base camp of the roadside marks, we broke left and right, walking a couple of hundred yards in each direction along the road, looking for any other sign of recent human activity. Nothing. We could only conclude that whoever had been riding that way must have stuck to the tar until forced off, perhaps, by some other approaching vehicle.

We marked the spot with a small slash on the bark of a young roadside tree, low down near ground level so as not to be obvious to anyone not actually looking for it, and moved on.

Base camp was abuzz when we reached it about half an hour later. George went straight to the ops room to report to the CO while the rest of us hung around, waiting to be dismissed to have a fag, a cup of hot tea, and take a welcome 'shit-shower-and-shave break'. After five days in the bush we were hot, dirty, unshaven, some of us slightly constipated, and all of us hungry for literally anything better than the *rat packs* we had been living on.

114

It was about four o'clock in the afternoon.

George came back to tell us that our track spotting had caused quite a stir.

"The CO has called in the Scouts to do a proper tracking job. They'll be here tomorrow. Meanwhile, just in case there are any gooks lurking around, we'll be having a full-on battle drill at five – everyone to their trenches while the mortar boys bang off a few dozen big ones into the surrounding terrain. So, well spotted Smuts, I think the CO is pleased. He almost brought himself to say so..."

The sale pens were set on fairly level ground beside a small stream, dry at that time of the year. On the opposite bank of the stream the ground rose very slightly and had at one time been cultivated, for it was now bare of trees, a barren patch that a cat could not hide in. On 'our' side of the stream, at our backs, so to speak, was the only feature that could possibly be used to dominate the camp, a granite hill, a sugar loaf, rising sharply from ground level to about 150 feet, surely too precipitous to consider as a good tactical spot from which to launch an attack on us. How would anyone get up there in a hurry? And more to the point perhaps, how would they get down under fire? Nevertheless it seemed to be the only possibility, and so that was the target of our afternoon mortar performance. There were two mortar pits, and it was from these that a bombardment began precisely at five while every other man jack in camp watched from the safety of the many trenches we had dug on arrival. Only the CO himself was above ground, directing the fire of one pit after the other, lowering or increasing the elevation to suit the placement of whatever imaginary enemy he had in mind.

It was not the most spectacular demonstration of fire power I had ever witnessed; mortars are not by nature noisy – as the bombs leave the barrel they cough rather than roar – and as we were about 500 metres from the point of impact, the explosion sounds that reverberated back to us were hardly frightening. Nevertheless we were impressed with our own arsenal. No doubt many of us went to sleep that night feeling confidence in our strength and organisation, and that it would take more than a few primitive gooks to rattle our cage.

I don't know why it was that I struggled to sleep. It was a moonless night and the camp was in complete darkness from soon after sunset. Lights were forbidden, so we hit the sack early. That was OK though because we had usually done such a solid day's physical work that the relief of sleep came easily, only to be reluctantly surrendered when an urgent shoulder shake meant that it was your turn at guard duty again. That day our stick had walked probably fifteen miles or more under the considerable stress of constant vigilance, and I was expecting to drift off as soon as my head hit the kitbag I was using for a pillow. Instead I lay on my sleeping bag worrying about my private life, Tina, Barbie, the business, my impending move to Psi Ops, Smuts and his move to the Scouts, and pretty well every other aspect of my rapidly complicating compendium of private affairs.

Carefully lifting the leather dial cover I peeped at my watch. Ten after nine. Shit! I thought, this night will never end. Then my turn on guard duty. What a relief. Back to the pit a couple of hours later; still no sleep.

I tried going back over all the places we had been in the past two weeks, all the huts we had examined, the women we had questioned, the hills we had climbed. Bored by that and learning nothing useful from the review, but still irritatingly wide awake, I tried to think of and count all the Shona words I could remember, starting with a simple sentence learned from an old Shona lady years before while making a half-hearted attempt to learn the language: *lo moto garry ino famba* (the motor car is going) or should that have been *ano famba?*

Now, at last half asleep but stuck like an over-used record on the Shona phrase, I dragged my fading consciousness to break the spell by looking at my watch once more. Five to two. Favourite hour of the burglar coming up, I thought, the hour when sleep is said to be deepest and alarm senses at their lowest. Could that be

116

true, I wondered, or is it just a silly superstition? Well, I'm awake am I not?

I was just drifting off at last when I heard, or thought I heard, a distant shout, a gabble of words which, in my befuddled half-dream state I thought was part of my Shona grammar puzzle. Next instant I was awake and shouting at my tent mates as I absorbed the terrifying truth that we were under intense gunfire.

Everyone seemed to be shouting at once, the whole camp was suddenly an alarming mix of humans barking at each other as we scrambled our way to the trenches, carrying only our weapons and ammunition, and the dominating sound of gunfire which itself was a compound of distant explosions and the crack, crack, crack of bullets as they passed, each breaking the sound barrier overhead.

Thank God our attackers, and at that point we had no precise idea where the firing was coming from, were shooting high. They must have realised it themselves because it was not long before the ground began to dance and sing all around us as we ducked down in search of the safety of the trenches, and there was now the persistent ping, carrion, bang and thud of metal slamming into metal. They had certainly finally found the range to our transport fleet, for the trucks were taking a pounding. Another word of thanks to the fates for the fact that they were not using phosphorous tracer bullets, if they had, the entire transport fleet might have gone up in one big ghastly blaze. By then all of us who could move had somehow got ourselves into a trench, most of us properly armed, but a few with nothing more dangerous than the pillows they were holding like shields in front of them. Three men would never move again; two killed instantly while still in their sleeping bags, the other one in flight.

Our Sergeant Major, Jimmy Rogers, dear brave bugger, was running from trench position to trench position, seemingly oblivious to the hell breaking all around us.

"Hold your fire until we know what we're up against. Hold your fire until the word of command! Stand by to be charged! Stand by, stand by! Save your ammo! And NO smoking. NO smoking! "

The ultimate folly of our afternoon mortar show was that it had prepared us, if only psychologically, for an attack from the wrong direction. Our first mortar reply in fact was to lob a few bombs into the same hillside we had so publicly destroyed earlier.

It is always difficult to keep track of time while you are mentally wincing with every overhead whip-crack in a bullet storm, but it seemed like forever before anyone on our side had worked out with any certainty where the attack was coming from, and then another eternity before they managed to get the mortars pointed there. If you can imagine a hundred Guy Fawkes Nights with every rocket and cracker a deadly missile pouring into an area about the size of a football field with you huddled in a small trench on the half-way line, it will give you a good idea of the difficulty in pinpointing our enemy. Confusion and distraction can muddle everything at first and only the coolest heads are sharp and clear under fire. Nevertheless our smartest brains were at work and in reality it was probably no more than a couple of minutes before our mortar men made the required U-turn so that our attackers found themselves now under fire.

Smuts and I were together with five others in the same trench. Throughout the attack conversation was limited. All you could hear from close range was *Fuck* and *Shit* and *Fucking Arseholes*. It wasn't pretty but it wasn't abject either; no one in the entire camp lost their nerve. We waited, straining our eyes and ears for the first indication of the feet of a thousand gooks rushing through the bush towards us with bayonets fixed. Many may have been frightened, none more than myself, I suppose, but as in my aeroplane adventure just weeks before, the idea kept on playing over to me "Don't panic, don't panic, try to be cool, don't show yourself off to be a cunt." Later on I asked Smuts what had been going through his mind at the height of the bombardment; he told me much the same thing, leading me to the thought that in the heat of any battle it may take more courage to be a coward than to do what is expected of you, so you just do it and hope to pull through.

I suppose the attack lasted no more than ten minutes. Once our mortar section started tossing bombs in the right direction, the gooks stopped firing. The incredible racket died down and soon stopped altogether except for the cough, cough of our own mortars. Finally they too were ordered to hold fire, and an astonishing silence descended on the scene. Whatever the gooks may have been doing or preparing to do it was clear that on this side of the divide the brass had concluded it was best to do nothing and await developments. It is difficult to imagine what else they might have done. They could have no idea of the size of the force opposing us, nor did they know how far they were away and what cover or reserves they might call on in the event of a counter attack. Above all, it was pitch dark, and to light a torch or lamplight would have been suicide.

And so we waited, holding our breath for the impending bayonet or machete charge that never came.

Jimmy Rogers was back in a while, dashing from trench to trench with orders, this time by torchlight.

"Company!" It was a stage whispered command. "Hold your positions, hold your tongues, and hold your fire! I and four details will now check for casualties, from tent to tent, vehicle to vehicle. You're still on high alert until stood down. OK?" And he was gone, into the black night, so dark still that we could only follow his progress by the occasional flash of his torchlight.

The night passed, and finally, in the grey light just before sunrise we began to make out the scene. At first all looked dimly normal, but with fast improving visibility we could see we had been badly mauled. All the trucks, Land Rovers, hyenas, every single wheeled piece of army property now seemed to be standing somehow askew. All had at least one flat tyre, some two or three. Word began to be passed round that we had three dead. And as the light got better we could see that our fleet had taken many hits. Miraculously not one windscreen was shattered, but it was clear that it would be some time before we would be going anywhere in our own transport.

Very soon the company was called to parade and the CO, Captain Manby addressed us. Very briefly he told us what we all knew – that we had been hit by probably the strongest individual force the gooks had yet assembled for a single action in this war – that we were bruised but unbeaten with three dead and no wounded, that we were the crème de la crème for dealing with the attack in such a disciplined way, and that specialist scout units would be arriving soon to take over the problem of tracking down and dealing with the 'riff raff' who had hit us in such a cowardly fashion in the middle of the night, blah blah blah. As he was talking we heard the distant sound of the approaching cavalry, Alouette helicopters, coming to our rescue with a dozen or more fit young men from the Selous Scouts and the Rhodesian Light Infantry.

If we had indeed been rat bait as some of our men claimed, the rats had a field day; they took the cheese and had a good feed at no cost to themselves.

Once our dead had been body bagged and packed off to Salisbury by chopper, and the scouts had done their scratching, all the fresh young men departed the scene by air on follow-up operations, and we were left to lick our bruised egos and review the proceedings.

The tracker team quickly located the enemy positions, anyone could have done so in the light of day because there were at least seventy well-armed gooks against us, neatly lined up in the old ploughed land. Most were using AK47 rifles, but there was at least one machine gun, apparently on wheels, a gun no one could identify from the tracks or shell casings. They had left behind a mass of AK shells as well as their own clear body imprints on the soil where they lay for the attack; it looked as if they may have been lying there all night, waiting patiently and silently for the zero hour. From the firing positions we could see they had formed up a slightly concave line facing our camp from a distance of less than 150 metres. In all, judging by the casings we collected, they had fired over 3000 rounds at us. It should have been carnage, a massacre, but we were saved by what we chose to think of primarily as their own shooting incompetence and the decision of their commander not to pursue his advantage.

We spent most of that day in the role of garage hands, jacking up the punctured vehicles ready to change tyres when new ones arrived, and checking for other damage, particularly to the radiators. Apart from bullet holes, of which there were many, the vehicles were surprisingly intact. Leaking radiators and sump pans could easily be repaired, and with new tyres all round we would be ready to roll in hours. As for following in search of our fleeing attackers it was decided, no doubt at the highest level, to leave all that to younger, fitter men. Whether we had achieved anything for the blood-price paid I can only offer the story that soon began to circulate in the wake of our defeat. It was said that our actual mission had been to measure the political temperature of the area with the long-term possibility that a 'protected village' was planned for the vicinity of our camp. If that was true then it meant, as we had discovered to our cost, that this was yet another NO-GO part of our country, a place where the guerrillas had already entrenched their authority and had become the *de facto* local government. The political implications of what was happening to us on the ground were lost to most of us at the time, lost to two greater imperatives in wartime army life – staying alive and getting home intact.

Chapter 17

As non-commissioned foot soldiers at the sharp end in the time of the Rhodesian war the two things we white occasionals wanted most − to stay alive and get home − were not easy to work towards ourselves, for the choices of where to go and what to do were of course never ours. All we could do in fact was to try to remain focused and alert, and absolutely switched on to the environment, which meant being wide awake always, intelligently observant and almost intuitively switched on throughout what were often long and boring working days. Many could do all of these for a while, few could hold concentration indefinitely against tedium, its bitterest enemy. With our final joint call-up rumbling on towards its close in the fifth week, Smuts and I were once more involved in an action which, but for his powers of sustained and intense concentration for hours and hours at a stretch, would surely have seen the last of us both.

After the fiasco of the sales pen 'battle' the company had moved on to a new camp deeper inside the same general area and we had been warned to expect more trouble, but for nearly a week had enjoyed the quietest time. While we daily probed our surroundings for evidence of a terrorist presence, we found nothing. Our new camp was on flat ground, and that, plus our new sense of watchfulness, made a similar sort of nocturnal attack unlikely.

It was Friday, seven days to go, when a group of us including Smuts and I, were sent on a seemingly risk-free mission to the nearest white settlement, which happened to be one of the smaller sugar estates, to pick up supplies, mostly for the cook-house, but also some vehicle spares. Our little task force consisted of two vehicles, a 5-tonner and a mine converted Land Rover, plus drivers, muscle and man-power, ten of us occasional soldiers in all. The route lay over a couple of kilometres of rough dirt road and then fifty-five on tar. The engineers swept the dirt track for land mines and we set off at about ten in the morning for what we thought would be a bit of a jaunt. At even the smallest of

122

the several sugar company premises we could expect a warm welcome; tea, coffee, good lunch, and the sheer joy of a few minutes of female company in the form of secretarial staff. It was pleasant to say the very least to be treated like heroes, which we always were to these people who lived every day under the threat of a terrorist attack. It was as if to them, everyone who came their way in the right uniform was a star member of the small force that was all that stood between their lives and a depressingly grizzly end. In a way, I suppose, that was true; certainly there was a powerful sense of team spirit in those days in the land, and the many black soldiers on the white side were always treated to the same warm welcome. In a crazy sort of way that element of black white togetherness created for many people the comforting notion that it was all of us, black and white, within this small idyllic but misunderstood country, against a world of communist motivated outsiders, and that, left to ourselves, we would soon come up with the perfect recipe for a peaceful future of racial harmony and economic progress.

We had an easy drive on our way to the estates, and as expected, we were only held up for the return trip, and briefly at that, by hospitality. The stores were soon loaded and we were ready to go when our hosts announced that they had done us a little something special for lunch. It was an invitation we could scarcely refuse, and in any case it would delay us up by no more than 30 minutes – we did not even consider it necessary for a radio check-back with camp, for we were not operating to a strict timetable. While we were enjoying an Impala venison roast the estate people added to our truck load with ten cases of free beer 'for the boys back at camp'. Though we had drunk nothing alcoholic with our lavish meal, we were in high spirits by the time we left and we set off with light and happy hearts. What could possibly go wrong with so many fabulous people all pulling together for the team?

Though much of the land in the Lowveld is flat, it was at the time fairly densely treed with Mopani, Msasa and Mvuti and a pleasant scattering of giant Baobabs. No doubt you could have kept an entire regiment out of sight almost anywhere along our route. But the sky was clear, the sun was shining, it was mid-afternoon, and we were no doubt a little relaxed under the influence of a good meal and friendly civilian company. The possibility of an ambush, though ever factored into our daily army life, seemed wonderfully remote on that wide tarmac road as we sped towards camp.

The supply truck was in front, the mine-protected and mildly armoured Land Rover behind with Smuts and I sitting side by side at the back providing rear covering fire-power. Two other men were watching out left and right. Besides the driver was the sixth man, scanning the front and immediate left for signs of possible attack. Everyone except the driver had weapons cocked and on automatic.

The truck ahead slowed for a bend in the road, not a hairpin, not even tight, just a gentle curve to the left. We slowed too, keeping our distance; I suppose we were doing a little under 20km as we made the turn. I remember consciously sharpening up my alertness for the bend, half thinking it might be an ideal ambush site, when I saw a uniformed man, a black one in dull khaki, step out of the long grass on the left hand side and turn towards us with something looking ominously like a massive shooter in his hands. I hesitated, in some way unwilling to believe what I could see unfolding. Then I shouted something and fired my FN at much the same time though I do not clearly remember the action or the result.

Thank God for Smuts. Seeing exactly the same thing that I did, he opened fire instantly and in the same instant shouted 'Ambush! Ambush! Ambush!' loud enough for the driver to hear, and the driver knew what to do – foot to the floor and drive hard through the killing zone.

In that first burst of probably no more than five rounds, Smuts hit the target twice, killing the man before he had a chance to do what he was there to do, to pump a rocket propelled grenade into our vulnerable rear end. Had he got the infernal machine to his shoulder before being stopped by an FN bullet we would have stood little chance, all of us would surely have been shredded; those grenades make a mess. As it was we were still in mortal danger for the main ambush was in front of us.

Everything was happening in perfect order in slow time: I saw the man step out of the bush, I can still see him. I hesitated, I heard shots, I fired at the man and I saw him fall. I was aware of the cries of 'Ambush!' I sensed the truck accelerating, I felt a very hard punch in the shoulder. I must have dropped my FN. I was in a panic to pick it up, I needed that gun. There was a lot of noise. I couldn't see the rifle anywhere. I was in the wrong place. I was trying to play golf. Who was I with? I put the ball on the tee but it became smaller and smaller until it slipped off the tee and into a crevice. I couldn't get to it with my sand wedge. No, it was Bezant I was playing, it was a game of Bezant. It was a stick I was looking for. There were Bezant cans everywhere. I struck out at one. The can exploded. They all did.

I am alone and very cold. Am I dead?

Chapter 18

I could feel someone holding my hand. It was limp but it was real, it was someone I knew but I couldn't put a name to the hand.

"Who's that?" I asked.

"It's Tina, I'm here. Why are you whispering?"

"Tina? I don't know. Am I whispering? Don't I have to? Where am I? Is it OK to talk? Who are you … Tina?"

"Its fine Hunter, you're in hospital here in Salisbury. You were hurt. They brought you in by helicopter.

"Hurt? I feel alright. Can't move my head. I've been somewhere, I don't know where, for a thousand years I think. I've been travelling, travelling. Man have I been travelling. I passed by whole crowds of people, everywhere. Just standing around, I thought they were watching me, but they weren't. I don't think they saw me. They didn't know I was there. No one would speak to me. What time is it? Why can't I open my eyes, why can't I see, am I blind?"

"You're going to be fine. Must not worry. You had an accident, you have a slight burn on the face and a bump or two so you're still strapped up. Bit of concussion. It's good that you're awake now. I have to go. I'll come by again tomorrow. The doctor will come soon to talk to you. There are some other people here to see you. Soon as you wake up properly."

I had a faint whiff of a gentle perfume as she bent over to give me a little kiss on my chin. I guessed everything else must be covered up. She was still holding my hand. She squeezed it a little, just enough to tell me I was OK and in friendly hands I suppose. I had no idea who she was. I slept deeply and dreamlessly.

When I awoke it must have been the next day, for it was light. I couldn't see anything because my eyes were covered under a bandage tightly bound, but I sensed rather than saw that it was light. Someone seemed to be fussing around my bed; a nurse perhaps, patting the pillows, tugging a little here and there at the sheets. I was very dopey. I wondered what they were giving me.

Then

"Mr. Hill? Mr. Francis Hunter Rowland Hill?"

A man's voice. I guessed he must be reading from a tag or a label. He didn't know me.

"Greetings, Good Morning and Hi!" Too cheerful for me at that somewhat confused moment.

"I'm Doctor Thomas. Ivan Thomas. I'm looking after you. You've been asleep for a while. How are you feeling this fine day?"

I said I was pretty good really, but it was a lie, for although I was in no pain or great physical discomfort I was awfully fuzzy and confused. Trying to remember why I was there was like trying to swim in a sea of cotton wool. It wasn't worth it. I lay back and shut my mind.

"Sorry about the very tight bandage and the strapping," he said. "We have to keep you more or less immobile for a while till the basic healing process is under way."

"What do I have to heal?"

"Don't you remember being in an accident.... anything about it?"

"I've been trying to remember. Was it yesterday, or before that? I know I have been sleeping for a very long time, and I feel as if I have been through something extraordinary, but I can't remember what. When I woke up just now it was all sitting in an orderly row on the edge; where I had been and why I had been there was one of many facts perched on the lip of my mind, like a wise old owl. I thought it was very important. But then it all disappeared like a puff of smoke. The owl was gone."

"Is that all?"

"Well, I know I was playing rugby and running for a high ball. Then I was lying on the side of the field watching other people playing. Then I was being carried away from there and struggling to be put down. That's all. Someone was in here to see me before, was it yesterday? She said I was burned..."

"There's a little more to it than that, but yes you did get a bit of facial burning, nothing too serious in the long run but it was close to your eyes and we have to be a bit careful round there. You also have a wound, and injury on the right shoulder that we've been able to patch up quite nicely and should give you no trouble, perhaps a bit of rheumatism when you reach 75.

"What's causing the memory difficulty is that you were concussed. Bang on the head. You'll have to ask your army buddies who were with you exactly how that happened, but I gather that you were in an ambush and a road crash more or less all at the same time. Don't you have any memory of any of that at all?"

Army buddies? Ambush? Road crash? I tried to fit pieces together but nothing would come.

"No. I only remember running to catch the ball."

I knew my mind was wandering.

"What ball?" he asked.

"No that's nonsense. I'm thinking of something else."

Doctor Thomas didn't appear awfully surprised at this. He put his hand on my good shoulder.

"A lot has happened to you," he said. "But let's leave it for now. You enjoy a good night's sleep and I'll see you again in the morning. Meanwhile there are a couple of people to see you, but I will tell them to come back tomorrow morning. See if they can spark something deep down in that big vacant black box of yours."

I heard him open the door but I was gone again before he was.

When next I became conscious, faint slivers of light, like mirror fragments, tiny and spasmodic reflections of my life and the people in it, started to flash across the screen of my cloudy mind. It started with a picture of Tina. For a brief instant I could see her face, but who was she? Then a flashback of Feinstein, grave and unsmiling. And who was he? I wondered. Though I could not put names to anyone at the time I soon realised that my mind was shuffling the deck of my important people; as well as Tina and Feinstein I saw Barbie and Jo, Smuts and Jimmy Rogers. My long dead father dropped in for the most fleeting visit of all, but I knew him instantly, I may even have whispered 'Dad!' Within seconds I had dozens of people clamouring for recognition, all of them as if saying 'Me. I can help. Remember me, remember me!' It was exhilarating having the parade, and almost fun trying to scratch around in my mind for clues as to their identity, but at the same time anxious and frustrating, for the only name that would surface immediately was my old man. The others remained stubbornly under cover.

When the doctor next appeared at my side I was making progress. I knew it because I recognised his cheerful salutation.

"Greetings, Good Morning and Hi!"

"Doctor Thomas I presume...."

"Well done," he said, "that's a very promising start today!"

He took my hand and felt for the pulse. Satisfied, he let my hand drop.

"Sister will take those bandages off your face now, let's see what you look like, and, more important, you can see what we look like." He laughed at his little witticism.

Sure enough, when the bandage came off and I opened my eyes I could see. Out of practice though, it took a blink or two for me to properly focus on these two beautiful people at my bedside. I had been a little apprehensive, wondering if they were telling me the truth, perhaps I was actually blind? But there they were, and I never saw such a welcome sight. They both looked warm, caring and friendly. I was momentarily overwhelmed.

"Thank you, thank you," was all I managed to stammer as I absorbed the scene. I was in a small room, obviously a hospital private ward, mine was the only bed, surrounded by the usual hospital gunk – metal bedside cabinet, a buzzer button within reach of my good arm, a simple trolley at the end of the bed, a single government issue armchair close by the cabinet.

I blinked a few times.

"St Anne's?" I asked. The name popped up out of nowhere. At least I could now recall the name of the only hospital I had ever been in.

"No, Andrew Fleming," he said.

"Can I have a mirror?"

Sister produced one. I looked at it.

"Is that really me?"

"That's you alright, Mr. Francis Hunter Rowland Hill. Minus eyebrows and lashes and plus those bits of gauze covering your small burns. How does it feel?"

"Is that my name?"

"It is."

"I'll have to get used to it."

I was struggling a little to take it all in. Was the face in the mirror me? The fact is that I did not know what I looked like, it had been ambushed out of me. I had no point of reference now, other than my old man and my name, and the name itself did not seem familiar. There was nothing else to remind me of who I was. The man in the mirror looked foreign. He, I, unshaven, but not truly bearded – a week-old stubble perhaps. His, my, hair, cropped short; no eyebrows, no lashes. Blue eyes, big chin line, no wrinkles, 'white' skin (only as opposed to 'black' or 'coloured', that much I knew).

"Good God, man," I said out loud, intentionally dramatic for the benefit of my little audience, "who is this fellow, for I know him not."

"No inkling? Not even a tingle of recognition?" Doctor Thomas asked.

"Complete stranger, I said. Looks pretty beat up. Friendly eyes. How do you do."

"That's alright for now," the doctor told me. "The people who are anxious to see you are back again now. I won't tell you who they are – let's see if a little charm and beauty can stir that old black box on your shoulders. Just let sister here tart you up a bit for the visit, freshen up those perfectly hideous gauze patches under your eyes. See you later."

He left the sister to change the dressing on my cheeks, which she did gently and speedily before brushing my more or less hairless scalp in an affectionate way with her hand, and disappearing with a thumbs up and a confident wave.

Waiting for my next visitors I dozed off, but I had barely shut my eyes before I became aware of someone else in the room.

I made a show of covering my eyes with left hand and peeping through my fingers. I didn't recognise the young woman I saw staring at me.

"Don't you know me," she asked.

Not even knowing my own name until minutes ago I felt bold and brazen.

"No I don't, but I wish I did. You are utterly gorgeous and incredibly sexy. Please don't tell me you are my sister or even a close cousin..."

She laughed and leaned down to kiss me, first a little peck on the neck, then, saying 'what the hell' she kissed me most voluptuously on the mouth.

"There," she said, "does that remind you of anyone?"

I wish I could record that my memory flooded back in that instant, but in truth it oozed in through the crack in the door created by this extraordinary woman's touch. My first recognizable thought was of the name Tina. But No! That was not her. If not Tina, then who? The widow Flanagan! Barbie! Office! Jo! Dog! Army! Call up! Ambush! Shoot man, shoot!

The oozing became a trickle, the trickle a flood until it was almost too much. I don't know how long it was before I could say anything. These things always seem longer than they are, but it was long enough for Barbie to nudge the question again; "Well? Anything happening in there?"

By then my brain was well at work. Stuff was pouring in, but still I was smart enough to recognise the advantages of a small dose of devious dissembling.

131

"Bells are ringing," I said. "I know that tooth paste... is it yours? Would you mind trying that again? But don't rush it. Definitely bells are beginning to ring."

She fixed upon me a distinctly curious look as if willing to believe that I was having her on, pulling her leg as they say in the army and everywhere else these days. But then she seemed to shake off the doubt and got down to the business of a perfectly serious kiss, could it be the first act of prolonged affection? I hoped so. Then her hand stole under the blankets and into my lap, looking for my hands. What she met there made her pause as if vaguely thinking once more that my amnesia was all entirely an invention.

"Don't stop," I said. "I think everything is coming back with a whoosh."

"Devious bastard," she said, without removing her hand. "You absolutely lovely scheming bastard, sod, swine. Does the doctor know what a charlatan you are? What about your beautiful nurse, did you plan this whole show with her?"

We laughed together. It was an intense moment. I didn't need physical relief. I was just happy to be feeling half-way back in the real world, and especially at the idea of having been brought back by a woman as lovely as I thought Barbie to be.

I told her it was all true and that until the moment she kissed me passionately on the mouth I was still deep in a shell of desperate unknowing. Whole years of my life had vanished.

"I'll write it up and send it to the Lancet. What a way to bring a man back from the dead! The kiss and touch of life. What a concept. What a talent. You'll be in great demand wherever men get knocked on the head. You'll make a fortune."

"Oh shut up," she said. "Just lose that part of your memory again, we need to talk business..." I did not need to be told to shut up or down. Quite suddenly the elation of seconds before was gone and a black fatigue rolled over me like a thunderstorm on a dry day.

I think I heard her calling the nurse and saying:" He's gone again."

I was gone a long time.

* * *

When next I was able to focus on the realities of my life, all had changed. It was as if recent events to do with my recovery had been wiped out, or re-sequenced to a new approved script. As to how long I was out on this occasion, the nurse would tell me only that it was 'days'. It is apparent that in that period I had had several visits from Tina; it may even be that she was by my side more or less the whole time. All I now know for certain is that by the time I was fully conscious again I was married again. According to Tina's version of what happened it was early morning and the sun was shining through the ward window, bathing me in a warm glow, when she noticed tears rolling down my cheeks. Thinking it evidence of recovering consciousness, she asked me what the matter was. Expecting a jumble of half-awake thoughts she was, she said, staggered to hear me confess all my sins against her and ask for her forgiveness. Whereupon it was settled that the past was past and that our future lives lay together once more – 'till death'.

I cannot say that I was shocked or even troubled by the news; I took it at face value, bearing in mind that face value for me in my recently wiped-out state was a very different kind of thing. Still troubled by guilt over the entire episode I was also, to some extent, relieved, as if a mighty burden had been removed from my shoulders and taken over by someone else.

Yes, I thought, Tina can take over the management of our joint lives; Tina can run the business, Tina arrange the loans, Tina pay the bills, Tina just tell me what to do and when. It had a definite appeal for a man still hovering on the brink of amnesia.

As if to cement the new arrangement, when I next saw the ward nurse she had a letter for me from my dearest widow friend, late widow lover.

"My very dearest Hunter,

"Tina came to see me at the office to tell me about your plans. I am delighted for you and believe me I will do everything I can to help you two make things work.

133

"As far as the office is concerned I am still very much involved unless I hear from you to the contrary, and then of course you can rely on me to make things as easy as possible.

Meantime I have been called to London on our mutual behalf. A big opportunity I think for a post-war situation. Don't know more than that right now but I do think it worth the trip.

"Jo is perfectly capable of looking after things until you are sufficiently recovered to get involved yourself, which I hope and pray will be soon.

"I cannot imagine that you will have any further military commitment, so why don't you and Tina take a break and go down south for a while. Do you good!"

Signed: two little crosses and a sweet little comic spider dangling on a thread from the word *"Flanagan"*.

Chapter 19

I did not have too long to wait to find out more of what had happened to me. A sergeant from the Intelligence Corps, a pale, depressed man with a bushy moustache whose name I forgot seconds after he introduced himself, arrived at my bedside soon after breakfast the next morning to 'debrief' me. I imagine his mission was to find out if I could shed more light on the way the incident unfolded. He was courteous and attentive and it was clear to me that he was after information rather than evidence. Why I had feared the reverse I am not sure, except for a nagging self-doubt; had I performed up to scratch in the affair? Had I been of any use to my side, or had I been an impediment, a wounded piece of baggage to be dragged out of trouble?

I lay back and told him all I knew from the time we left camp that morning to the moment I saw the gook go down under fire. I told him of my own hesitation on seeing the man step out from tall grass with a gun in his hands, and my last certain recollection of hearing Smuts calling out the dread word 'Ambush!'

He was making notes. They must have been very short, for there was little to my part in the incident; as far as I could recollect it was over quickly for me – seconds rather than minutes I suspect.

I mentioned that.

"In this war contacts seldom last long," he said. "For the gooks it is usually a hit and run affair, and there is nothing wrong or cowardly with that strategy and it is important that we all recognise that. They know they cannot match the quality of our manpower, communications, ordnance, transport and so on. Hell they can't even get to their men when they're down. No aircraft, no vehicles, no radios even. But what they can do and are doing very successfully, is to tie us up. They don't have to fight big battles to win this war, they just have to bleed us to death economically by keeping us very busy with frequent little hits."

"You feel some sympathy with them?" I asked, with, I hope, not the slightest hint of disapproval, which anyway I certainly did not feel.

"I suppose I do in an abstract and intellectual sense," he said. "I'm on call-up just like you. I'm a teacher and I teach black kids. The ones I teach are not communists, guerrillas, terrorists, or even just plain gooks, but they soon will be all of those things when they leave school. We teach them maths and we teach them history along with all the other subjects, but from those two alone they know that life in Rhodesia does not add up. It's hard to explain to a child why it is that he and all his kind are considered inferior, not good enough to vote when they grow up, even though they are educated and may eventually have university degrees recognised all around the world. I can't do it! I won't do it because in any case I don't think they are inferior. So how do I explain to them what's going on in their home country? It is a hell of a dilemma for anyone who thinks about it."

"You could tell them it's just a cock-fight between Robert Gabriel Mugabe and, say, Bishop Abel Muzorewa assisted by Ian Douglas Smith," I said. "Nothing but a cock-fight to see who runs the roost. A power struggle. They'll know about that. Forget the underlying issues for the present or you will go mad."

He seemed distressed. Though he obviously liked to think of his standpoint as abstract and intellectual, I could see that he was deeply involved emotionally. I wanted to put my arms around him, cheer him up, give him a hug, but it was only a fleeting thought, a reaction you see; I was lying there with my one arm trussed up like a fowl. He should have been thinking about me. I gave him a gentle nudge.

"Do you know the outcome of my contact situation? Was anyone killed?"

He cheered up.

"Three gooks altogether," he said, "including the one you and Smuts shot at. Only one hospital casualty on our side and you know who that is, The Leopard vehicle was pretty badly fucked. You should never have done that trip with just two vehicles. Three would probably have put them off. As it was, you guys were just an invitation to a twilight bullet fest. Still, no good worrying about that now, nothing else much was available after the night attack on your camp position.

"I don't know at what point you were wounded, but we think you must then have been flung out when your vehicle veered off the road and up the embankment.

"It was while accelerating madly out of the ambush *Kill Zone* that the driver lost control and hit this embankment, causing the vehicle to come to a sudden stop and then tip over on the slope. Incredibly, none of your guys were killed when that happened, but somehow the way you were thrown out got you concussed and burned. Luckily the driver had managed to get you a couple of hundred metres away from the main ambush site itself by then, and with three of their number already killed, the gooks gave it up when your pals managed to regroup and fire off a few FN bursts. Someone had the presence of mind to pull you to safety in a ditch beside the truck. By that time you were well and truly out of it, quite unconscious and unable to react for yourself. At what point in the incident and with what result you fired your FN no one has so far been able to work out.

"All your mates, Brander, Cleve, Tyler, and the others, were badly shaken up and bruised but not badly enough to get them off the rest of the call-up. You all did well and I expect you will get some kind of recognition for your efforts eventually. Their call-up ends is over I think. No doubt some of them will be in to see you if you are still here."

Packing his notes into his impressive briefcase he vanished with a plaintive squeak:

"See you again soon, when this is all over, perhaps."

Chapter 20

Including the head bash in the ambush I have been concussed three times in my life. I have already passed over the rugby 'accident' which I so badly mixed up with the ambush story – out for four days. The other time I was eight years old, helping myself to some peaches in a neighbourhood garden when the owner surprised me and I fell out of the tree, striking my head on the gnarled old tree trunk. Out for three days. This time? Out for at least four days. I am thus able to say with some authority that you learn very little from an amnesia inducing smack on the head. On the other hand, the experience offers the unique opportunity to get to know who you are again.

Having had some time to absorb, and in turns to like and dislike the realities of my newly discovered persona, and especially the prospect of returning to married life, I was lying in bed the following Monday morning pondering the possibility that I might actually be insane when the ward door burst open and there, in full camouflage kit, was Smuts with four others from our mutual ambush squad, freshly released from call-up.

It was a wild scene for a moment, much shouting of 'Hey', and 'You', and 'Look at that!', and then boyish hugs all round to demonstrate we were really all very pleased to see each other, and especially for them to find that the sole actual victim on our side was alive and apparently well. Then the lads just stood around for a while and, one by one, slowly peeled off with a wave or a thumbs up or some other undefined hand signal suggesting solidarity or team spirit or whatever. At length I was left with Smuts. He pulled up a chair and sat down at my bedside.

"Sorry about all that," he said. "They insisted on coming to wish you a speedy etcetera, etcetera... Nice guys. A good bunch to be in the shit with I guess."

Before I could reassure him that I was in fact perfectly happy they had all showed up, he went on; "now you old dog, how are you really? The docs say you are doing fine, but you are very pale and seem to be taking strain. Are you alright?"

"Pale," I said. "Is that all? I'm head sick and quaking inside. I don't know if I am losing my mind or maybe I am already absolutely certifiably insane."

I told him the story of my recovery so far, or at least what I could recall of it, giving him everything that I actually remembered and that which I did not – in particular the bits about my sick-bed confession to Tina and the consequences.

"I cannot doubt Tina," I said. "She just would never do something dishonest like that to me. But still it doesn't altogether fit because I know that when I first came to the point where I knew who I was, Barbara was with me and I was like freshly in love with her all over again. So happy. But I think her visit had the effect of another kick in the head and I must have passed out all over again. So now Tina and I are together again, The Widow has been nicely spoken to and she has buggered off (I showed him the note), and I'm lying here trussed like a fowl on one side and just not sure what really comes next.

"Not that I am against going back to Tina, I am just a little confused at it all being decided while I was out of control. Why the fuck can I not remember that part?"

"Guilt?" he suggested. "Deep seated guilt that you can't cope with, and so your brain simply makes the whole thing disappear."

"Thank you Doctor, that makes me feel fucking wonderful. Guilty, guilty, guilty."

"Hey!" he said. "Don't panic, it is just a mechanism, and if there is nothing behind it, it will pass. Face facts Dog, nothing has really changed, you're no more chained to Tina than you were before. Actually, when you leave this place you leave as a brand new man. I'd say congratulations. Lucky Dog."

I perked up.

"OK. That's all good. Now have you got time to tell me how the action went? I know more or less nothing. A guy from the Intelligence Corps came to see me but seemed to be more interested in what I could tell him, which was nothing really. I saw the gook, I heard your shout. I think I saw him go down but I'm not sure. What the fuck was I doing while you buggers were all fighting off the ZANLA army?"

"Don't worry Dog," you were there in the thick of it too. We both fired at the man with the RPG and then just carried on firing until we ran out of magazines. The important thing is that we got the man at the back. Another split second or two and he would have taken us out. A Land Rover Leopard is no match for an RPG at ten paces from behind.

"Another thing. Everyone in the Leopard kept up a great firing rate and I think that was vital in saving our skins. It all added to the general racket and I am sure must have been unsettling for the buggers waiting for us in the killing zone a couple of hundred yards beyond where we were first attacked.

"Let's face it though, I think we were all lucky. The result could have been very different if either of us had not had our eyes on the road at that precise instant. I get the shivers just thinking about it. Flip of a coin, man, flip of a coin. Life or death."

"Wish I could remember more." I said rather lamely.

Around about then there was a timid little knock on the door and Tina looked inside.

"Come in, come in, join the party," Smuts told her. "There's nothing to drink but the conversation is OK."

The ready banter lasted only a few minutes before Smuts excused himself, leaving me alone with Tina. I smiled at her and reached out my hand to make sure she felt truly welcome, but she did not immediately respond.

"I hope I never have to see you in that uniform again," she said.

"Well sweetheart," I replied, striving not to be confrontational. "I am still in the army, and I am not sure the damage is enough to get me an immediate discharge on the grounds of health."

"Oh let's forget all that. How are you feeling today?" she asked in a breezy, cheerful and, I thought, utterly artificial way.

"A bit cloudy," I replied, "but clearing. At least I know who I am, where I come from and what I do. How I got here is also no longer a complete mystery thanks to a visit from an army bloke yesterday, and Smuts has filled me in on the missing story of the ambush. The outlook is great."

A little kiss and an even briefer hug and Tina was gone; off on a mission to add cement to the mix we were trying hard to make.

Fade to black. Fade to the droop, fade to loss of interest.

The rest of the week played out its way to the end. Visitors came, stayed for a while and left. I have no doubt whatsoever that those who knew me best and cared for me most will have left whispering to each other that I was greatly changed, and wondering if, perhaps, I had suffered more severe head damage than the medics were giving out. And it was not an act on my part. I was indeed much subdued. I felt listless, unmotivated and idle. My room was a maze of flowers, chocolates, books, magazines; there seemed to be hundreds of gifts and cards, testifying to the enormous circle of my friends and business associates. In earlier times, perhaps even as little as a few weeks before, I would have been humbled but happy by the show of affection and good wishes; now each item seemed to me yet another limiting clause in a complicated contract setting out the terms of the sale to society of my soul.

The strange thing about this vile flood of introspection and misery was that it did not, for a second, make me regret my part of the deal – being back with Tina. That arrangement was now fixed, I thought, a steady pole angled like earth's axis, around which my life must now revolve in timeless harness to truth, honesty and sterling effort. I supposed and accepted that sometimes I would be in summer, sometimes in the cold; that one day there would be a new spring, another the horrid depths of winter. Just as I imagined how the thoughts of my visitors might be running, I took it for granted that my abject mental state, so unusual in my old easy-going nature, was a side effect of this particular concussion, or of the pills I was taking to wind back time and unscramble my brain.

Chapter 21

Nurse talking. "There's someone here to see you. He says to tell you it's Ross."

It was the following afternoon, I had been half hoping for a visit from him, if only to talk about what would happen next in my army career. I didn't want out, I hoped the accident wouldn't prove terminal.

"Ah," I said, "the fixer at last, show him in, I can't wait!"

Ross was smartly dressed in his finest civilian suit, obviously not on army business, I thought.

Men didn't hug each other much in those days, but he tapped my good shoulder with the back of his hand and then gave it an affectionate squeeze.

"Still having a good loaf in bed I see Hunter" he said. "I thought by now you would have been back at the office directing some new additions to your harem..."

"Harem be fucked," I retorted. "For some reason that I have yet to fathom I am being kept here on a diet of brief waking hours, and hours and hours of pill-assisted sleep. I wouldn't be surprised if it works out at that I'm spending 20 hours a day lost to the world."

"Ah," he said. "Feeble brains need lots of that, especially after far too much sex and a bad bit of jostling. How you feeling otherwise?"

"I'm alright, pretty good really, great. Physically in good shape and the old brain box is OK too. There were a few blanks but between Smuts and an army guy who came around for a chat I think I am now as fully in the picture as I am ever going to be. I am only sorry that I missed half the action. Have you got any news for me?"

"I have. Your transfer to Psy Ops has gone through. You're in. As it happens the next induction course is quite soon and if the doctors say you're fit enough for it, you will be included. And by the way, you are now Sergeant Hill. Can't have mere Riflemen writing speeches for top brass."

"Will that be my job?" I asked.

"Not really," he replied. "But our writers do get asked to do all manner of things – from rubbishing Mugabe to polishing the marbles of some dodgy politicians."

"Shit, straight off the rim of the frying pan into the sizzling fat."

"Don't worry about it. It will be a breeze. You may even enjoy it," he said as he got up and left the ward with a cheery wave.

I was not alone long, however, for Smuts dropped in for what he called a flying visit – "literally".

"Quick test of your memory," he said. "When I came yesterday I completely forgot to mention something that may be important.

"Remember the night at the Quill Club when you introduced me to Norton; there was some narrow minded little prick who took exception to us being on friendly terms with Norton because he is black. Do you remember that incident, or is it buried now beyond reach?"

"Absolutely I do, no bloody problem. Still irritates me endlessly just thinking about that arsehole."

"Well, after we left the club that night he checked us out through the staff, got our names, and made some kind of disparaging report about the incident at his army unit. Not quite an official complaint – more of a nudge to Intelligence. Obviously he thinks we may be batting for the other side, or just careless dummies giving away military secrets to the opposition.

"The most potentially damaging part of his report is that he claims I passed myself off as an army officer and, worse, introduced an unknown African visitor, a Zambian journalist, as a Captain of RAR. His company Adjutant passed the info on to our Adjutant and his guys called in the MPs to check the story out. They were at the Depot waiting for me when we were stood down, which delayed me a bit but they were quite open and straightforward about the whole thing. Of course I denied the bullshit and gave them a statement of my memory of the evening. So now I'm waiting to hear if anything will come of it. They will very likely call on you when the doctors think you are well enough.

As a sort of media person what do you think of that? Anything for us to worry about?"

"Rubbish," I said without giving it much more than a cursory thought. "Surely no case. Won't go far, and certainly not to court. But it probably will waste a lot of time and I'm sure it won't do either of us any great harm as far as our newly integrated Army is concerned anyway. Ross was just in to tell me that I have been accepted by Psy Ops now if I can pass a medical. What about you and the Scouts?"

"Might hurt a bit I suppose, the Scouts are sensitive to the media. I have set my mind on the unit, not only for now but also as something that will be useful for my future. Being in the bush so often has grown on me, and if this war ends while I am still young enough I may give up my so-called mining supply career and go into the bush business, here if possible, South Africa or Zambia if not. I want to have a few years learning how to hunt and track and then start a safari lodge, bring in hundreds of wealthy American tourists and show them this incredible piece of the world with all its wild-life treasures. And then retire by the time I get to 50. But what the hell, if I lose out because of this cunt I'll take it as a hint from the universe.

"I'm ready to go head to head with the complaining bastard. I don't think you are implicated in any way other than as a witness to what passed that evening. Apart from the general complaint of talking too loosely there is nothing specific against you. You don't have to be included in whatever follows if you would rather stay out of it."

"Fuck no. Of course I'm in it. If the MPs don't come to me I'll go to them, soon as I'm up. And as for the bush life, whey hey! Can you use a dog with half a good brain, messy shoulder and slightly burned eyebrows? I want to come too. Unbutton all my personal shit and start living again! Count me in if there's room for another dog in your bushy future. "

145

Chapter 22

It was to be almost three weeks before I was discharged from hospital. My brain and my facial burns had caught up, but the doctors worried that the bullet wound might turn nasty if left to its own devices in civilian life. As much as I begged and pleaded to be let out they insisted I stay. I was anxious about many things but mostly about the challenge of a return to the quiet married life of my past which now seemed so many years ago. Tina was a regular visitor, Smuts came often, but of my partner Flanagan there was still no sign, I assumed she was still involved in Zambia. In her place to give me occasional updates on how our business was going came Jo in her fresh young vitality. On her first visit I told her how much I had always cared for Tina and that the accident had brought us together again. Her reaction was a simple bright smile as if to say that she was ever so pleased for me, and we left it at that. I thought I passed a test of some kind.

Smuts and I enjoyed hours of mainly small talk, idle chatter about the war, our hopes and dreams for a post-war future, starting up a safari business on the banks of Lake Kariba, stuff like that. What we did not discuss in any depth was my return to Tina and the married state. I do not know if it embarrassed him or perhaps he had some sixth sense about it. The nearest we came to a conversation on the topic was when he said something about 'all you wonderfully happily married people'. Rather taken aback at the connection, I think I just stared at him in dumb amazement. He put his arm on my good shoulder and said quietly and without any particular emphasis "Wish you both well, don't give up". There was nothing to say but a mumbled 'thanks'.

My ward was rather big for just one patient, a fact I was just mulling over early morning after being woken before daylight, when it became clear that I would soon have company. An extra bed was wheeled in and prepared for a new arrival.

Sometime around noon he arrived. No one introduced us, and he had nothing to say for himself, being quite unconscious at the time. The two orderlies who wheeled him in and moved him to his new bed said nothing. Later, a nurse who had come in to check on him was slightly more informative. To my enquiry she would say only "RLI Fire Force. 19. Badly wounded. Shattered pelvis and other injuries. Out of danger now. Just coming round from another op. You guys go out and get shot very quickly and we, slowly, slowly, try to make you well again. Some, like poor young Humpty Dumpty here, we never can quite put together again."

Humpty's steady, even snoring was infectious. I soon slipped off myself, and slept soundly through much of the afternoon. I was wakened by the sound of my new neighbour burbling away happily like a child in a cot, obviously still very much in a semi-anaesthetised state but gradually becoming aware of his surroundings. When I went to the bathroom and stopped by his bedside to see if he was awake, he pierced me with two soft and beautiful blue eyes and a curious, enquiring little smile.

"Hello," he said, not much above a whisper. "I'm Wallace. I've been wounded you know."

"Hello then Wallace, I'm Hunter. I'm your neighbour. Slightly wounded myself, but I'll soon be out of here. Do you feel like talking?"

"I'm fine, only a little woozy."

"What happened?"

"Oh," he said, "it was just a chopper contact. We were coming down to be dropped off. Funny thing, it wasn't sore, more like a heavy punch, knocked me off my feet and I couldn't get up. I'm glad I was the only one. My friends got all the bastards," he almost chortled, "every one of them. I can't walk but the doctor says it's OK I will be able to soon."

He was a wonderfully good humoured casualty. He laughed all the time. I didn't know what at, but I presumed it was the memory of things he had seen and done that amused him.

We talked again next day and I learned a little more about him; talking was a thing he liked to do as much as laughing, because with him, talking always led to something to laugh at.

147

He told me he was a South African from a small town in the Western Cape. He had come to Rhodesia to join the police not long after leaving school because it seemed like a nice job and he didn't want to join the South African army – 'too dangerous'. The day before he was due to sign up at Police Headquarters he met up with a bunch of young *troopies* of the Rhodesian Light Infantry having a wild bash in their favourite drinking place, Salisbury's *Round Bar*. Hooking up with them in their feverish pursuit of pleasure was cheap and easy, and the next day it was even easier to switch his proposed enrolment from the police to the RLI. It was something he said he never regretted, even now that he had got such a bad bullet wound 'in the nought'.

"Nought?" I asked, when he first said it. The tag was new to me.

"Yeah, you know, bum, ring-piece, arsehole, nought." He laughed at the rich variety he was able to conjure up for that body part. Then he became momentarily very serious and in a confidential sort of way.

"The doctor says I will probably be impotent forever, but I don't really believe him. Still, a bullet in the nought can definitely slow you down. I know that much."

He wasn't much interested in my story but I didn't mind that; I had rather lost interest in it myself. I must have seemed like an old man to him; his war was all about sharing adventures with boys of his own age. Good old Wallace.

When about a week after Wallace's arrival the doctor told me at last that I could go I was sorry to say goodbye to him with his irrepressible good nature. He had made my problems seem slight and self-centred.

I called Tina and told her I was to be discharged next day. Since my car was still at the depot there was no point in coming to collect me. I would get home myself. She seemed concerned.

"Are you sure you can manage?"

"If I couldn't they wouldn't be letting me out."

"OK then. See you later."

148

Leaving hospital was not simply a case of walking out and making my own way back to the depot. I was irritated to find that I had first to be delivered by ambulance to the Army offices so they could formally sign me out. Technically I was still on call-up, a military patient, army property, and must be delivered back to the army like any other item of equipment. Only after that would I become once more a civilian, a free citizen capable of making all my own decisions.

I packed the few items of my kit that had been salvaged from our camp in the bush, reflecting as I did so that soldiers at war are mercifully free of the garbage that so marks civilian life; my sponge bag, car keys, change of clothing, three pairs of socks, four of underpants, a few ball pens, a book, that was all I now had, my *impedimenta*.

The formality of being stood down was short, usually a matter of picking up your pay for the period and handing in your rifle. My rifle, of course, might be a bit of problem, I thought, since I had lost it along with my memory. That was something they were not aware of at the armoury when I went for the formality of a release signature, but they quickly found out and apologised for the 'inconvenience' of their ignorance, becoming ever so respectful. To them I was the latest member of the 'wounded-in-action' club. From now on my views on any subject would count for so much more and I should never again need to wait in any kind of queue. That, at least, was the impression they managed to convey as they scooted around at speed, stamping my forms and clicking their heels.

At length it was all done. I was free to walk out. Somewhere in the gigantic car park was my car. I hadn't forgotten that I had driven myself to the depot at the start of the stint, Tina not being around in my life at that time.

I wondered if the old Volvo would start, wouldn't the battery be flat by now? When I found her she was covered in a thin layer of dust, nearly two months' worth. I felt an urge to apologise and to complain. I wanted to scream at the car. I wanted to shout out loud 'sorry about the dirt... but don't you know what's been going on? Don't you care that I could have been killed?'

Instead I wrote with my finger in the dust on the rear windscreen 'Wash me'.

Somehow it made me feel whole again. At that moment I started looking forward to the rest of my life.

Chapter 23

I had a few hours to get used to being back before Tina came from her work. I showered and changed into T-shirt and jeans. It was good to be home. Everything Tina had taken with her when she left me was back in place. It was as if nothing had ever changed, no dust had settled there. By the time she arrived I was in the perfect mood to meet her. My mind was a blank, I was relaxed and content. I was like our comfortable couch in the lounge. I was part of the furniture. Now our situation would need no introduction or discussion, there was no thick ice to be broken.

As I heard her car coming up the drive I went out to meet her. We kissed before going inside and it all seemed fine again, on the surface at least. Nothing was said about the past. We looked at each other a lot and smiled. Sometimes I laughed out loud. Tomorrow I would go to the office. The thought made me flinch.

As I look back on these things now I can see that I was in a somewhat weird state of heightened euphoria, almost certainly caused by the growing realisation of quite how lucky I was to have survived 'the accident'. I was lucky to be alive, lucky to be wounded where it would heal quickly and without lasting damage, lucky to be whole. Like any other drug, the euphoria shielded me from fears and worries, and enhanced the pleasures of everything else. In my case those fears and worries could be summed up in the two words that still had the capacity to make me flinch - 'the office'. The mere mention, the most fleeting thought about 'the office' put me into an immediate mental panic. I was not ready to face up to and deal with the conflicting emotions the place involved. In an instant I decided to follow Barbie's advice. Tina and I would go away for a while, take leave.

I wondered whether Barbie was back from her trip and in command of our joint business venture. I didn't really want to ask. Yet it was only if I could now rely on her to run the business that I would be able to go away. The irony of it all made me flinch some more. I would check tomorrow and make the arrangements by telephone, I wouldn't go near the place.

At breakfast next morning Tina asked if I would be going in to the office. I told her I didn't know. I ducked the subject. She seemed ready to do that too, and fled the house without further discussion.

Later when I called the office to discuss my taking leave, to my pleasant surprise, Barbie was back.

"Good to hear you," I said. "How was England? I've completely lost track of time, have you been gone long?"

"Oh just a week. Had to get back in case you were laid up a long time. "

"Bravo." I said. "I wish I could say I knew you were the one from the very first time I clapped eyes on you, but that would be a lie. It was the second time."

"Very funny," she said.

I told her Tina and I were thinking of going away for a while.

"Good idea," she said. "Get your health back, don't worry. It will be good for me to have to deal with whatever comes up. If I need you I can always ring."

Then "why don't you make it a second honeymoon?"

The comment, for it was a comment more than a question, broke the spell I had been trying assiduously to weave.

"Because that's not what I want or need," I said in the quietest most controlled voice I could muster.

The weight of all the emotions I had pushed back broke the flimsy dam I had erected.

"What I really and truly feel like at this moment is some slightly longer-term form of selective amnesia. Or, to put it another possible way, what I wish for is to be able to forget the magic few weeks you and I had before my call-up. For all this second honeymoon bullshit I'm not over you. I'm just trying to do the right thing. Going away may help, but it won't be a second honeymoon."

"Sorry," she said.

"It will take a while to organise our holiday. Call me if you need me, I'll be here at home." Ever so slowly I put the phone down. But it rang almost instantly and the subtlety was wasted.

It was Barbie ringing back.

"Sorry about that. Forgot to tell you the Military Police were here this morning half an hour after we opened. They want you to call when you get in so they can come for a chat. Didn't say why. I imagine more questions about the ambush."

"Not quite, but what the hell. Did they leave a contact number?"

"Yes."

"Please call them for me. Tell them to come here to the house. Tell them I'm on recuperation leave. Tell them I won't be back at work for at least a hundred years."

She laughed.

"I hope we see you a little sooner than that..."

About an hour later two burly MPs, one large, the other extra-large, arrived at the house in a khaki Land Rover with red Military Police labels splashed all over it. They wore red and white crested headgear and small white gaiters above their incredibly highly polished black boots. They looked aggressive and belligerent, but that may have been what I was projecting when first I saw their vehicle – they say many people have the same response to the mere sight of anything labelled 'police'. In fact they were soft spoken and polite, maybe a little too precise, but I couldn't fault them for correctness.

The one I labelled *Extra-large* opened proceedings.

"We have a complaint against Rifleman S. Brander to the effect that he led people to believe that he was a commissioned officer in the Zimbabwe Rhodesian armed forces. The complainant says this took place in your presence and that a black Zambian journalist by name Norton James, was also there. This incident was said to have taken place at the Quill Club in the Ambassador Hotel.

"At this stage please understand that this is a report only and no formal accusations have been made. It is possible that a charge may be laid arising from our investigations. Are you happy to talk to us on that understanding?"

"I have been expecting you," I said. "I have been told of the story, and yes, I was present at the Club with Mr. Brander that night, and yes I am happy to set the record straight as far as I can. I believe I have a pretty clear recollection of events that evening. I certainly remember being incensed by the intrusion of the person who I suppose is your informant."

"I believe you have lately been involved in a military contact and that you were badly injured, including a severe concussion followed by a complete blackout from which you have only recently recovered?" he continued.

"That is true, or something very much like it," I replied. "But my memory loss was confined to the short period immediately surrounding the ambush and the head blow. I expect a medical report will confirm that. So if you are worrying that my version of events may not be clear, I'm sure it will be, but in any case there are other witnesses you could ask for confirmation. For a start there is my business partner Mrs. Barbara Flanagan who you must have met at my office this morning, she was there. And then the waiters at the club – one or two of them will have heard the whole thing."

"Good, good, good thank you. So then Sir, can I ask you to say what actually happened, what took place for this report to be made? Go ahead, I'm not recording this, I'll make a few notes but nothing more than that."

"Look," I said, "I'm a member of the Quill Club. I'm not actually a journalist myself but I was once and my work in Public Relations means I mix a lot with journalists. I happened to be at the club that night for a social get together with the Zambian man you mentioned, Norton James, who I had recently met and formed something of a friendship with. Barbara Flanagan came a little after I got there and we got Mr. Brander to come and join us. I felt sure he would be interested to meet Norton who is such a polished and urbane man – not the sort of African we meet here all that often, as a matter of fact not the sort of man you meet every day – black, white, yellow or brown.

154

"So we had a few drinks and were chatting away about this and that when this oaf of a man, probably a bit pissed at the time, came over to our group and chose to make an issue of us being on such obviously open and friendly terms with a black fellow.

"As you must know better than I do, the army has quite recently started commissioning black officers, they are becoming quite a common sight on television and even in the streets of town. But even forgetting that simple fact, it was an incredibly irritating thing to do to us. Mr. Brander took considerable exception to the intrusion, but he was very cool as he always is. Basically he said to this oaf something like 'what has it to do with you? For all you know this gentleman here could be a distinguished officer in our army. Black does not automatically mean enemy.'

"Mr. Brander has quite a commanding presence and this incident brought it out to the full. He was clearly angry but he did not lose his temper. Instead, after that little speech, he put the man down ever so effectively, I thought, pointing to his untidy appearance, half-loose tie hanging drunkenly around his neck and so on, and telling him to 'get a grip when you've been drinking, and smarten up'. It was, I suppose, mildly intimidating, probably a bit embarrassing for the guy. But if that amounted to passing oneself off as an officer then I'm a wheelbarrow."

"What do you know about this man Norton James?" the large MP, the smaller of the two, asked. "Do you know who he writes for?"

"I had just met him. Mrs. Flanagan apparently knew him a bit in Zambia. I think he said he worked for a Zambian paper but was also a stringer for some English crowd, or maybe an American wire service – it's quite common for journalists to work for more than one news organisation, especially out here in Africa, it's the only way they can make a half decent living."

"Is that what it means, being a stringer, like moonlighting?"

"Sort of. Sort of reporting on the side. You provide additional editorial cover in your territory for some organisation that can't or won't actually employ a full time correspondent of their own there.

So they pay you only for what they can use of what you send them. Occasionally they will ask you to do something particular for them and then you'd expect to be paid whether they use your stuff or not, plus expenses. Stringing can be very lucrative at times."

"You seem to know all about it."

"I told you, I was once in that world, I've been through all of that myself."

"But you're not writing for anyone now?"

"Nope."

Extra Large wrapped it up: "I think that should do it, we'll probably look in on Mrs. Flanagan, maybe try to get in touch with Mr. James too. Do you remember where he was staying?"

"Meikles. He must have been on a decent assignment otherwise he would have been staying with friends somewhere. Someone must have been picking up the tab."

"It didn't bother you talking to him knowing he was a journalist?"

"Of course not, I have no special information he could have got from me and used against this country if that's what you mean. If he had tried to quiz on anything sensitive I would have known, but actually we talked about nothing current, strictly in the zone of common philosophical speculation. Heavens above, at the time I probably didn't even know the exact date of my next call-up."

"Just checking..."

They were scarcely out the door when I called Smuts to tell him about the visit. He was not surprised. He had already been questioned, but he wanted to come around right away to talk it through more fully.

When he arrived we compared notes and concluded that our versions of the events were broadly the same, differing only perhaps in emphasis; so no trouble there.

"I think we can forget it," I said. "Although I suppose they will now do a very careful check on Norton – more thorough than they must have done when he came into the country I guess."

"You know, Dog," he said, "when you think how easy it must be for the gooks to find out everything they need to know about our

156

movements and our handling of this war it is really rather fatuous for our guys to start scratching around among the likes of us for fifth columnists. They really don't need to go digging into the behaviour of guys like you and I, or the credentials of a visitor like Norton. Even if he was a spy he could find out more by talking to any cook or housemaid in the country than by cuddling up to you or me. This country, Rhodesia, or Zimbabwe Rhodesia, whatever we choose to call it, still relies on a black workforce. Apart from the mechanics, the painters, the carpenters, teachers, nurses and so on, pretty well every white household has at least two black servants, most of them three.... cooks, maids, gardeners. They live in our back yards, and on high days and holidays they take off for their tribal homes. Once there they come under the influence of ZANU or ZAPU political commissars. Each and every one of them probably knows more about the real progress of the war than most of us do. And you know what, they come home from those weekends in their tribal areas and they say nothing. No servant of mine has ever once come to me and told me how it was when they visited home. Has anyone ever said a word to you?"

"Not a word, although my gardener Shadreck, who hasn't been away to his tribal home for months and months, once explained that he didn't want to go because of 'trouble that side'. I tried to press him on what kind of trouble he meant, but he just shook his head sadly, and said nothing. I know he is devoted to us and to me personally, but nothing will persuade him to get involved in anything that might be taken as informing against his own people."

"Wherever his heart is, he knows like they all do that, come the revolution, the price of collaboration will be high," Smuts answered.

"For all that, I suppose the MPs will visit Barbara to ask her version of our night out; maybe to grill her about Norton. I'll ring her when I leave here, maybe ask her out to dinner."

"Ouch." I said with feeling, "ouch, ouch and ouch."

"Sorry for that Dog, would you rather I didn't?"

"No, no, it's OK. Only that the heart wound is still a little open, maybe a little raw. It is quite something to do what I'm trying to do... Tina and I worked hard, we're still working hard, to have the business and a fairly decent home, and until I met Barbie we were fairly solid I would have said, boring, but solid. Actually it was not until that stag party after we came back from my first call up, that raunchy performance in the industrial sites, that I signed up to be a bastard. I guess Barbie might always have been a challenge, she has so much of everything: vitality, looks, brains, experience, a very colourful past, plus, for me at any rate, pure animal attraction, but as it was, and the mood I had got into, she was irresistible. It took a heavy blow on my head with lots of force to make me see how my desire could affect and perhaps destroy the little world that Tina and I were building together. But even now I fluctuate.

"Right at this moment I'm looking forward to Tina coming home from work, but I'd equally like to be finishing my work and opening our little office bar for a drink or two with Barbara and Jo, and you and maybe Norton. It's still a bit of a mess you see. There's nothing else wrong with me physically now, I'm shirking. I could easily be back at the office. I'm putting it off in the hope that I will be building up my resistance, or maybe suffering a total memory loss...."

"Ah Dog," he said. "You say it well, and I do understand. But I'll call her all the same. I need to know more about Norton James..."

I saw Smuts to his car and watched as he disappeared down the drive and out the gate. His plans for the evening had unnerved me a touch, I was a little on edge. I was trying to keep my balance.

Chapter 24

I suppose it was because I was consumed with fear rather more than curiosity that I phoned the office next morning as soon after Tina had left for her work as I judged there would be anyone in to answer the call. Jo was in and we chatted idly for a few minutes about my health and how busy Mrs. Flanagan was and how all our clients had expressed their best wishes to me for a speedy recovery.

"Thanks Jo," I said. "Tell them I'm getting better fast. Should be in at work any day now. Any chance of a quick chat with my partner?"

"Should be in soon. I'll get her to call you first thing."

Three hours later I was still waiting, and quietly steaming. Four hours later I could control my curiosity no longer so I dressed for work and drove into town.

Barbara was at our little office bar. She was entertaining people I had never seen before: three men aged somewhat over fifty. From the look of them I could see they were there on business; they had all come out of the same dressing machine, immaculately clad in dove grey suits, white shirts adorned with soft blue ties. One was balding, the other two must have had their hair done professionally that morning by the same stylist. Lawyers, I thought. Or maybe accountants, bean counters. I glanced around for their brief cases. Surely there would be an identical set of expensive leather briefcases? There was, neatly arranged – one at the foot of each of their three bar stools. I felt certain that if I looked closely I would spot the same elegant identifying logo on each one.

The office was very much an open plan arrangement: three square rooms in a line interconnected by open arched partitions. What went on at one end would inevitably be seen at the other. On my unexpected arrival, Barbara left her guests with some brief explanation that I could not hear, and came over to me right away. While her back was to the guests at the bar she mouthed something to me that I could not grasp but understood enough of to be guarded in my remarks.

Then, loud enough for all to be part of, Barbie continued: "this is an unexpected pleasure, Hunter. Come and meet the gang from Whitmore Hughes." There was no time to say more, but I knew the name to be an international audit partnership.

She introduced me simply as her colleague and chief partnership writer. Too quick for me to remember the three names.

"Hunter is still recovering from a very bad bout of the flu," she lied. "I didn't expect we would see him for a week or so more. But it is an excellent chance for me and, with your permission gentlemen, I'd like to fill Hunter in on your mission?"

In and around the three expressions of pleasure at meeting me, I heard the bald fellow agreeing to the digression.

The gang, the delegation, these three men, were from South Africa. They had come especially to brief a couple of PR companies on a project, as yet secret in detail, that would rapidly be put in place more or less the very minute that there was an agreed cease-fire leading to a political settlement in our war. It was not, we must understand, an offer of a contract to work on this project; more of an expression of interest in our company, and an invitation to put a document together to convince the principals of our abilities. This we were being invited to do within a few weeks of that day's date, for which we would be recompensed what was then a substantial sum in US currency, plus a monthly 'retainer' fee thereafter, subject to review every three months.

Baldy took up the story from Barbara's outline.

"What I have to stress," he said, "is that there is as yet no indication that your war is about to end. We have no inside information on that at all. However there are interested people in the larger world, and I am thinking specifically of Britain, America and South Africa, who believe the end is now in sight and they wish to be prepared so that they can play a constructive role in, shall we say, the reconstruction period.

160

"I cannot tell you much more than that beyond saying that our principals are not politicians. This has nothing to do with the politics of Rhodesia, Zimbabwe Rhodesia, or whatever else the country may one day be called. Let us just say that you don't have to be clairvoyant to predict the many business opportunities likely to open up once your country is back within the international fold. The people we represent would like to be among the first to be involved.

"In the meantime they wish to prepare themselves and their operations for that day. I am aware of the wartime restrictions that must apply in our coming communications. You will never be asked to divulge information that your government will deem classified. What we will ask of you is a general outline plan to deal with a number of communication possibilities and the likely costs to us of anything you do.

"Lastly I must stress that your government knows of our mission, so we are here with official blessing. You are free to share with them all the information we have shared with you today. Any questions?"

Between the two of us we asked a few; enough to show we were excited by the prospect and flattered at our selection. Then the three robots picked up their briefcases and trooped out the door. I angled myself to get a closer look at the brief cases. There it was. A discrete W-H in gold emboss just below the genuine leather maroon handle.

I saw our guests to the lift and then ran back to the offices in time to peep out of the window down to the ground floor entrance and watch them emerge from the building. They trooped across the street at a pedestrian crossing. I thought they look like the Beatles crossing Abbey Road. Then they were shown into a large purple Mercedes Benz by a snappily dressed chauffeur. Barbara was peeking too. Only when they disappeared from view did we risk what had obviously been on both our minds:

"So what was that all about?"

We looked at each other and shook our heads as if they were joined by a string.

"Well then," I said, "where did they come from? What brought them to our door? Is this the first fruit of our new association?"

"I wish I could claim it," she said. "The truth is they called very early this morning while I was alone in the office. It was so early Jo had not yet arrived and when the phone rang I thought it would be you, but it turned out to be these guys. I must have been talking to *Baldie*. He was very precise, He wanted to come round right away but I put him off because I had to meet Feinstein at 9 and I had no idea how long that would take."

"Carpet baggers," I said. "I suppose we must now get used to the idea that businessmen from all over the known world will be lining up for the opportunities that will develop if this war does end. Still, it is an opportunity for us and the retainer will be handy. Do you think Feinstein might have had a hand in getting them here?"

"I told him about the call when I saw him this morning. He didn't say much, so I asked him straight if he had any dealings with Whitmore Hughes."

"What did he say?"

"He said, and this is an exact quote, 'I talk to a lot of people'."

"Probably not him then, maybe just a routine enquiry through our Ministry of Trade and Economic Affairs, although the money angle might be against that. Someone must have pumped quite hard for us."

Of course my heart and mind were only half in this conversation. As if my very future depended more on it than any trivial subject of the future profitable operation of our company I itched to know from Barbie what had taken place last night when she and Smuts went out for drinks and perhaps dinner. But I found it ridiculously difficult to ask the question direct. So I took a wild roundabout shot.

"Is it remotely possible," I asked, "that this enquiry has something to do with Norton?"

"That's odd," she replied, "Norton keeps coming up. I saw Smuts last night and all he wanted was to find out what I know of Norton, who he really is, how I met him, and so on. Then again this morning, that's why I was with Feinstein. Army police contacted me yesterday and wanted to talk to me about guess who? Norton James.

"For anything to do with the military or any other kind of police I wanted to have someone friendly on my side. Feinstein has an infallible memory and in any case he always takes notes. So I told the MPs to meet me at his offices."

"And?"

"Couldn't tell anyone much really. I met Norton in Zambia after Jim had been gone about a year, I was impressed by his manner, his education, his speech, and of course his size; he's big man by any standard – must be nearly six foot six I would say. Stands out in any crowd. We had lunch together once or twice. I didn't see him again for about six months; actually not until I bumped into him at Meikles. He asked me to join him at the Quill club for drinks which was the night I bumped into you there and there was that vaguely racial incident which turned out to be the matter of interest to the MPs. Some kind of trouble maybe for Smuts although he doesn't think so; says it will all blow away. They asked me what I could remember of that incident. It wasn't much. I do remember being irritated by someone obviously drunk, and I remember worrying that it might lead to some kind of a scrap, but nothing more really."

I brought her up to date on my visit from the MPs. After that there was little more to say on the subject of Norton James. Yet I remember thinking that there could be further developments in the affair.

Barbara and I exchanged warm farewells. As she hugged me she said "I meant to give you that earlier but I thought the visitors might be alarmed. Are you fine? Are you better? Can you stay for a while? Don't answer that, I have to go myself. Appointment with another new client. This time definitely one of Feinstein's vast list of friendly and incredibly wealthy contacts. Later I'm meeting Smuts, hopefully to finish the chat we didn't finish last night. Join us if you can, bring Tina if you like. We'll be at La Bom from about seven on."

Well that did it. Though I had no justification for it, I was once again shattered at the thought that my widow woman might soon be someone else's.

What a mess, I thought, you're heading once more for an almighty mess.

Hurting unjustifiably and deeply, I said good-bye to Barbara as easily and confidently as the lump in my throat would let me manage, and she left.

It was still early, much too early for me to go home, so I thought I would stay in for a while and if nothing else, rummage around my desk to see what state I had left it in so many weeks ago. I stopped off at Jo's desk to tell her what I was doing and please not to send any calls my way.

"I'm not really here," I said more than half-truthfully. "I'm utterly somewhere else. It's far too early to go home and much too dangerous to hit the Hole. Probably wouldn't take more than a teaspoon of whisky to have me on my knees... I don't remember when last I actually had a drink, it seems so long ago. Actually I do remember now, it was in the army on our call up. Smuts and I were playing Bezant. We made some money. Have you ever heard of Bezant, Jo?"

"Only as a can of orange juice. Odd flavour, but quite more-ish."

"If anyone asks you to play a game of Bezant, don't do it Jo. You could lose your head."

"I believe I'll do that anyway," she answered. "Can I start right now by pouring you that teaspoon of whisky?"

Uh uh, I thought to myself, stop, take a deep breath, and think. Here comes trouble. But the trouble with that kind of trouble was that it was lovely, eagerly awaited, longingly looked forward to trouble, and now something to take my mind off Mrs. Flanagan.

"Fetch it Jo, let us waste no further time, let us drink to the future, the next four or five hours of it anyway."

Inhibitions now firmly locked up, she brushed close past me as she went to pour the drink, pausing briefly to kiss me gently on the forehead as she did so.

One of the few memorable pieces of advice from my father when I was in my final year before leaving school, now so long ago, was to pledge to be always true to myself, to never hide or disguise my own motives from myself, and to try to be guided by the resulting revelation which, he said, was always sure to come at moments of moral crisis. In that moment with Jo I knew very well that what I was about to embark on was more in protest at the apparent loss of Barbara than the perhaps inevitable loss of Tina.

I felt confused and hurt but I wanted not to look that way. I wished, as I always did, to look like Paul Newman's *Cool Hand Luke*. But at the same time Jo was beautiful, Jo was sexy, and Jo, it seemed, wanted me. So for all the alarm bells my father had set ringing in my head I went ahead anyway and plunged right in.

Jo brought the bottle of whisky to my desk. She was already half undressed. She had a teaspoon in her hand, and she sat very deliberately on my lap, poured a spoonful of Scotch, and, pretending to be my nurse, proffered it purposefully towards my slightly parted lips.

"Here's your medicine," she said. "Best taken often in mixed and loving company."

That was one other thing I liked about Jo: she did not beat about the bush.

I made quite a show of getting drunk on the teaspoon of alcohol, then brightened up.

"Why don't we do this in style?" I suggested. "Let's book into the Jameson Hotel and have some fun? I've got a suitcase somewhere in the cupboards here; we'll arrive at reception and just book in as man and wife. Drinks on the balcony, a shower before dinner, which we will have delivered to us by Room

Service. A couple more shots of Scotch, and then all the love that we can manage. How does that grab you? Come on, let's do it!"

Jo needed no urging, all the while through my short speech muttering 'yes yes yes' and then rapidly slipping back into her dress before disappearing to the office bathroom to put on some lipstick to make herself look more like a wife than a wayward secretary. I scratched around for the suitcase; found it and filled it with old newspapers and magazines to give it a bit of bulk in case the hotel porter insisted on carrying it in for me. My car was parked in the street outside the office, just across from the hotel and we could have walked right over in less than half a minute. But I wanted the car parked away from the office just in case Tina should come to look for me, so we jumped in, drove around the block and pulled up outside the hotel reception. Leaving Jo in the car I walked to the desk and, as casually as I could, booked in for the night as Mr. and Mrs. Hunter; I chose my own first name in case of bumping into some acquaintance who might greet me from near or afar. Far-sighted duplicity indeed, Mister Hill. Oh shut up, I said to myself, you're not my father.

A hotel driver took the car away to be parked while Jo and I, both rather too obviously striving for invisibility, followed the porter to our room on the first floor. I tipped the man and went straight for the mini-bar. My brassy veneer of just minutes before was beginning to wear thin, and but for the magnet of Jo's still unexplored body I might have come to my senses and fled home to the safety of my wife. As it was though, I poured us each a stiff enough drink, coughed the frog out of my throat and carried on like, I thought, any other soldier on leave from the front line. While Jo lay curled up on the bed with her glass I performed my next miserable but vitally dishonest act. I called Tina to tell her I would be home late and not to wait up for me. I was, I said, 'with the boys', and we would 'without doubt' be drinking too much but otherwise enjoying a perfectly innocent evening away from the burdens of war and peace. Tina asked only one question. Was the widow with us? Quite truthfully I was able to give her the reassuring answer that Mrs. Flanagan was out on an entirely different mission with my best friend Smuts.

As I had chosen to believe in my frequent fantasies about her, Jo proved to be an enthusiastic and uninhibited lover. Unlike most of the women I had known in this particular sense, she was neither shy nor awkward about the moment. What she wanted me to do she whispered in my ear. "Leave the light on," she asked when I made to turn it off. "I like to look. When I look down at what we are doing is when I explode with a rush of feeling like no one else has ever had before. Please, please, oh, yes please." She did not cry, bite, scratch, tear or scream. She caved in delightfully, folded, cuddled up and dissolved.

By the time we had worn each other quite out it was late. The planned showering, dining and drinking of wine had been overtaken by more urgent events. We were spent, and, I think, indescribably happy. In love actually. Even if for only a short time to come.

I could not possibly go home in that state; my infidelity would surely gush from every pore of my body. I would go back to the office and try to recover my balance.

I asked Jo to stay over in our hotel room and I would come to fetch her in the morning in time to open the office as usual. She understood, bless her, so I left, stopping off to pay the bill at the reception desk with the explanation that I was going out for a few minutes only, 'for supplies'. I expect the young man at the desk presumed I meant condoms. I didn't care, it was all the same.

At the office I tidied up a little, drank three whiskies fast, checked my face for any signs of evidence, and went home. It was coming on for midnight. The house lights were still on... Good, I thought, Tina is still awake.

I let myself in the front door and turned to scan the lounge, adopting, or so I thought, a suitably goofy, slightly inebriated mien. The act was wasted, for Tina was already in bed and our two bedside lights were still on. I went in, and there she was, propped up against the pillows, seemingly fast asleep with an open book beside her. I stood quite still, only swaying slightly, trying once more for the appearance of an elegantly drunk state of person-hood, fixed foolish grin and eyes suitably focused on the end of my nose. I imagined she must have heard the car and was now feigning sleep, her eyelids perhaps fractionally open, enough to examine her wayward husband for signs of the true nature of his night out 'with the boys'.

If she was awake she chose not to reveal it and I undressed and slipped into bed beside her, naked except for my shorts.

* * *

Still filled with the excitement of my few hours with Jo, I found it difficult to sleep, but when at last my mind tired of the endless replays and moved on to more peaceful thoughts I slept soundly and dreamlessly. Some part of my subconscious remained on duty however, for I awoke early, well before Tina's usual time, and set about an attempt to recover lost ground from the late night. I got up and made her a cup of coffee and a couple of slices of toast spread lavishly with anchovy paste, her all-time favourite.

"So you *were* out misbehaving," she said with an impish smile after I woke her with a little kiss on the neck and placed the tray beside her.

"Oh yes indeed," I said, "hideously. And I'm not feeling too good in the head this morning, I can tell you. Will a simple sorry do?"

It turned out the simple sorry would indeed satisfy her and I breathed a heavy sigh of mental relief, at the same time all too conscious of the fact that in less than 30 minutes I would have much more infidelity to be nervous about.

The romp ended more or less as planned: I went to the hotel and found Jo still in bed waiting for my return. Temptation easily got the better of me and we spent another extraordinary hour together. It was well past office opening time before we were ready to leave the hotel, so I suggested she take the day off, which would be easier for me to explain than if we arrived late, separately or together.

When at length I did make it to the office, Barbara was there.

"Anything to tell me?" she asked after our formal hug and kiss of a greeting.

"No," I replied. "Have you got something for me?"

"Only that Jo isn't in and I can't get hold of her."

"That's because she is taking the day off. She asked me just after you left yesterday afternoon. A close friend of hers has arrived, or is arriving from Holland, I can't exactly remember which, and she said she wasn't particularly busy. Sorry, I hope that isn't inconvenient. I knew you were out so it was pointless trying to call to check with you first. She will be in tomorrow. OK?"

"Sure. That's fine, I was just a little perturbed at having no one in to answer the phone."

"Yeah, Silly of me. Guess I'm not yet thinking straight."

Liar, liar, your house is on fire, I thought. But on reflection I settled for the view that the truth, if broadcast, had the potential to spark a greater conflagration either at home or in the office than any bullshit I chose to peddle just now.

Chapter 25

This, my peace-time kaleidoscopic train of events had flashed by in a rush, all in little more than a week since my discharge from hospital. My gunshot wound was healing rapidly, the concussion appeared to have left no sign of lasting damage, and I was certainly not suffering from anything like post-traumatic stress. Looking over it all I concluded that if I were to continue at my current rate of peace time performance I would be in greater danger than ever I could be if surrounded by the enemy in the bush, the ambush notwithstanding. Indeed, it was my new lifestyle itself that posed the gravest hazard to any hope of an ordered future. I was a loose bazooka, and I was only too well aware that I needed to be checked.

But what was I to do, where would I start?

Why not chat it through with Smuts I sensibly asked myself?

I called and we arranged to meet at *La Boheme* after work although I did not warn him that he was in for a session on human behaviour.

I waited until we had settled down with our first glass of Scotch before tackling the main issue.

I'm in trouble Dog and I need your help."

"My God," he said. "You must be in big shit to come to me. Is it money? Are you in trouble with the fuzz? Have you had a rape?"

"No, no, Dog, take this as a real cry for help. I need you to help me pick through the present absurdity of my life. Maybe you won't have to say anything, just help me by listening."

"Hit it," he answered. "I'm sitting on the very edge of my seat..."

"Let's go find a spot away from the mob," I suggested, "I need to concentrate, get away from this noisy bar."

We moved to a distant and quiet corner.

"OK," I said, when we were settled in that nook by the band stand, which would be anything but quiet in an hour or two.

"So Dog, here's the background.

"You remember I rang you about nine weeks ago, before our last call-up. About the poison of testosterone and all that delightful troopie shit..."

"Can I ever forget it?" he replied, "don't tell me you have been poisoned again?"

"I have indeed and it could be terminal this time. But joking aside, you know that when I came around from the amnesia of the concussion, which recovery incidentally, was brought about by a particularly wonderful piece of manual therapy wrought by the Widow, I was nevertheless in quite a muddled state of mind. I'm not sure that I was at all able to think or act rationally. So, though I was utterly smitten by the magic of the widow woman, I was equally won over by my own wife when she came to visit. I felt very much in love with her for coming to see me, sitting holding my hand, apologising to me for leaving so suddenly before, and promising to be a nicer person and a better wife if I would have her back. In seconds I was helpless. I was the bastard when she walked out, I really was. I had surely given her cause to go, but then there she was taking on the blame. Her sincerity, her humility was enough to make me shed a tear. I may even have cried more than a bit.

"I did. And I thought that the wonderful cocoon created by the mood of the moment would last us forever. It was easy to say 'I love you', and even easier to promise to be a better man and a husband forever. Well anyway, that's what I surmise, for much of what was said and done I have no real memory myself. It all comes from Tina."

"And....?"

"I was barely out of hospital before I was in the sack with someone else."

"Not Barbara surely?"

"Not Barbara, although perhaps it should have been. It was my secretary person, Jo. I bloody nearly spent the whole night with her, and worst of all, I loved every minute of it. I loved the excitement of booking into a hotel as man and wife, and the whole dreadful, wonderful mess of it all.

"Lucky bugger..."

"That's not helpful, Doctor Dog."

"Doctors also have urges in the lower zone."

"Thank you Doctor. Now, to continue...

"It was a pretty good night really. Unfortunately the kind to make me want to keep coming back for more, but maybe not only with Jo, probably with Bar. Or even worse, any woman at all I'm attracted to. I don't know how to carry on. I am afraid I could easily get right out of control, lose my marriage, lose my business, lose everything important. I seem to have lost my sense of proportion, my sense of right and wrong. And the worst part of it all is that in general I don't care a fuck."

"Well that can't be true or you wouldn't be talking to me about it.

"As I told you once before," he continued, "and I don't need to be a doctor to know this, this kind of behaviour is not unusual even in the most stable and peaceful background situations. The wartime bomb and bullet environment, I think, can make men doubly horny and half as inhibited. It is a lethal concoction, and really, Dog, the only thing I can say is that basically we're all in the same state. Take me for an example..."

"Wait, I haven't finished yet," I interrupted, "what I want is for you to tell me how you would do what I have got to do."

"Which is?"

"Not sure yet. Break it up with Tina again? Move in with the widow and commit? Or just do nothing and float with the tide? I have not the slightest idea even how to start the conversation with Tina. And as for Barbara, I may already have blown that prospect to pieces and I am not sure how to try to pick them up again."

"OK now?"

I nodded.

"In the first place, my dear fellow, there are at least three and a half good reasons why you should ignore anything I advise. I'll list

them when I have said what I think, as a kind of closing caveat –
to help you.

"So, my counsel, my honest advice to you is to go away
somewhere by yourself for a day. Take a bottle of something, go
fishing or something. Spend the time thinking about your life and
what's important in it.

"Think of yourself as a buyer, a buyer of a house or an expensive
car. Put a massive mental microscope to work on your worries,
which, by the way, amount to nothing less than your entire future.
What are you going to get for the huge amount you're going to pay
or lose? Memorable sex? Better company? More affection?
What?

That should take you most of the day, especially if you have a
snort or two and maybe land a good fish. So then, towards
sundown, when you have mellowed out a bit, that's the time to
bundle it all together and say: THAT! That is what I want to do!

"And then, Dog, just do it. Come home and do it. Don't fuck
around. Say nothing if you decide to stay – it will all become
apparent as you go along. But If Tina has to go, she has to go
quickly, or rather YOU have to go and go right away, immediately!

'If 'twere done, and if it were done and dusted when it were done,
'twere well it were done quickly".

"Julius Caesar?"

"Mac the knife, with apologies. Tell her straight. Tell her you're
out of love. She won't want to stay if you just say that one small
but vitally important thing. I love you Tina but I'm not in love with
you any longer and there's nothing left to keep me faithful and in
check. Whether it is the war and the ambush and everything, or
just that I have become an unreliably randy turncoat bum, I have
to live the rest of my life quite free.

"As for the rest, I think once you are on your own again, free to
do whatever you want, you'll probably settle down to life much as
it was before, only with a change of sexual scenery. Being on the
cusp of what you think is an inevitable breakup is a very unsettling

173

thing. No wonder you're after Jo and whoever else you can get your hands on.

" But whatever you do in the excitement of new bodies and fresh, exciting humping, don't make any kind of quick commitment to anyone else. OK?"

"Thanks Dog," I said rather slowly. "That is exactly what I hoped for from you. A good and sound line of reasoning. Should help me put some order back in my rather jumbled state of mind. Whether I can put it into action I'll only know when I try. But before I piss off to do some fishing, you said there were exactly three-and-a-half reasons to ignore whatever you might prescribe?"

"I did, and here they are.

"One. I'm a man at war like you, so it is highly unlikely that my thoughts are as subjective as they ought to be, especially when trying to help unravel the complications of war-time masculine urges and fear-driven horniness.

"Two. I like Tina and I don't want to see her hurt.

"Three. I like Jo and I would like to see her happy."

Then a long pause; long enough to make me prompt him.

"That's three. You said three and a half...."

"I very much more than merely 'like' Mrs. Flanagan myself. If you don't move quickly to make something of your head start with her, don't complain if I do."

My turn to pause.

Chapter 26

As a matter of fact I did take a day off to go fishing; I went to a favourite place on a favourite river, not too many miles away from town but far enough to be sure of relative peace and quiet. It was there, when I was a schoolboy, that I caught my first few fish. The situation was perfect for a few hours, days, or even weeks, of solitary confinement; a deep pool a few hundred meters long, neatly bisected on the near side by a huge protruding whale-back rock. An ancient wild fig tree grew right out of the centre of this rock making it a shady spot to sling a hammock or hang a tent against the heat of a summer's day, or leafy cover against the cold of night when camping. In my youth the pool was home to the occasional hippopotamus and enough fish to keep small boys, big boys, and old men interested. Now the larger wild life was all gone and to be truthful just at that moment I was not particularly concerned whether there were any fish left either. I was after something else – peace of mind, or a plan, or was it merely re-assurance?

Among its other attractions for those in the know was a reasonable access road cut many years before by miners looking for a good water pumping site. By the time of my latest visit the mines had all gone but their memory was kept alive by an old rusting donkey engine and a few bits and pieces of the pipes it once kept filled with good clean water. The important point was that it was still easy to get to in my faithful, left-hand drive red Volvo.

I had brought with me a couple of bottles of beer and two of the best white wines I could find. These I carefully immersed in a shallow spot of the running stream near enough to where I planned to sit with my rod, and soon I was relaxed and happy, dangling enough bait for any serious angling business that might come my way. I shut my mind and thought of nothing more than the immediate bliss of the situation. I lit a cigarette and flicked the dead match into the stream.

Nothing would come to me, no fish to distract me, no constructive thoughts to justify my idling. I tried starting a mental process artificially by just calling up a name; Tina first, then Barbie, then Jo. Obstinately they remained only names. I was far from them, they were all good people, they all meant a lot to me, but they would not perform in competition with each other. I gave it up and opened a beer. I took a deep swallow. I didn't care much about anything else.

The second beer soon followed and I dozed for about an hour before tackling the wine. By the time I had swallowed half a bottle I was ready to go home. All I had managed to come up with was to go ahead with the idea of a South African holiday. I knew Tina would like that and I felt confident I could play the part of faithful husband without difficulty. Well, at least I would give it a go. If I came back from SA still undecided that too would be fine, as long as I did not carry on hopping from one bed to another.

I drove home in glow of personal well-being. Although I was sure I had not achieved all that Smuts had suggested I should aim for, I felt I was half on my way.

No need for Tina to ask where I had been when I got home, the fishing tackle and the cooler box told her.

"Catch much?" she asked, affably interested.

"Only one good idea," I said.

"Oh what was that?" she asked.

"I'm staying away from the office until we go to SA. What do you think of that?"

"Good boy."

Both Jo and Barbie treated my hermit act with extraordinary tolerance, telling my clients that I was still recovering from war damage, and, as far as I could tell from the distance, running the business rather more efficiently than I might have done on my own in the old days.

Those 'good old days', by the way, were still less than a year in the past. At that time so much was going on in the country that it seemed whole years were being packed into a few months.

Our growing civil war had moved in a direction that everyone should have expected but no one did, or so it seemed. Perhaps it was too horrifying to contemplate – *civilised people would never do that...b*ut civilised people went right ahead and did do that.

They shot down a civilian aircraft shortly after it had taken off from Kariba packed with week-end holidaymakers.

It was a hell of a story, making headlines around the world. Among all the other damage of the incident itself, those headlines, naturally, were fatal for the country's tourist industry; ultimately fatal too for whites' hopes of a compromise ending to the war. It was then that many white people made the decision then to leave as soon as they could, but others, in a strangely perverse response, hardened their attitudes and chose to think of the Viscount hit as a bit of a fluke and an open invitation for the government to increase the tempo of the war against the guerrillas by a series of attacks beyond our borders.

For our South African trip Tina and I arranged to drive to Johannesburg and then on to the South African coast for a few days rest at the holiday home of a distant cousin of mine with whom I had kept up a desultory but still affectionate correspondence for many years. Iris was her name, and Iris was extremely wealthy; some of our more envious relatives claimed it was because her grandfather had somehow hogged for himself all the accumulated family treasure when his father died, leaving the rest of the family more or less with nothing. Whatever the truth of the story, Iris was kind and generous and always willing to share her own good fortune.

On the eve of our departure the buoyant Nationalist forces struck again, proving their recent successes were nothing like the lucky strikes many supposed them to be by attacking Salisbury's main fuel depot and starting a devastating fire. Thousands of dollars' worth of petrol were being lost every minute in a conflagration visible for many miles around.

Tina was busy packing for the trip and I was sitting, lost in thought, on our lovely veranda. My reverie was interrupted when

Tina came through and, pointing to a mounting column of dense black smoke on the horizon, said "what on earth do you think that is? "

I looked up and instinctively realised it was bad news indeed; the war was now on our doorstep. The fact of the story spread rapidly; one phone call and I was to learn that a unit of Zanla fighters had simply assembled in the vulnerable city industrial sites and launched their lightning attack with grenade launchers, anti-tank missiles and machine guns. It was all over in minutes and they were able to disperse without casualty, leaving many red faces among the military security people. It turned out that the site was only partly walled and feebly fenced. A schoolboy armed with a pair of pliers could have breached the fencing in five minutes. At each corner of the site was a two-man army tent. Of the eight men who lived in them, little was ever seen, though it was said they were on patrol night and day; nowhere near enough boots on that vital piece of ground to prevent the ZANLA strike.

The resulting blaze burned on brightly for five days. Tina and I were not there to see the end of it, we left for the south early the next morning. But we were witness to it for long enough to know it was a publicity coup for the nationalists and an ominous warning that the war would no longer be fought entirely amongst the black population in the rural areas. Until that incident most urban whites did not feel particularly threatened in their daily working lives. It is true that a bomb had been detonated in a small supermarket some months before, but there was no quick follow-up and so the incident was a talking point for only a week or two before getting lost in the larger mix of easy peace and civil order in the cities. After the depot attack however, many young white Rhodesians began to think the unthinkable – the nationalists might win and Zimbabwe Rhodesia might soon become just another failed black state. Having thought the unthinkable they began to prepare for a faraway future: South Africa, Australia, New Zealand.

The road from Salisbury to the South African border began, if you like, in the southern quarter of the city, very close indeed to where the petrol depot was burning so crazily. As we headed off that Monday morning we were at first quite chatty and happy, looking forward to our holiday, but gradually, as we got nearer the epicentre of the inferno, conversation in the car dwindled in inverse proportion to the ever enlarging view of black smoke billowing before us. Even Tina, normally so judicious with her words that even *gosh* was unusual, was finally moved to let out a quiet *fuck*. I knew what was in her mind. The holiday was a waste of time as far as she was concerned; we could serve our future better if we turned back home to pack up, sell, and bolt.

Journeying on that summer day all the evidence was on Tina's side, though, as a soldier, albeit part-time, I found the unfolding scenario fascinating.

After an incident on the route some months before, the government had introduced a protected convoy system for vehicles travelling between the border at Beit Bridge and the small mining centre of Umvuma, 'purely as a wise precaution'. This meant that something like two-thirds of the total distance was involved, and cynics might thus comfortably have deduced that two-thirds of the country was now more under the control of the nationalist forces than the government. It did not strike me that way however, for like many white Rhodesians I clung to the forlorn hope that the war was under control.

It was not compulsory to travel in the convoys; many people went their own way according to their own timing. If you wanted to be part of the convoy arrangement, however, it was necessary to gather at pre-arranged times at points along the route. I had not discussed this with Tina, nor had I thought it necessary to go with the convoy, but as we drove on through the countryside towards a town called Enkeldoorn, and with the blazing fuel tanks still much in my mind, I began to doubt the wisdom of my casual attitude. When we passed the blackened shell of a reasonably recent model Mercedes Benz, the alarm bells rang. I accelerated so that we reached the next assembly point just in time to be part of the onward convoy. Arriving so late though, we would be at the back of a very long line of cars, buses and trucks; no great problem except that we would probably be the last to make it through the border formalities at Beit Bridge.

At exactly the advertised time the convoy began to move. Dear old Tina sat there tight lipped as the evidence of a hostile environment mounted. At the front, back and in the middle of the convoy line, armed military vehicles took up positions. These were little more than half-ton open backed trucks with a machine gun mounted behind the cab manned by a standing uniformed soldier looking as nonchalant as his obvious vulnerability allowed.

As we drove along at a steady speed, these three armed trucks performed a sort of barn dance, exchanging positions from time to time in clearly choreographed moves; while the lead man pulled off the road and parked in some conveniently shady spot, the other two raced ahead, middle becoming leader and back marker becoming middleman, and so on. At the same time a small propeller driven fighter aeroplane in grey and khaki camouflage circled and wheeled above us, occasionally diving towards the terrain before pulling up again in a brilliant display of aggressive aeronautical dash. Had there been any terrorists lurking with intent to ambush, interdict and slay, that little fighter alone would surely have been sufficient to keep their minds on other things.

For me it was almost fun, boys playing well-rehearsed and spectacular games. The reality of actual danger at the heart of the thing managed to elude me. Not so for Tina however, and the futility of our little charade was driven home anew with every passing piece of military muscle. While the five-hour drive must have been to her interminable, to me it went by so quickly that it seemed but minutes later that we were gathered before a series of friendly white border control faces on this and that side of the Limpopo River.

And then we were through, formalities complete, speeding towards Johannesburg.

Tina was immediately a much changed mortal.

"You can keep your war," she said. "I prefer this," by which she meant travelling in peace and tranquillity along good roads any place other than war-torn Rhodesia.

I rubbed my wounded shoulder and pushed the harsh reality of our differences out of my mind and out of the picture.

And so I bumbled through the journey, happy enough, reasonably good company for my wife if we didn't mention the war, and both looking forward to whatever life might bring. Personally, I was at that moment in no great hurry to embrace once more the twin excitements of my life back home: the impending move to the Psychological Operations Unit of the army, and a marvellously convoluted personal and business life.

We spent a quiet two weeks at Iris' seafront holiday cottage, swimming, lying on the beach, eating plenty of sea food, and generally behaving like a couple who have been married too long without children. That is to say we got on fine together without any of the frills of affection, love, or sexual intimacy. There were times when I wanted to reach out to my sweet wife and break the bonds that were holding us in this weird state of unbliss, but on every such occasion malicious circumstance seemed to intervene to delay and eventually prevent the action – a knock on the door, a telephone call, and once in the night while we were both in bed, she reading, me just lying there, there was a complete electrical blackout that I had to attend to immediately for the sake of an unfinished chapter. That was it, underlined by the fates, the clearest writing in the sky, telling me, telling us that our love had perished from lack of use. We had simply forgotten how to begin to make love to each other and the fates would do nothing to help.

Tina showed no outward sign of a similar rotten frame of mind. She was in her element, getting up early every day to go to the local sea food market, making friends with everyone there, paging through cook books, preparing ever more wonderful sea food dishes, and finally, reading all the popular novels that were not available at home.

Whatever else might have been going on in our hearts, when the time came to go back home we were both tanned and healthy.

We stopped off and stayed overnight with Iris to thank her and return her keys. In the morning, still lying in bed and thinking it was time to be making a move, Tina snuggled up to me in what I thought at first was a rare show of affection.

"This is it Hunter," she said. "I'm not going with you. I'm done with the war and Rhodesia. I hope you will come to the same conclusion in due course, though I know it won't be soon. I will be here in Jo'burg waiting for you. Don't make me wait too long I beg of you."

It was a shock if not a surprise, rather like the first dash of ice cold water you throw in your own face to wake up on a cold winter morning.

"Where will you stay, what will you do?" I asked, knowing that any protest would merely expose me as the hypocrite I felt I had become.

"Iris is giving me space for a couple of weeks, I will apply for a temporary teaching job, I've got money. I will be fine."

I knew she would be, for she was determined and tough, the more so at this particular moment in life with her opposite minded and uncooperative husband.

I kissed her gently at the back of her neck, got out of bed, and began my preparations for the lonely drive home.

"I'll call often," I said as I left her.

The journey passed without incident, and being on my own I felt no particular need to join the convoy from Beit Bridge. I took my time, stopping overnight at the Lion and Elephant, a popular motel on the banks of the usually dry Bubi River. It was quiet there with few guests; the fuel depot attack had all but dried up the flow of tourists from South Africa. The only other customers in the bar in the evening were all in uniform. I joined them for a beer or two and then a whisky or three. It was good to mix with them. I felt at home back at war.

Chapter 27

Back home I was in no hurry to settle the basic platforms of my life. I made a few calls and planned to put in an appearance at the office the following day or the day after that, there was no urgency to anything. I was still in limbo, and to be truthful, not entirely sure how to go about the business of letting my colleagues and friends know that I was yet again alone. It was becoming something of an embarrassment.

I called the office to find that Barbie was out. After a short chat with Jo, and a long one with Smuts, I decided to stay home another day and let the news that I was back marinade among those it might reach. I did call my old pal Ross to check that my army transfer was still on the cards. He confirmed that all I needed was for the medics to say I was alright in the head, a request I thought quite reasonable under the circumstances. I made an appointment with the army medics for the following week.

Once I was able to tick off these few 'issues' I shifted all of Tina's most personal belongings to suitcases and boxes, and made the house as much my new home as I could. Then I went shopping for a good book, some beer and a bottle of whisky. I meant to have the approaching weekend to myself, to keep my mind as blank as my diary.

It didn't work out that way. An hour or so into my retreat Smuts arrived, armed similarly with refreshments, so that the beer flowed early and it was not long before the alcohol loosened us up and we started to think it was time for an afternoon barbecue and impromptu party.

Smuts took over, quickly calling a parcel of our closest friends, organising food, bolstering the bottle inventory, and mobilising my music centre. Slyly, I thought, I did not get involved in the list of invited friends and looked forward to seeing his choice, particularly of the female component.

First to show up were Barbara and Jo with male companions, neither of whom I had met before. Next, to my total astonishment, were Norton and a young black girl he introduced as a teacher, a recent graduate from university to whom he was somehow related. Two army friends who had been in the ambush with Smuts and I arrived with their wives, and the party was complete when I answered the door to find my old friend Ross, standing there with a bunch of roses and a case of beer.

Back in Rhodesia in those days the barbecue, better known by its Afrikaans name of 'braai', was a lopsided and informal way of entertaining friends to a meal. It required no culinary skills at all since it consisted mainly of raw meat cooked over a charcoal grill – usually outside in the garden. 'Lopsided' because it was possibly the only catering event in white Rhodesian life that was left entirely to the men. It was absolutely a masculine thing, but since then it has devolved, and now, if you follow the smoke or the compelling odour of sizzling cuts of meat in search of a party, you are just as likely to find twenty girls having their own kind of social fun around an outdoor charcoal grill.

So that, more or less, was the setting of the little afternoon party that Smuts and I concocted together. And what a convivial occasion it was, justifying, I suppose, the commonly held belief that *the less planning the more pleasure*. When Norton and his black female companion arrived I confess I did have a twinge of apprehension that the unexpected black element might lead to some sort of racial incident, but our mutual friends being largely a reflection of ourselves, I need not have feared. In fact the two black Rhodesians were the stars of that particular ball. Norton I knew to be a man of distinguished bearing and presence; his young niece showed herself to be from the same mould, quietly confident, fluent, and most surprising of all, exceptionally ambitious. If she felt underprivileged or racially disadvantaged there was no sign of it.

We stood around the charcoal burner, we men and women, drinking a little, smoking endlessly, and talking, talking, talking. When the flames died down and the coals were perfect for their intended purpose, Smuts and I shooed everyone away and set about grilling the many slabs of meat as best we could. So far there had been no real opportunity for a private natter.

"I had no idea Norton was back in the village," I said.

"Neither had I," he responded. "When I got hold of the Widow she told me he was in town and staying at Meikles again, so I called him. Told him it was a home-coming party for you, and he didn't hesitate; asked if he could bring his niece and lo and behold, here they are. I haven't had a chance to catch up with him yet. I suppose I should tell him about developments in our little incident at the Quill, though I would just as rather not. What do you think?"

"Mm. Yeah. I think tell him. Maybe make a bit of a joke about it otherwise he might think we have become worried by the connection."

"I'll get him over now while we are still busy burning the meat."

He strolled off in the direction of the mob, waving his braai tongs and shouting for liquor. I saw him work his way over to Norton. When he came back to the fire, Norton was with him.

"The Hunter at work turning harmless raw meat into expertly browned bits and pieces you can eat when added to enough sauce," Norton joked.

"Glad to show you how it's done," I replied, "For an appropriate fee of course."

"Ah," said Norton, "the dread spectacle of the fee. Now, if you white people had let us dark people show you how to cook when you first got here, there would be no question of payment, but of course if the chief didn't like the result, bang, you'd be on the fire instead of messing around with it."

We laughed, and Smuts said "speaking of which, do you remember the evening we had a bit of a row at the Quill Club the night we first met?"

"I remember it well," Norton replied, "by the time we left I was Lieutenant General James of the Selous Scouts, or was it Court Marshall? More likely the latter I think..."

"Yeah well the man who started it all then ran off to his army buddies complaining that I had impersonated an officer and improperly introduced you as a member of our army."

Norton seemed quite unfazed by the news.

"And now? Do I need to make a bolt for it, get a body guard, or what?"

"I think the thing has been dealt with, and I am sure you are not involved. But you never know... I suppose someone somewhere may have scratched through the files to find if there was anything odd about you but so far as I am concerned the subject has been closed. I only mention it so you know in case it ever does come up again. I'll be in touch if there are any further development this side..."

"Well, if it does re-surface, here's my Lusaka number. Get in touch at any time. I'm quite well connected with the popular black politicians of the moment....."

"Good to know that," Smuts replied, "but I don't think any of us will hear of it again.

"By the way," he asked, "are you married? Do you have a young family back home?"

Norton did not answer right away. His little pause gave the impression he needed to think how much he should say.

"No wife, no kids. There is a girl waiting for me to make up my mind. Norwegian. I haven't seen her for a while. I wouldn't be surprised if she has given up the wait..."

"A bit like my own short story," Smuts replied.

Before Norton had a chance to press him on the story he shut that thought down.

"Now," he said, pointing to me, "I think this dog has burned the barbecue as far as the meat can tolerate, it's time to eat."

The afternoon passed in a contented blur, but as the sun dipped below the tree line of our heavily timbered suburb the party began to break up; first to go were Norton and his niece, then another couple and another. I lost track of the comings and goings and eventually found myself quite alone, slightly pissed, slightly unsteady on my legs, and very much ready for bed.

Chapter 28

Whatever the time of night or day I always loved walking into *La Boheme*. There was something vaguely forbidden to me about the place. Though it was very far from being the first night club I had ever been in, each step across the threshold induced in me a furtive feeling of something mildly contraband, of breaking rules, as if I was wandering for the first time out of bounds. It was like slipping out of the house illegally after dark when you were still too young to be allowed any such freedom; hiding in the alley, lighting candles you had lifted from the pantry, and matches surreptitiously slipped from your father's pocket; smoking cigarettes similarly obtained, a sense of adventure, excitement, danger, and perhaps even tears.

For a start *La Bom* was ever in darkness. Night or day, walking in from the north side pavement in Union Avenue it was always darker within than without. Only the bar itself in the far right hand corner was anything like lit, a waist-high strip of subdued twinkles bouncing gently off the mirrors behind, barely drawing attention to the astonishing array of alcoholic offerings lined up like little soldiers, each with its own special uniform, on a shelf within easy reach of the barman. For me it was the Galliano that always stood out among the multitude of bottles, the brightest decoration in that little parade, and I would often end the evening with a shot of it as if paying homage to the crown prince of the bar.

Each of the many tables, always perfectly laid out for four, with clean linen, expensive silver, and eight wine glasses, was marked only by a tiny centre candle. The effect was strangely intimate even before the crowds arrived; when they got there it was the busiest little secret in the world. Whether it was because I had always enjoyed myself there or that it had a warm and welcoming personality of its own I cannot say, though all my friends and acquaintances were agreed, *La Bom* was the place to be after dark. In those days it was also known for its cosmopolitan entertainment which added to its popularity. You could usually expect a good stripper to do two shows a night at *La Bom* - It was there that I enjoyed my first 'tassle tosser' shoe. And the music was always good.

That was the location of my meeting with Smuts that Monday evening so many years ago. I arrived early and ordered a beer. He came in soon after, a smiling, happy man; my most excellent friend. And boy oh boy, did he have a story for me. A story and a proposition. Unexpected, novel, some would say outrageous even. I'll give it to you the best way I can – in Dog's own words as far as I remember them, without my many interjections, my 'shits' and my little 'well bugger me's'.

Do you remember that 'Snoopy sent me' night in the industrial sites shortly after our first call up together? Of course you do, who could forget it. And you will remember I was not even there for the whole show, I had to leave early because I had a date at The Hole. You will find this hard to believe, I suppose, and you will wonder why I never mentioned it before, but that date was with Barbara, our now mutual friend The Widow Flanagan. It was not exactly a blind date, more of a first date, and as we know, she didn't show up at the expected time, or perhaps I had mistaken the time. In any event, that was who I was there to meet that evening.

I did not know her well, certainly not intimately. I met her one night in Lusaka some years before. I was there on mining business. She was one of a dozen other business people at a cocktail party after the conference event I had attended. Of course I was struck, almost blinded, by her. Not so much her great beauty as her very vivid choice of clothes. It seems to me now, as I think it struck me then, that for her clothes sense alone, Mrs. Flanagan deserves to be on the front cover of Cosmopolitan, she would stand out in any crowd, anywhere, London, Paris, Kicking Horse Nebraska or Naboomspruit in the Northern Transvaal.

On that occasion we did no more than shake hands and exchange cards, and, despite her obvious attraction, I put her out of my mind, imagining she was married and unavailable. A few nights later I was taken for a few drinks to an extraordinary nightclub in the main Lusaka township. Saigi Dhaka's Nite Bar was like nothing you have ever seen, or at least nothing like I had ever seen. It was throbbing – several hundred revellers at the very least. It was already dark when we got there and so my view of the entrance was hazy; it appeared to me to be set up in a great tent, something like those huge tents favoured by evangelists on the road in America.

Finding a waiter, or even a functioning bar was a mission, food was totally out of the question – as indeed was conversation. Yet somehow my host found me a decent drink and we sort of settled into a tiny open space on the fringes of a fully occupied dance floor. At some point in the noisy proceedings a young man popped up next to me and asked me to dance, a lovely fresh faced young boy with, I thought, not a single ulterior motive in his shining black head. He just wanted to dance with someone, to make a show of moving his body in rhythmic time to the repetitive and ear-shattering music. I was fascinated by the scene, so much so that I was paying no great attention to my friends at the time. Perhaps he noticed that I was not intensely occupied with anyone else, so he hit on me. That I was white may have been an added attraction, a chance to widen his circle of influential friends. Naturally I accepted his kind invitation – what else could I do without risking being thought to be either racist, homophobic, or even worse, just not with it?

So there I was, stomping away with my new best young black friend, feeling, I must say, somewhat foolish, but trying nevertheless to give the appearance of having a good time, when blow me down if Barbara Flanagan didn't suddenly and most miraculously appear. Smooth as silk she cut me away from my partner and I found myself dancing rather more conventionally with by far the loveliest woman in the room. You can guess how I felt: the night, suddenly, seemed alive with possibilities.

I could barely make out what it was she was shouting in my ear; the music level had reached the outer limit, but I heard enough to understand that her breaking in was to be taken not as a pass but a kindness to an outsider caught in a difficult social situation.

She thought I should be rescued without offence to my erstwhile partner, and returned pronto to my own little group.

She left me with this advice: "If he comes back for more, tell him you have a headache and your feet are killing you." Laughing madly at her little witticism, she left me and waved goodbye, a picture of bubbling self-confidence and happiness. The last I saw of her was just a glimpse as she was leaving in the company of a tall rather distinguished man in a Tweed jacket. I guessed he was a safari type, possibly a white hunter, out with a client. But what marked him more than that for me was the bright red polka dot silk scarf tied in a tight knot around his neck, and a yellow rose in his jacket lapel. The Barbara signature touch! Surely the colourful lady had marked her man.

And, yes, you have probably guessed it, that was Jim. As I found out much later they were on their way that very evening to pick up Barbie's young cousin. A week or two later Jim was dead.

Of course I knew nothing of all of that at the time.

The evening broke up soon afterwards and the entire episode receded to the distant horizon of my memory where it stayed until quite recently, a couple of months ago – just before I found you on our first call-up together.

Smuts paused.

"Let us drink a little more before I move on," he said. "We are getting to the meat of this matter and it is thirsty, worrying work."

Needless perhaps to say, I had sat there spellbound by Dog's revelations, so much so that I had not noticed what was going on around us in *La Bom* that night. To my utter surprise I looked up to see a half-naked young stripper in the closing stages of her act. Incredibly, I had missed most of it. I wondered what was coming next to keep me so transfixed.

I had been to Bulawayo on business a few months ago, Smuts continued, *and I was driving back to Salisbury. I was quite sleepy and decided to stop in Gatooma to fill up with gas and get something for a quick refresher.*

Would you believe it...? I'd just stopped at the only service station on the main road when Barbara pulled in to fill up too. It turned out she was in Gatooma, which is where she grew up, to pick up her ailing old mother. Anyway, she seemed pleased to see me, even remembered my name. Of course I was chuffed myself. It was rather like Buzz Aldrin bumping into another human being on the moon, the unexpectedness of the meeting alone turned us into instant dear friends.

We chatted a few minutes on the forecourt and agreed to meet in Salisbury, where she said she would be spending a week or two before going back to Zambia to pack up and move down here more or less permanently to look after the old lady. I left her my number, cheerfully enough, but doubting somehow that I would hear from her.

A few days later she did call and we met one evening at Brett's. She couldn't stay long because she was without a car and needed to get to a house in Avondale where she had installed her mother. I drove her there and on the way she told me her husband had died and she was leaving Zambia, partly because of her mother, but also to get as far away from what had happened as she could.

We kissed and hugged, more like really old friends than possible new lovers, and made a date for a week later at the Hole. I was looking forward to the meeting, I suppose partly because I imagined her to be free, and of course because I was very much on the loose myself and I was powerfully attracted to her. I thought I would take the opportunity to chuck my hat into the ring so to speak, and I was looking forward to it more than most things then occupying my free space.

But that was the date that never happened. She missed, I missed out, and you broke in.

Seeing my lips struggling to articulate complex questions Smuts held up a pointing finger and asked me to wait a while.

"There's still much more you need to grasp before you rise to speak, even on a point of order," he said, "and I know you are itching to ask me why none of this came out at the time. Patience my son, all will be revealed, all will be revealed."

Of course I contacted Barbie the next day to ask if she was alright, wondering why she missed our date, which, of course, she said, she had not. After waiting a while she was just about to leave herself when something important happened, she said. A stroke of fate!

She didn't mention any names. Why should she? She had no idea that we were friends or even knew each other. She said only that she had bumped into someone from her distant past, that she was meeting him again that evening and that, in a word, she was sorry she wasn't free for the moment etc. etc. etc. A charming brush off, but a brush off nevertheless.

I was disappointed, I had built up quite some expectations for sure, but I wasn't actually in love with her and I quickly got over it. All that remained was the minor agony of unresolved lust.

It was quite some time before I found out that you were the man she had met that night. Even when you told me what was going on in your life and that Tina had left you, I didn't put the pieces together. Nor did Barbie, not until you actually introduced us. By then it had become too complicated to talk about our connection. You obviously did not notice anything, but when you actually presented the lady to me I looked at her and she looked at me and I think our jaws dropped together. I blinked my eyes, and damned if she didn't do exactly the same. It seemed astonishing that none of us had joined the dots, not even you.

And once the surprise had worn off nothing further needed to be said. Barbara and I more or less forgot the complication and just got on together as part of your circle of friends. It was all going great – until the battle in the bush and the temporary disruption in your memory muscle.

Well, you know what I mean, that was when life got really awkward. When you recovered enough to know what you were doing it appeared that you were going back to Tina, and it sounded to all of us as if that was what you most sincerely wanted. So, after a while, I thought what the hell and I tried lighting the old candle to see if it would burn. It sputtered a bit but did not take, which was not immediately encouraging. Then when you went off to SA on holiday I tried again.

Barbara was available for the occasional dinner date and we had a few good evenings together with lots of laughs, but at first she was quite blunt about the bedroom – not open for recreation. And that, I discovered, wasn't a form of sexual blackmail; she was just being careful about jumping from one battle zone to the next. Still, I could tell that she liked me and I thought it was just a matter of time and patience.

And it happened.

It was the day after the attack on the fuel depot. I think that was also the day you and Tina left for South Africa. Barbie called me to find out when I was going off on my Scouts course and while we were talking about that, you came up in the conversation. You always come up in conversation with that lady.

I had no particular news from you but, craftily suggested we meet later that day at this very venue to drink a toast to your good health and future happiness. So at five I pitched up and very soon after that she did too.

No beating about the bush this time, after several fairly stiff whiskies for both of us, I told her how I felt and asked her if she was willing. She laughed at what she called my distinctly Australian foreplay technique and said she was. So I took her home and made love to her. Simple as that. She stayed the night. I asked her to come back after work and she did. The only problem for me was that she wouldn't discuss anything longer lasting. She insisted that we wait and see. Wait and see what? I asked, to which she just repeated: wait and see.

And what did happen? You came back from South Africa alone, without a wife, that's what happened. Straight away I realised, understood, that my deal with the Widow was not sealed. Barbie expected some development, some resolution to come out of your return. She didn't say it, but I was convinced that if you wanted her back in your life you could probably have her. Actually what I really thought was she wanted one of us and it would be the last man standing, the one who didn't throw a tantrum and go off in blind jealousy.

So that's it my friend. If you now feel huffy because I have had a scene with the woman you rejected, you can forget her. And equally, if I get all funny because she still fancies you, then I will have to forget her.

Get the picture?

I did get the picture although I did not particularly like it. Enlarged, I could see two half-wits fighting over one woman. It did not appeal to me. I preferred an image of Barbara and I together in the foreground with Smuts behind, scooting off to be alone somewhere. But my great love of the man quickly trashed that for what I guessed was a much more likely sight: a snapshot of two losers hitch-hiking together away from a smash, differing only about the right road.

I wanted to have a drink. I wanted to have a lot to drink.

But Smuts was not finished. There was nothing devious about him and, as I should have expected, he went straight to the core of our mutual complication.

"As I see it there's only one thing to do about this. Barbara must choose one of us or, perhaps, kick both of us out of her life right now. Why don't we ask her to choose? We'll do it together. Tonight. Straight. Loser walks the plank. One, or both. OK?"

I was so surprised by the prospect that I could think of no alternative. Still mentally reeling from the story I ummed and ahed and bit my lip.

"What the hell," I said. "What the hell? Let's give it a swing. Now, can I pour you a drink?"

I already had a date with the Widow for that evening, and of course she was expecting only me. Instead, when she opened her door, she found the two of us, each with an exactly matched bunch of flowers, dressed in matching dinner gear, complete with maroon bow ties, deliberately slicked down shiny hair, heavily mascaraed eyes, and grinning from ear to ear. While putting down a few Scotch whiskies we had warmed to our coming task and rehearsed a little show in an endeavour to keep things reasonably light, and to amuse this woman we both found ourselves in love with.

"Madam," I said.

"We have something important," Smuts said.

"To say to you," I added.

"May we come in?" Smuts continued.

"You may need to sit down." I finished.

And so it began. By arrangement we kept the pitch as bright as we could, even though the outcome was serious enough to both of us.

It went something like this.

Me: "Can I pour you a drink?"

The Widow: "I may need a whisky. Go ahead and pour us each one."

Smuts: "Dog and I aren't drinking right now."

Me: "A little later, maybe. A lot a little later maybe."

While I poured one for Barbie, Smuts pressed on: "It may have come to your attention, Mrs. Magnificent, that I have been deeply in love, with your amazing person from the time that we first met."

Me: "Ditto, if you allow a certain latitude regarding our farmyard fascination centuries ago."

Smuts: "Whereas this Dog and I might in ages gone by have resolved our impossible suit with handbags at dawn, he is much too good a friend for me to dispose of in such heartless fashion, and in any case the law will not tolerate such a solution. I must therefore appeal to you, Madam, to shake him off for me. Dispose of him. Choose me. Tell him to be off, to be gone, that thou and I should be free to set up home together and live happily ever after."

Me: "Not so fast, Shakespeare. Choose me, rather, Barbie Doll. I'm better looking than he is, I have good prospects, and besides, you are already my partner in working life. Not only that, but he is heading off to the sticks to eat lizards and snakes and stuff while I will be eating caviar. Choose the one with the better breath. Choose me! Choose me!"

At this point the game was becoming harder to keep going for we had only rehearsed so far. We looked at each other, our expressions loaded with meaning, got the clue, and shut up to allow the Widow to speak, both striving for the angelic, hopeful look of two young men on stage who have both forgotten their lines.

"Good show," she began. "Good show."

"Silly bastards, no choosing. Rubbish idea. Love you both. Let us disappear together now and go and have a drink in some congenial hostelry in town. How about a couple of looseners at the Ten Thousand Light Bulbs and a bite to eat at the Charioteers?"

As all who ever crossed that threshold will remember, the *Light Bulbs* was in fact *The Ten Thousand Horsemen* at the Monomatapa Hotel, wonderfully sophisticated meeting place and wartime haunt of the Rhodesian rich and famous. Smuts and I ruffled our hair and removed the mascara while Barbara slipped into her black leather trousers and coat of many colours. We made an exceptional threesome, I thought. My opinion was confirmed at some point in the evening when a stranger came over to our table and asked quite seriously "are you two boys airline pilots?" no doubt taking Barbara to be the hostess on our stopover flight.

Smuts was onto it instantly, measured him, weighed him and slaughtered him, slurring his words for emphasis. He was having an anti US moment.

"Yes," he said, "TWA. But we've gotta stop drinking soon. We take off for Kennedy International in forty minutes. Join us, I can get you a free ticket and an upgrade to first class if you like. Sit with us, I'll show you how to fly a jumbo. Easy really, flies by itself if it hasn't had too much to drink."

"No no no, thanks a lot, some other time. I have to...." the stranger answered over his shoulder as he left our table in a hurry, his parting words and plans lost to us and posterity for ever.

"You can be a bit of a shit you know," Barbara told Smuts as our guest was disappearing out the door. "He was only trying to be friendly."

"No he wasn't," Smuts replied, "he was trying to be smart. In any case who wants to be a fucking airline pilot? Why couldn't we just be a pair of fairies, out with a queen?

It was a happy, well lubricated evening, full of fun and good humour. No one would have guessed that behind it all there were two would-be alpha males locked in a battle for the right to link up with the most desirable female on the planet.

We did not speak of these things however, and when at length we left, flagging a single taxi to be dropped off, one after the other, the only thing on anyone's mind was a good night's sleep. First to be deposited at home was Barbara.

"Same time tomorrow?" Smuts asked

"Check with me in the morning. My head may not stand it."

"It will have to," Smuts laughed, "it's my last night out before I go off on my snake and lizard diet..."

It was a far more sober little party to say goodbye to Smuts the following evening. I think all three of us felt that, entertaining as it was, our little show of the night before had somehow spoiled whatever spontaneity there might still have been in our oddball triangular relationship. Red faces all round I would have thought, but Smuts appeared unconcerned and distant. It was hard to get any joy into our evening. I think he was preparing himself mentally for what must surely be a trying time ahead. Success would change his life in a way that neither Barbie nor I could hope to do. Failure, on the other hand, would no doubt be taken in his stride, for as I have earlier observed, he was a wonderfully well balanced man, ready for any challenge, steady in any adversity.

I hoped that in the two weeks that he would be away on selection for the Selous Scouts my own militarily career future would be decided. I was only out of my regiment because I had requested a transfer – the doctors agreed that I had totally recovered from my wound and concussion, and was once again fit for active service. I was pleased with the classification because I was undergoing physical therapy which included a busy regime of monitored exercising in a gym, and I could feel myself daily making progress; actually I was already feeling fitter than I had ever done before.

Chapter 29

Psy Ops, more correctly known as '1 POU', had accepted me subject only to the medical, indeed I had been promoted to Sergeant, and now they quickly arranged for my participation in their own forthcoming induction camp. It proved a lot tougher than I had expected and encouraged me think more highly of my new outfit. Not so much a selection course, it was in fact a crossover induction/training exercise in which the new arrivals were reminded on the one hand that they were uniformed soldiers in the army and needed to know something about their weapons, and on the other encouraged to think and contribute creatively to ideas for the psychological promotion of our side of the argument in the national struggle.

The centre of POU operations was Cranborne barracks in Salisbury. That was where we mustered and did most of our work in a long corrugated iron hut, of which there were many ranged in lines and looking, let us face facts, rather decrepit and tatty. They had been there since World War Two when the site was a training base for Britain's Royal Air Force, and now needed a coat of fresh paint at the very least..

My induction began just a few days after Smuts left for his life-changing test, so our personal lives, and in particular, our battle for the hand of the crocodile hunter's widow, were very much on ice. In the thrash of my new surroundings, and the busy bustle of learning new tricks, there was little time to relax and let the mind roam free. Only a few early nights gave me time to wonder and worry about what was going on elsewhere. The rest of the time we were kept busy until late.

For the main body of the course we were based near Darwendale at Inkomo barracks, much the same in layout and style as Cranborne, but more comfortable and not particularly challenging for those many of us who were past the usual military service intake age. We had a day on the shooting range; quite an intense day I should say, for we had the opportunity to use a variety of weapons; the standard issue FN, G3, Sten gun and Uzi.

200

Also, for the first time in my life, I had to handle and throw a live hand grenade. That particular exercise took me a little by surprise and I made such a pathetic first attempt at it that I was called back to do it again.

The 'drill' that we were all individually to follow began in a standing position behind a low earth wall at the weapons range, accompanied only by the training officer and pile of grenades sitting in a box, looking like toys. He would then hand you a grenade and indicate where he wanted you to throw it beyond the wall. First you had to check the point of aim, then pull the pin, count to ten, toss the bomb in the agreed direction, see it land, and then duck down below the wall and wait for the explosion. All of which went well until a few seconds after I had pulled the pin. My count to ten was too hurried and it could not have taken more than three seconds before I hurled the grenade in roughly the indicated direction and dropped immediately to my knees behind the covering wall. No amount of tugging from the training officer would get me back on my feet. After the explosion he remarked quite kindly; "bit quick to get down old boy, were you frightened?"

"Yes, but only when I realised I had hashed the count. By then I had lost track and was too afraid to get back up," I explained. "Happens a lot," he said. "That's why we do the thing live. Rather you fuck it up here than in a real contact situation. Come back when I call and we'll do it again."

Second time round it went off perfectly, almost too cool, for I was counting very deliberately, indeed too slowly, so that when I reached eight, he said to me "CHUCK THE BLOODY THING!"

I saw it land, counted slowly to four and dropped to the ground to find he was already there. The bang was immediate, and I heard the whoosh of what I imagined to be the grenade base plate zinging directly overhead. Had I still been standing I would surely have been decapitated. It was a lesson of sorts.

"Fuck," said the Officer. "That was a bit tight."

I was much pleased, especially to reflect that he was surely now unlikely to think I wasn't up to the serious side of soldiering.

201

The same evening we went out on a map reading exercise which was, I think, also planned as something of an endurance test. We were parcelled off into threes, given a map and a map reference target, and dropped off an hour before dark on the eastern side of the Great Dyke near where the road entered the hills. Whoever may have thought that POU was for pussy-cats should have been with us on that mad ramble; it was quite a test, for my little threesome at least, largely because the last part of our direct marching route took us up the steep hills where once there had been considerable chrome mining, and there were deep and dangerous pits all around. Avoiding them and maintaining a fair rate of progress was not easy. We were allowed no lights other than cigarette lighters and matches, so the climb in the dark was difficult and challenging. In addition, although we carried a radio, we were on radio silence, to be broken only upon reaching our objective, or if we thought ourselves to be in imminent and serious peril.

Our instructors had set up their own little tented camp in a delightful glade among a cluster of giant Msasa trees, and there they expected to spend the night untroubled by any of their charges, for they fully expected everyone to have to camp down for the night *en route*. My team made such rapid progress for the first hour that by fading light we were already near enough to the chrome mine pits to see most of the more dangerous ones and to plot a route round them. We wanted to surprise the instructors by arriving long before expected. In this we were successful, but the prize turned out to be a lemon.

Expecting a warm pat on the back and orders to come down off the mountain to enjoy a hot dinner with them in their comfortable camp in the glade, we radioed our arrival as soon as we hit the top of the mountain. We were met with disbelief and instructions to keep the radio link open, to keep a close watch on the ground immediately below our rendezvous point for possible terrorist activity, and await further instructions. The exact wording of the radio transmission was lost in the static, but we clearly understood that the instructors thought we must have made a massive map reading error and were still miles away from true destination.

Developments were not long in coming. By that time it was dark and windy, and we were so far above ground level that we could hear little, even of the occasional passing traffic whose lights we could see way down below. Then, as we kept watch, we saw the lights of a vehicle coming out of the camping site area and travelling parallel with the hills for a mile or so. When the vehicle was directly below us it stopped and the lights were turned off. Presumably whoever was in it had got out, for very shortly after that there was a burst of machine gun fire that we could hear well enough. They were firing tracer bullets at us, but high, the shots passing over our heads with a crack, crack, crack.

And then the radio came to life with a query for us.

Anything happening in your sector?

Some bastard firing tracer at us.

That bastard is your CO.

Thank you Sir.

Well done on reaching your objective. Make camp where you are and we'll see you at first light. Come in for coffee and a bush breakfast.

So much for our winning ways.

Although Travis and John, my two companions, and I were a little disappointed at the outcome of our monumental effort, we had from the start more than half expected to be spending the night under the stars without blankets or sleeping bags anyway, so it was no great shock. With the wind beginning to turn quite chilly we looked for a bit of cover and found it in the lee of protruding rock. Heeding instructions to keep lights down to an absolute minimum, we used one or two matches to bed the spot and then settled in as best we could for the night. Though we doubted the likelihood of any enemy elements being at the top of the same mountain at the same time, we took turns of two hours to stay on watch.

It was a long, cold and miserable night. The falling temperature and the gnawing pangs of our empty stomachs contrived to prevent sleep from making it all pass quickly. As the first faint rays of the sun hit our little turf we wiped all traces of our stay away and headed off downhill towards a cup of steaming coffee and, we hoped, a round of rather more robust congratulations.

If anything, our descent in the half light of dawn was more difficult that the climb in the dark. It was steeper by far, but still beset with the shafts and adits of years of chrome mining, so that we had to pick our way gingerly lest we slip to our deaths in one of the many gaping holes hidden from our view by the steepness of the gradient. It was a challenge well worthy of far tougher troops, and it made me think of Smuts. I wondered how he was getting on. Hungry as I now was, I killed off my yearning for food by imagining my friend hunched over an early morning fire roasting a helping of scaly lizard on a forked stick. I had no real idea of what the would-be Scouts might be subjected to on their selection course, but the stories among us run-of-the-mill occasional soldiers had it that they were reduced to some quite disgusting dietary choices.

With my two companions I made my way down that steep mountain, slithering and sliding, and when going too fast for comfort, grabbing hold of some small bush or sapling as an emergency brake. By the time we reached the road at the bottom, our hands were red and sore and we were quite out of breath.

After a short smoke break we pushed on. From radio contact we learned how to find the instructors' camp and we were soon there, to be met with a fairly cursory 'well done' from the CO and a hot cup of coffee. Breakfast consisted of a cold boiled egg and a half-tin of bully beef, but never have I enjoyed such plain fare more.

It turned out to be a day of serious loafing, the only real reward for our winning performance, since there was nothing to do but await the arrival of the other teams, and a few of them were slow in getting there. When all were safely home, a couple of army Bedford trucks arrived and we were carted back to Inkomo for a late afternoon exercise in the real work of the unit, a series of lectures on *How to alter attitudes and influence choices.*

For the rest of our two weeks at Inkomo we enjoyed a busy and active schedule, at one moment being soldiers, the next trainee teachers. That aspect of it was mainly about coaching the civilian population on both sides of the colour divide to understand what our side thought the war was about, to bolster their flagging confidence in 'our' side, and to convince them that a great future awaited all who would sign up to the concept of harmony between the races.

When the day came for us to pack up our kit and get back to the real life business of the unit I had to admit to myself that I had enjoyed the exercise, despite the nagging conviction that we were preparing buckets of water to douse a major conflagration. It had been much like a Boy Scout camp: plenty of physical exercise out in the open, making new friends and telling tall stories around a smoky fire, watching the billy can boil and brewing up a cup of ridiculously sweet tea. As for whatever we may have learned, I did think then, as I do now, that the Psy Ops concept was a good idea come too late and thus perhaps, a mere distraction. The war situation was spiralling out of control and the government had already been forced to make one concession after another. Gone were the days when the Rhodesian Front believed they could handle the insurgency, gone were the days when they believed black Rhodesians could never be trusted to govern the country. Now it was a case of trying to influence the choice of which particular group of blacks would next govern the country.

For myself and most other male white 'Rhodesians' serving in one capacity or another in the war, it was still simply the future versus the present and the past; the past had been great, the present was a bit rocky, but the future looked bleaker by the day as it became more and more obvious that the war would not end until the, for us, 'wrong' blacks were in power, people we had convinced ourselves, if no one else, were hard-line communists likely to bring only death, destruction, and chaos to what had been such a wonderful and productive land.

Chapter 30

For all the clear indications that our national conflict was approaching some form of resolution, the war was still very much with us occasional soldiers, and our call-ups continued throughout ceasefire and peace talks then taking place in London. After my training exercise I found myself at work each day, tasked to produce leaflets for distribution to the black population at large, and some directed particularly at guerrillas. To my many questions as to how we would deliver these I received little enlightenment.

"Surely," I said. "If we know how to place these pearls before those swine, could we not just as easily deliver them a speeding bullet each?"

It was a good point, and one to which there was no real answer other than the possibility that the messages would somehow be passed on from good fellow to bad fellow. So those of us involved in writing and illustrating the leaflets simply churned them out without little hope of success. We had our own copying machines, and it was all easily done, but I suspect it was a mounting tide of effective publicity for rather than against the people we were striving to destroy.

The leaflets were not our only weapons. We had a clandestine radio station, air shout equipment, and most important, money. We were able to offer considerable rewards for treachery of one kind or another, including handing over weapons of war. I was not involved in the reward machinery, but I don't think much was ever earned or paid out – one more testament to the team spirit that was so surely developing around the 'nationalist guerrilla armies' as they now more regularly were described by the media rather than the 'terrorists' of old.

I had not been long employed in this curious creative industry when I was chosen to go with a group of intelligence officers to a small trading centre in the north-east. To one side of the surrounding district there was a substantial community of European tobacco and maize farmers; on the other a heavily populated Tribal Trust Land, a hotbed of nationalist fervour. Not surprisingly there had been several 'hits' lately against the farmers in the form of land mines, roadside ambush, and midnight attacks on lonely farmsteads. The casualty list was growing, and the farm community was worried and angry.

There was to be a protest meeting at the local sports club. All the farmers and their families would be there. They wanted to know if it was time to pack up and go. A senior army officer would brief the farmers on the current war situation, try to reassure them that although there would still be casualties, the guerrillas were actually losing the war. Then a farm economist would talk about the rosy economic future awaiting us all if a political settlement could be agreed at a conference then taking place in London.

My part was to be present as a member of the Psy Op unit, to speak from the platform if necessary, but mainly to circulate and let the local public know that we were doing something different, trying a creative approach to the longer term problem of protecting them and saving an entire way of life. I had no illusions myself; I knew it was no easy thing trying to talk away the constant threat of violent death. Yet at the same time I thought it all rather remote and unlikely. Despite my own experiences of land mines, gunfire and ambush I could not quite believe that the combined machinery and resources of the Rhodesian military machine might one day be swamped and a brand new order forced on us as the losing side. In my head I was drifting through this all; nothing was personal. But nothing could prepare me for the personal shock coming my way in that far corner of the land.

Whether by coincidence or astute military planning, the night before the meeting a large gang of guerrillas had attacked the well-guarded and strongly fenced home of one particularly prosperous farmer in the district. He was a man of something over 70 years of age, but he was fit, very active and entirely without fear. He and his wife and a young assistant were asleep in the house when the attack was launched just after midnight. They were well armed and mentally prepared for just such an eventuality. After the first hail of bullets the three of them calmly made their way upstairs to rooms on the second story of the building giving them all round surveillance. Having established roughly where the firing was coming from they waited for the next burst, and then opened up a devastating return fire themselves. The ensuing battle did not last long. The guerrillas withdrew, leaving a number of their comrades dead in the bushes beyond the fence.

In the morning when the local police and a stick of scouts arrived at the scene they found the bodies and loaded them up on the back of a truck. They were going to drive the gruesome cargo to the police station for possible identification and other forensic work, but decided to stop at the club to show off the trophies of the shoot-out. By the time I arrived for the meeting there was quite a crowd around the truck. I didn't particularly want to see what the fuss was about, but then someone said something to arouse my interest and I half-pushed my way through the throng to the side of the truck.

There were four bodies. Three were dressed in rags – tatty clothes chosen, I imagined, for a dirty night's work. The fourth was more or less naked, with only a pair of slightly muddied snow-white boxer shorts for cover. It was the body of a big man, as big, I thought at first, as my friend Norton James. It was lying with its back towards me and I could not see the face which was partially obscured by an arm of one of the other dead guerrillas. Some dread premonition made me edge my way around the crowd to get a better view from the other side of the truck. I leaned forward, looking closely at the features I knew too well. Norton! Norton James! I stifled an involuntary scream of pain, turning it as best I could into a sudden bout of coughing.

"Something wrong?" the person next to me asked in evident concern at my very obvious breakdown.

"I'm OK," I gurgled, "just a sudden bout of hay fever I think."

Stunned as I was, shocked, saddened almost to the point of tears, I yet realised that this was no place for the revelation that probably only I could make. For the first time among my own people I worried that I was in a hostile and unsafe space. After my first strangled cry, some animal instinct took over and told me not to say anything in public. For Norton's sake as much as my own I should go about this business in a quiet and measured fashion. Thus it was that I approached the senior intelligence officer of the small 'squad' I was part of.

He was in the Club hall shuffling papers when I found him.

"Excuse me Sir," I said after a brief salute, "can I have a word? It may be important."

"Go ahead Hill."

So I told him, though I found the words difficult.

"I recognise one of the dead on the back of the truck outside. They are all supposed to have been killed in an attack on the Truffleby farm last night, but he is a Zambian journalist and I know him reasonably well. There is something very wrong here I think but I don't know how best to deal with the information."

He looked puzzled. This was not his usual kind of problem. He didn't know right away how to deal with it. It was out of his range of possibilities.

"Come and show me," he said, "but say nothing for anyone else to hear. Understand?"

"Yes Sir."

We were just in time for me to point out Norton's body because the truck was on the point of leaving, presumably to take the load for close ransacking and eventual disposal somewhere secret. Though I looked again as closely as I could, I saw no sign of a bullet wound on Norton's body, although it was entirely possible that I would have found something if I had been able to turn his corpse over.

When we were back inside the Club I drew attention to the odd fact that only Norton was in such a state of near-nudity. The other three were fully clothed, albeit somewhat tattily.

"That is odd," he agreed. Then "leave it with me for a while, and do not whatever you do mention this to another living soul. I am sure you will appreciate that this could be explosive news if it comes out, and let me remind you that you are under the Official Secrets Act."

That was something I was only too well aware of and I wondered what might have happened had I refused to sign at the time. Oh well, no sense in dwelling on that.

I didn't hear anything further until after the so-called protest meeting which went off very well, partly perhaps because of such a successful outcome to the Truffleby Farm attack. The other reason, of course, was that the farmers had little choice but to see things through. Any ideas of packing up and leaving soon came up against the stark reality of *nowhere to go, nothing to go with*.

After a drink or two in the Club bar most of the farmers and their wives were gone by about four in the afternoon. They wanted to get home well before twilight time.

At length I was called to the Clubhouse office for another private chat with the OC. He was no longer out of his depth. He had taken advice.

"Well Hill," he said quite affably, "it turns out you are wrong. That gook was no journalist, he was the gang's political commissar. The security people have known of him for some time and they have been after him for months, a dangerous man and a committed communist with the war name of Killboy Jonas."

I started to protest.

"It's impossible...

"I don't think you heard me properly Hill. The body you saw was that of a gook called Killboy Jonas. He was a dangerous, devious political commissar well-known to us. Thankfully we've got him and that's the end of it. Do you get my drift?"

I did indeed, and I said so, even apologising for my extraordinarily idiotic and inexplicable error. I hoped he would spot the irony behind my exaggeration, but he said nothing further and we drove back to Salisbury in our little convoy of army cars, arriving sometime after ten that night.

The most enjoyable part of being with Psy Ops was that call-up nights for Salisbury based members could be spent at home, but I was not looking forward much to this particular night for I planned to phone Barbara and tell her of Norton's death, to hell with the Official Secrets Act. By the time I got back from Cranborne it was nearly midnight, but I called her anyway. I was in a hell of a state about our mutual friend.

She answered right away.

"I'm sorry to call so late, but I have really bad news about Norton. He's dead."

"What? Oh My God NO, what happened to him? Wait. I'm coming round. Make some coffee, lots of it."

We spent the best part of the night talking about Norton, trying to puzzle out some sort of reasonable explanation for what had happened. I did not accept that the body I had seen and so closely looked at was not Norton's; I felt I knew him as well as a brother. There was no mistake on my part. The only questions for me were how he died, why he should turn up among a load of gook bodies after a night attack, and why he alone was in such a state of undress. Barbara listened to all I had to say. Neither of us could come up with any plausible explanation except one. She suggested the possibility that he might have been doing a hand's on 'African Guerrilla battle' report for one of his client papers. He would have had the right contacts to facilitate such a mission, but would he have agreed to be part of an attack on a lonely farm family? I doubted it, but then of course he may not have known what the intended target was to be. Every answer only led to more questions.

Coffee, and our great affection for Norton, kept us going through most of the night. When at last we decided it was time for bed it was already near dawn and we were both exhausted. I persuaded her to stay over and we shared a sibling hug before slipping off to separate beds in separate rooms. It was too sad an occasion for anything more personal and intimate. In any case, after the duet with Smuts there was an unspoken reserve between the widow and I that I would make no attempt to break in his absence. But we needed to talk a bit about the office, and so at seven the next morning I knocked on her door with a tray of coffee and a few slices of hot buttered toast. She was sleepy, but revived rapidly under the influence of coffee and a busy stomach.

"Maybe we should do a little digging," I suggested. "Do you think we can find out when Norton left Meikles at the end of his last visit? Did he in fact check out? And maybe the hotel can tell you if he left a forwarding address?"

"I'll call them. No, I'll go there rather."

"Great, just don't say why you need to know."

"I'll tell them he left some dry cleaning with me and it was late coming back."

"That should do it. Now, I have to be at Cranborne in an hour and I don't know when I will next be able to get to the office, so maybe before I go you can give me a quick run-down on anything going on there that I should know about?"

"Nothing critical," she said. "Nothing, that is, that I can't easily handle myself. I had a letter from the Whitmore Hughes people asking for some local demographics which made me think they probably do represent one of the consumer product groups rather than a political party. I'm dealing with it. Other than that, nothing much of interest. Maurice Feinstein popped in yesterday for a brief chat and I could see he was ever so pleased with himself. He is a little like a proud father and he thinks our splendid offices are entirely thanks to his vision. Silly bugger. But incredibly clever and very supportive, and I have to admit that without his approval I probably would never have joined up with you, much as I wanted to for my totally subjective self."

"Mad woman that you are..."

And so we nattered on until it was time for us both to head off for the day. In our shared pleasure neither of us had forgotten Norton, we had just pushed the bleak thought aside for a few minutes of being together. But as I drove off to Cranborne in my faithful red

213

Volvo I could think of little else but what had really happened out there on Truffleby farm in the middle of that awful night.

I was to get no answers from anyone at Psy Ops. I could not mention it myself, and the subject did not come up through anyone else. I had the impression that if anyone even knew of it they were doing their best to ignore it.

Chapter 31

After a nondescript day printing the latest bunch of slanderous war propaganda leaflets at Cranborne I called Barbara to ask if we could meet, and more particularly, to ask if she had any luck with the hotel in tracking Norton's movements..

Before I could say much more than hello she told me that Smuts was back from his selection course with the Scouts.

"He got in this morning and called me as soon as he was home. He had a wonderful time, he says. A 'hell of an experience' is what he actually said.

"I didn't tell him about Norton. I thought I'd leave that to you, so I asked him if we could all meet this evening. I did say there was something desperately important, which was probably silly because he will immediately have thought it had something to do with our complicated three-way future. On second thoughts, maybe not such a bad idea, no reason for him to spend time worrying. He's coming to your house at about seven.

"About Norton. I went to the hotel but there's nothing unusual to report. He checked out at least ten days ago and he was heading back to Zambia via Johannesburg. I have his forwarding address in Lusaka if we need it. Anyway, I'm coming over to you now, get the Scotch out and a bucket of ice...."

She arrived promptly and Smuts not long after. I heard his car, and by the time he was at the front door, I was there to open it for him with a welcoming glass of scotch and soda. He took a quick sip, put the glass down, gave us both an affectionate hug, and said "OK you two, what's the important news?"

"Norton's been killed."

He was shocked.

"Crash?" he asked.

"No, murder I think. Assassination. Contract killing... God knows, could have been an accidental shooting, almost anything except natural causes..."

I went on to tell him the story. I left nothing out. He listened without comment, but I could see he was deeply affected. He too had grown attached to our giant black friend.

"You know what," he said. "Of course I am shocked, but there's no explosion of any kind inside me. The news hits me like ink onto blotting paper. It just sinks in, and spreads. I guess that's what the war has done to us.

"But as for trying to find out what happened, I don't think we will ever know. It is an incident of war. Whether he was killed by our side or his side or even by accident, it was really just another in the long list of casualties.

"I don't want to think our people killed him. It would be such an insane murder – unless he really was Killboy Jonas, and I don't see how that could be true. Political commissars stay with their charges for ever. They have to, they're there to whip them into line constantly. As far as we know, Norton kept up a full time job as a correspondent. He could hardly have been much use if he was moonlighting as an occasional gook.

"What is fascinating is that he was stripped. Who by, and why? Not surely to find out who he was. Perhaps to prevent others from finding out too easily who he was. If he had been a part of the guerilla group as their political commissar he wouldn't have been going into an attack with so little clothing. Same if he was doing a story, so I guess he was probably stripped after death and his body dumped where it would be found. I think he was killed by his own people, I really do, but I know there are still terrible holes in that possibility."

"Why would his own people want to kill him?" Barbara asked.

"Because his own people are not by any means all his own people, not at one with each other by a million miles. There are two armed groups and possibly a third, each representing a different political party. If elections come soon they will be at each other's throats to form the next government. Norton's death could be part of a coming bloody election campaign.

"All these thoughts. So many maybes. That's why I think we'll never know the truth, and especially for us at the moment because we can't go out and ask questions."

"And since nobody has yet been interested enough to ask me how my selection course went off, let me add another weird dimension to this story..."

Barbie and I were both clamouring our protestations of deep interest, but Smuts just laughed.

"I jest. I know. I had a good one, but my story was trumped by yours. But here it is anyway, and it has just become something else to be factored into the bigger equation.

"I didn't make it into the Scouts. Rejected! But only because of the incident with Norton. I got through the course alright, actually I did rather well. But in the meantime the brass received a report - from the MPs probably - about our 'case', and in the end it was decided that nothing would be done about my actual transfer until there is a decision whether to charge me with impersonating an officer or not."

"Bugger me," I had to say. "That is just so bloody typical of our side. Losing out on a technicality. Following the rules of cricket when we're playing a deadly game of war."

"It isn't that bad for me personally," Smuts argued. "I've learned what I really wanted to, the war seems to be nearly over and I can use more time to work on my own future which, by the way, is definitely going to be in the bush.

"One thing I would like to suggest though is that we think about how to let Norton's family know what we know. Can't be done while the war is on, but I think one of us at least should go and break the news to them when we can. Incredible to think that the death of a man like that should go utterly unmarked, his passing unknown to his family. No one to cry for him but us."

After a decent pause I begged Smuts to tell us all about the selection course.

"Did you eat a snake?" Barbara asked.

Smuts was reluctant.

"It was just physical," he said. "It was a test of physical endurance in the first place and of ingenuity and determination. I learned nothing about the Scouts that I can share with you, but I did learn a lot about myself. As for the eating of snakes, I think I can say with some safety that you would much rather not hear about some of the things you can eat when you have to. Any snake would be considered a luxury, good white meat like chicken, a pleasant enough bite if you're hungry enough to shut down the thinking about it believe me."

We left the subject alone and decided to go out to dinner, somewhere we felt we could be with our absent friend, at least in spirit. And so we chose Meikles where he so often stayed and obviously enjoyed.

With dinner done we went on to one of our own favourites, *The Hole,* where we drank a lot and danced a little.

"There is much to be said for a woman having two best friends as best friends and escorts," Barbara said as we prepared to leave. "The attention is incredible and there is never the slightest chance of a fight breaking out. Come on you two useless creatures. Show a little fight. Make a girl feel special."

We had all had a little too much to drink, but we remembered to close the evening with a toast to Norton.

"Goodbye proud and noble dude," said Smuts. "Goodbye."

I looked at Barbie. I think she was crying.

Chapter 32

There are, I imagine, many dozens and dozens of news clips in archives around the world showing the general euphoria of public reaction to the end of World War Two. Every now and then the TV stations air one or two of them for an anniversary or war documentary, and they show happy smiling faces, strangers kissing each other in exuberant excess, balloons flying, and such a level of excitement that you cannot fail to be dragged in to the joy of the moment yourself. There was no such public exhibition in our country the day we learned the war was to end.

It is true that the news came as a process from ceasefire to final whistle. The various sides gathered together to talk about the future in London. There they argued like mad. Some threatened to walk out. Others did the same. But in the end something approaching animal instinct for self-survival kicked in and an agreement was reached – there would be elections in the new year, supervised by the British ar*my. In the meantime the various armies separated, promising not to attack each other or anyone else. On our side, black and white soldiers stayed more or less where we were; the guerrillas retreated into holding camps.

It is incredible now, years later, to reflect that this elaborate but rickety arrangement worked. Despite one or two incidents and any number of official complaints and threats to call the whole thing off, it worked.

In military limbo as he was, Smuts was off the hook right away, his soldiering days ended as soon as the agreement was signed, for he was no longer a member of any army unit and was never called up again. Not so we propaganda merchants in POU; we stayed at our task, courageously writing rubbish from the safety of a private billet in the city. That 'billet' was actually the seventh floor of one of the city's biggest hotels, given over to the army for the remaining duration of the war presumably because the proprietors couldn't fill it with visitors. There we kept our growing army of printers and photo copiers busy cranking out many thousands of leaflets in an attempt to bolster the election chances of an amiable but ineffectual bishop who had become Ian Smith's latest way out.

I was on call-up in the immediate run-up to the elections, and while they took place. By that point there was no longer any real work to do and we just sat around chatting about the future. We had managed to convince ourselves that Bishop Muzorewa would win; he was of course the man we favoured because he alone of the contenders was not at war with us. We had also done such a good hatchet job on Mugabe that we truly feared him ourselves, being quite certain that if by some extraordinary late development he won, we whites would have to go, run away with our tails between our legs. We imagined columns of refugees streaking towards the border, protected by the British army and whatever was left of our own.

Against this new background of enforced idleness in uniform I was at least able to spend most nights at home and most evening with Barbie at her flat, ostensibly catching up on the work of our firm, but in truth trying to make sure that I was still very much a contender for a long-term romantic future connected to the delightful widow. With Smuts around and free to come and go all day without military let or hindrance, the competition was always much on my mind, though in fact it took no visible form. It was as if, having made our proposals clear, and neither of them having been accepted, or actually rejected for that matter, an amicable cease fire had come into force. Smuts, dear man, took no advantage of my absence in the army, and I, equally, made no capital of the fact that business gave me privileged daily access. I think we both knew instinctively that there would be no significant shift until the current uneasy national peace was cemented through elections, a new government installed, and the future for whites reasonably clear. Nevertheless I am sure neither of us wavered in our ambition; I was mad about the widow, and I am sure he was too.

The elections were to be held over several days because of the distances involved and the difficulties of policing the process. On

220

Day Two, back now at Cranborne, we at POU were called to a briefing, the shortest ever.

In essence we were told to our absolute shock and amazement, given how we had managed to convince ourselves it could not happen, that in their very great numbers up and down the country, the people were voting 'joyously' for Mugabe. There was no question of the outcome, and no protest possible. Our bête *noire* would be the next prime minister of our country, which it now became crystal clear would no longer be known as Rhodesia or Zimbabwe Rhodesia, but simply Zimbabwe. We were instructed to burn everything left over from what we had ever worked on, original papers, carbon copies, and all the stencils we had accumulated from the beginning.

We found an old petrol drum serving as a rubbish bin and in this appropriate receptacle over a period of two days we burned every piece of paper we could find. Someone must have been taking copies as we produced them however, for it was not that many years later that much of our handiwork appeared in a book devoted to Rhodesian military clandestine operations. I think it true to say that the revelations produced not the slightest ripple at the time, and I never heard of any come-back for our work at all.

When everything had been reduced to ashes we shut up shop and went home. No farewell parade, no medals, no sadness, no regret. At some point in the future we would no doubt have to hand over our uniforms, boots, caps and all to whatever new national army should emerge, but I felt sure there would be no need for the occasional soldiers like me. In the first place we were on the losing side and in any case there were now hundreds of thousands of much younger men willing to serve the new cause.

Barbara and Smuts and I went out one evening, more to commiserate than to celebrate. The official results of the election were not yet out and we had no idea what the victors would say or how much time they would give us to go if go we must.

Norton was still much in our thoughts and Smuts had interesting news.

He had taken advantage of his free time to call on the MPs to find out if they had made a determination in his case. They had indeed. There would be no charges, he had no case to answer. The decision was being communicated to his original unit and no doubt he would be on call-up again 'quite soon'. Since then, of course, events had moved quickly and he knew he would never again serve another day in the army. More important from our point of view was that the MPs said they had not thought it necessary to interview Norton since he was not suspected of any part in the issue.

All of this was reassuring on one point. If true, it meant that Norton had not been in the hands of our security people over the Club incident. No one had mentioned the fear, but I am sure we all shared it - that Norton's death was perhaps the consequence of an interview gone very wrong.

Smuts had also been in contact with someone at Norton's Zambian address and found out that although no one knew where he was at that precise moment, he had arrived back from his last assignment as usual. Last, he had found out from close friends in the Scouts who had worked in the area, that Killboy Jonas was indeed the name of a local commissar. Whether that was an alias for Norton no-one could say. The likelihood was against it, however, because Killboy had been particularly active in the district over the past six months, at a time when we knew first-hand that Norton was coming and going between Salisbury and Lusaka. He would not have had the time for a commissar's job.

"Which," said Smuts, "leaves us with little more than the possibility that he was indeed part of the gang who attacked Truffleby, whether as insurgent or insurgent supporting feature writer. None of us have seriously questioned your identification so far Dog," he continued, "but are you absolutely certain the body was Norton's?

"No question of it," I said. "Even if he has a twin, the body I saw was his. I am certain it was."

"Who then will come with me to Zambia?" Smuts asked. "Someone must make an effort to tell his family. I can go as soon after the elections results are announced as it is possible to travel freely again. That way I can combine the trip with a look into safari camp opportunities there."

Both Barbara and I volunteered, but after more thought agreed that one of us should stay to see after the welfare of our company. We tossed a coin and it fell to Barbara to go with Smuts. I wasn't worried. I knew it would be fine. The silent ceasefire would last at least until the mission was over.

Election developments on the ground were moving forward at what seemed to us lightning speed. With nine parties contesting the election and all needing promotional leaflets and press stories, our business did well. A day after burning documents at Cranborne, Mugabe's party was declared the runaway winner and he became our new Prime Minister. Getting over our shock and alarm at this outcome was made easy for us when our new head man made a calm and reasoned acceptance speech calling for reconciliation.

With good money pouring into the company coffers and my steady attraction for my business partner growing daily, I found myself extremely reluctant to leave the country. Making it even easier to stay was the fact that our former arch enemy now appointed three whites to his new cabinet and asked our army commanding officer to stay at his post to help supervise the integration of the opposing forces.

Easy? It was a piece of cake. What people now describe as a 'no-brainer'. You did not have to be any kind of intellectual wizard to know what was good for you.

Metaphorically holding my breath, I called Tina in Johannesburg to tell her that I was staying. Even as I dialled the number I was unsure how I would react if she said she would like to come back. The conversation was cool, but not too cool; friendly but not warm. I was not tested.

"I have not much missed our life up there," she said. "I've got used to things here and I am starting to enjoy myself a little. I think I'll wait a bit longer if you don't mind. You never know, things may change."

"Probably best," I said. "This national reconciliation talk may be just talk. We'll see what happens when the British go home and our new masters are truly free to do whatever they wish. I do feel safe enough though. I'm sure our fears of a bloody end to the white occupation of Rhodesia have been put to rest. The business is doing well and I can send you whatever you need."

Tina needed nothing, so we talked politely about each other's lives, learned little, and agreed to keep our relationship on the books for the moment. No immediate divorce. I was happy enough with that. To all intents I was unmarried and free to do anything and go anywhere; I was reasonably prosperous, childless and happy. My new country Zimbabwe appeared to be on the brink of a bright and harmonious future. Above all I had two wonderful friends, one of whom I might eventually marry. What could go wrong?

Chapter 33

I do not want to give the impression that we were obsessed with what had happened to our friend Norton, yet he was much in our minds. Smuts, in particular, would not rest until we could make an effort to find his family and tell them of his death. In this determination I suspect that Smuts was deeply influenced by his own unusually close family background. Being an only child, he felt himself to be one of a charmed circle of three. His parents loved him as much as they loved each other, and the idea that, had they still been alive they might not know at every moment of the day where he was and how he was doing, filled him with a kind of guilty dread. He wanted to meet Norton's Mom and Dad if they could be found, and hold their hands for a while before passing on the sad news of his d*eath. I did not ask how far he intended to go with the narrative; I assumed he would handle the business tactfully and kindly. He would be their other son.

It was not long after the formation of a new Zimbabwe government that Smuts was able to make the trip to Zambia. He and Barbara set off in a station wagon he had bought as a war-end present to himself. I was there to see them leave, a little disappointed that I could not go with them, but full of the new-found joy and hope that peace had brought to our lives.

Barbara had friends in Lusaka and they would be based there while busy tracking down the elder James family. All they had to go on was the fact that the old man had once been a parliamentary secretary in the days of the Federation of Rhodesia and Nyasaland.

"Shouldn't be too difficult," Smuts said to me before setting off, "the old chap must still be a respected sort of elder statesman if he is alive. And in any case Norton's office people will surely be useful. He once mentioned he had a Norwegian girlfriend. I'll call her too if anyone has her number. There may be letters at the office. We'll have to see."

It is only a day's drive to Lusaka, and I rather hoped for a call from them that first night. It was days before I heard a word. I was talking to Smuts. The news was disappointing but not terminal.

No one at Norton's office had any information on his family at all, and his surname was not James. This they gleaned from unopened letters waiting for his attention addressed to James Mahembe. In itself the fact was not unusual – some African names are too long or difficult to pronounce for a workable pen name in an English publishing environment – but it made the business of tracking down Norton's family more complicated.

The hunt had eventually led to the National Archives where they found a reference to Parliamentary Secretary Laurent Mahembe.

Trawling through telephone directories was a lengthy process but eventually yielded an entry for 'Mahembe L' in a distant town called Chingola. Calls to the number had so far proved worthless because they had been answered by someone who could not understand English. Now their idea was to get a Zambian friend to call in the evening and hopefully get some coherent answers. At the same time Smuts was taking the opportunity to talk to investment officials about his other great interest, the safari business. He felt sure that he and the Widow could wrap up both assignments and be back home within a week.

The fates, however, had other plans for the three of us.

Anxious to get on, Smuts and Barbara decided to separate for the speedier resolution of their two projects; he to deal with the search for Norton's next of kin while she talked to government contacts about the formalities of investing in the country's tourist industry and getting the necessary licenses. They went their various ways.

It was on the way back to Lusaka from a day's trip to Chingola that Smuts was badly injured in a collision with an overloaded firewood lorry. He was driving at night and the broken-down lorry had been abandoned where it came to a halt – only half off the road. Though badly injured, Smuts was alive and conscious but pinned inside the car by the crumpled framework. He endured almost two hours waiting for anyone to come to his assistance. Another few hours passed before mechanical assistance could be brought to the scene to free him. By the time he was ferried to hospital in Lusaka he was in a state of severe shock in addition to other injuries yet to be identified.

Still conscious and ever forceful he managed to find a pen and scrap of paper to scribble down Barbara's name and telephone number for his rescuers. She was soon at his side. It was from the hospital office that she telephoned me. She was calm but deeply worried.

"The doctors here say he is at serious risk of infection because of the prolonged state of shock. They think he has broken bones as well, though so far they are trying to deal with the risk of infection first and don't know exactly what else may be wrong. He is on a drip, pale as death but still chirpy. In fact he says he's going to be fine so I mustn't bother you to come. But I think you should drop whatever else you are doing and get here as fast as you can."

I promised to get going immediately. I wondered whether Smuts had seen the Mahembe family.

"I haven't asked him yet," Barbara said. "Everything but his recovery seems utterly unimportant now."

"I'm on my way. I'll drive through the night and try to be with you first thing in the morning."

"And you watch out for firewood trucks," she said. "They're everywhere in Zambia, the charcoal capital of the world. They've already cut down all the trees for miles around the charcoal pits along the roadsides, so now they are trucking wood in from miles away and they are dangerous."

I found my passport, packed a bag and left almost immediately, hoping only that my beloved old left-hand drive Volvo would continue to serve me faithfully and deliver me safe to the two people I cared most for in the world.

The drive went off without incident, and by first light I was at the border post at Chirundu on the River Zambezi. When I told them my story the officials on both sides were friendly and helpful; the entire procedure took no more than twenty minutes. Then I was on my way again, keeping myself awake by opening all the car windows and letting in the chilly dawn air.

Arriving in Lusaka at the height of the morning traffic I stopped at the first service station I could find, not only to fill up, but also to ask for directions to the hospital – I had forgotten to ask Barbara.

By the time I got there, vast crowds of people were converging on the place. There were many nurses among them, and judging by the stethoscopes round the neck, many doctors too. But by far the greatest number were patients or visitors arriving to see patients. It was as if everyone in Zambia that morning to had business at Lusaka General Hospital. I wondered a little fretfully how my friend could possibly get the care he needed against a background multitude like that.

But I found my way to his bedside in no time at all and I was surprised to see how cheerful he looked. He greeted me warmly and apologised for the inconvenience. Barbara was already there of course and she laughed.

"Inconvenience my foot," she said. "We're here to make sure you keep your hands off all these beautiful black nurses."

Although it was early in the morning and nowhere near visiting time, those wonderful nurses allowed Barbara and me to sit with Smuts for almost an hour. When we had worked over the details of his ordeal for perhaps the tenth time I asked him about his visit to Chingola.

"It was great, I guess, in a way. I found the old man living more or less alone on a little farm outside the town, looked after only by a couple of young girls, apparently distant relatives, both utterly illiterate as far as I could make out. His wife died years ago apparently and he is unfortunately very deaf and his mind wanders a little.

"I told him I was a friend of his son Norton which seemed to make little impression, but he did order up some tea and was very friendly. We sat out on his exquisite veranda and quietly drank our tea. Then I took his hand, just as I had imagined I would, and I

228

tried as gently as possible to break the news to him that Norton was dead. To my great surprise he knew already.

"'You don't have to worry about that my son,' he said to me. 'Some people from Lusaka came to tell me about it not so many weeks ago. They told me he was killed by the Rhodesians while doing a war story for the newspapers. Always doing a story that boy. Always doing stories...'"

"I stayed a few hours with him, I didn't want to hurry. He was a gentle soul, untroubled by anything really: he seemed to take his personal tragedies philosophically. We talked of his days in the Federal Government. He seemed proud of his part in that. By the time I did leave the day was getting on. It is a long drive from Lusaka."

"I did not tell him the circumstances of Norton's death, nothing about the attack on Truffleby, nothing about being taken to town on the back of a truck like a load of dead meat, and I certainly did not mention the fact that he was nearly naked. I decided he did not need to know anything about that."

Barbara and I sat there listening to the story in silence. I was living it all again, and Barbara, I suppose, was once more pole-axed, this time by the dreadful truth.

Just then a doctor stopped by the bed and told us we would have to leave. Smuts, he said, was to be prepped for an operation. His right leg was broken in two places and needed to be set. There was also some suspicion of internal bleeding that they would look at and fix 'quite easily'.

We were just saying our goodbyes when Smuts interrupted.

"Don't rush off," he said. "I've been thinking so much about Norton's death and how he came to be almost naked. I think I know what happened. Won't take a minute. Came to me in my wreck of a motor car in the night while I was waiting for help.

"Like our beloved Widow here," he said, squeezing Barbara's hand. "Norton was a natty dresser. He loved good clothes and he always looked good, as if he had just emerged from an appointment in Savile Row. So I have absolutely no doubt at all that he went off on his last story impeccably dressed, probably in the very latest safari gear from Willis & Geiger. Beautiful clothes that anyone, maybe even Killboy Jonas, would have been delighted to get his hands on.

"Seriously, I think it was someone in the gang who stripped Norton's body after he was shot, and kept all that magnificent gear for himself. And I think that someone might very well have been the smart commissar.

"Killboy Jonas. Think of him rather as Stealboy Jonas..."

"Sherlock!" I had to say, for it made so much sense.

"That's it Sherlock Dog! I think you have hit it on the head even in your frail and feeble state. And stripping the dead in war is nothing new, not especially shocking. It has been going on for as long as there have been wars. What the dead have no use for, the living can still enjoy."

On that surprised but illuminating note Barbara and I left for her friend's home where we waited impatiently to hear from the hospital. We called a few times but Smuts was either still in theatre or coming round from the anaesthetic. Ultimately it became clear that we would not be seeing him that day, and so we settled down to stay another night.

It was in the night, in the darkness before morning, that Smuts died.

A post-operative embolism killed him. It is, I am told, somewhat like a stroke. The tiniest scrap of clotted blood makes its way to the brain and kills you with the deadly efficiency of a rifle bullet fired close up. What a waste. What a sad waste of a precious and much loved man.

Chapter 34

We buried Smuts in Lusaka. There was no one else but us to mourn him, no reason to bury him anywhere else.

When it was all over, we made our way back to our business in our home city, now called Harare. Getting back to a new city in a new land now at peace with itself at last was cheering in a way, but when I drew the car up outside Barbara's flat she was anything but cheerful.

"I don't want to go there. I don't want to be alone. Please can I come home with you?"

And then, when we reached my place, she said: "You don't know it and Smuts did not either. I'm four months pregnant.

"Four months pregnant," she repeated slowly. "And one of you two wonderful men is the dad. The hell of it is that I do not know which."

It was a shock, partly I suppose because Barbara delivered the news in a rather flat and matter-of-fact way. As well as she now knew me, she did not know how I would take it. I'm not sure she was thinking of that though, we were both still in a state of shock at the speed that our three lives had gathered coming up to this defining point.

"I'd like to stay the night," she said. "Then I will take long leave.

"I don't want anything from you right now, maybe a bunch of beautiful flowers when the baby is born."

"Don't worry," I said. "I will be there with the flowers. And a priest."

And that is exactly what happened. My wonderful Widow Flanagan produced a boy, very red in the face and with a remarkably flat nose, but then that, I am led to believe by people with more experience of it, is the inevitable consequence of the child's emergence from an exceedingly tight spot. We called him Smuts.

We were very happy with him, and with his two younger brothers.

Smuts is now a grown man with a wife of his own and a son called Hunter. His wife is expecting their second child soon. Barbara is sure it will be a girl. I don't mind. A boy would be very nice too.

Printed in Great Britain
by Amazon